THE SILVER HOOD

THE
SILVER HOOD
A NOVEL

JUSTIN RICHMAN

NEW YORK

LONDON • NASHVILLE • MELBOURNE • VANCOUVER

THE SILVER HOOD
A NOVEL

© 2019 **JUSTIN RICHMAN**

Published in New York, New York, by Morgan James Publishing. Morgan James is a trademark of Morgan James, LLC. www.MorganJamesPublishing.com

The Morgan James Speakers Group can bring authors to your live event. For more information or to book an event visit The Morgan James Speakers Group at www.TheMorganJamesSpeakersGroup.com.

ISBN 978-1-68350-894-6 paperback
ISBN 978-1-68350-893-9 eBook
Library of Congress Control Number: 2017918796

Cover Design by:
Megan Whitney
Creative Ninja Designs
megan@creativeninjadesigns.com

In an effort to support local communities, raise awareness and funds, Morgan James Publishing donates a percentage of all book sales for the life of each book to Habitat for Humanity Peninsula and Greater Williamsburg.

Get involved today! Visit
www.MorganJamesBuilds.com

For my son, Aiden.

CHAPTER ONE

B lackness consumed me. I couldn't move. I tried to breathe. I couldn't.
What was happening?
Panicked, I again tried to breathe.

I couldn't.

The earth beneath me was rough. Sharp stones bit into my skin. I was wet. Cold.

Still there was nothing but blackness.

Someone was pounding on my chest, crushing me. My sternum and ribs screamed in pain.

Was I dying? Was someone killing me?

Then the sudden urge to sit up and cough. My body wretched out water. Spasms wracked my body. The water that spewed forth tasted like dead fish.

Light filled my world again. But pain. So much pain.

I wanted so badly to breathe.

Water continued to pour from my mouth.

There was a large, firm hand pressed against my back. A man was speaking to me. "You're okay. . . You're okay." His voice was soothing and strong.

The spasms subsided.

I gasped for breath. Precious air filled my lungs.

My stomach hurt and my throat was on fire, but I could breathe again.

I took another deep breath but that caused another round of coughing. I was choking. Water again filled my mouth. I spit the foul water onto the ground. I took another breath, shallower this time.

"Take it easy, take it easy."

My lungs heaved in breath after breath, alternating with coughing.

As the coughing ceased and my breathing quieted, I turned to see who was with me. A police officer was kneeling next to me. I tried to read the name on his uniform. I blinked hard to focus. It said, "D. Reed."

His expression was somber. "Can you tell me your name, Son?"

The words meant nothing. I glanced around me. I was sitting on the bank of a river. I looked up and saw a road. A single image flashed through my mind. Headlights.

I had been driving home on Highway 151. It was around midnight. Headlights blinded me. Without warning, a car swerved into my lane.

I blinked.

The memory was replaced with the scene above me. Part of the guard rail was dangling 25 feet above. Another part of it was missing. My eyes followed the dangling rail to the river below. The water was still, as if nothing had happened. But along the bank, there were jagged car parts everywhere. Shards of glass reflected the moonlight.

My car. I turned my head from side to side looking everywhere for it. "Where's my car?"

The officer pointed to the river. "It's submerged over there."

I squinted at the water. Surely, I would be able to see some hint of my car. Nothing. The water held its treasure in secret.

"Now, I need you to concentrate," he said. "Can you tell me your name?"

I stared into the river in front of me. Unformed questions flooded my mind as the officer tapped me on my shoulder again, looking for a response.

I dragged my gaze away from the water and met his eyes. "Devin. My name is Devin Shephard."

"Devin, thank you. I want you to remain calm, okay? You've been in an accident. I need you to continue talking with me."

I nodded my head. I began to shiver from the cold.

"Good," Officer Reed continued. He wrapped a blanket around my shoulders. "What can you tell me about your accident?"

"Where's Lara?" I croaked.

"Who's Lara?! Was there someone else in the car with you?"

I blinked, trying to think. Then I remembered.

"No," I breathed. "No. She's okay."

Everything came back to me in a flash.

If Officer Reed was still talking, I didn't hear him anymore.

CHAPTER TWO

I t had started with snow.

Just a dusting, I thought. No big deal.

It was playoff night.

I weaved my way down to the Liberty Arena in Decker City and found a parking spot. I was an hour early, but I still had to park at the far reaches of the earth.

I trudged through the black slushy snow to the front door. My co-workers were already there.

I was the last one to arrive, so we proceeded through security and into the arena. It was already buzzing with music, people, and lights. The teams were warming up on the ice.

The scoreboard was set. The Decker City Devils were playing their most hated rivals, the Forsyth City Firestix.

It was game seven. Each team tied at three games each.

This was it. Tonight would decide the series.

We had tickets behind our team's goalie, right behind the glass. Best in the house. Courtesy of the investment company I worked for, TruGuard.

Out of nowhere, our beautiful receptionist Lara appeared and sat beside me.

"Hey, stranger," she said to me with a shy smile.

"Hi," I croaked. I mentally noted my usual suaveness with the ladies.

"Great seats, huh?"

I nodded, but not just because I agreed with her. It was because I wanted to explain why I was staring into her eyes. They seemed to change color from blue to green, depending on the light. Today they looked blue.

Strangely, her hair looked gray today. Why would she dye her hair gray?

I mean, I knew she was constantly dyeing her hair different shades of blonde and brown. In her words, she bores easily.

Lara frowned when she caught me staring at her hair. "It's grayish blonde. You don't like it? It's all the rage."

"No, I love it." I smiled to reassure her.

She beamed.

Phew, she believed me.

Lara was easily my favorite person at work. I would walk over to her counter to talk with her every chance I got. During our many conversations, we discovered we had a lot in common: hockey, zombies, and greasy diners. It was always fun gossiping about the same TV shows we would watch the night before.

We became good friends. I had always wanted to ask her out, but I had never found the courage to do so. I hoped that the game would be a great opportunity to get a little closer to her.

The hockey game was incredibly intense. At the end of the third period, it was tied 2-2.

Overtime. Whoever scored first, that was it. It was over.

The crowd was out of its mind. They were cheering and banging on the glass in front of us. It was a great time. The music filled the arena and the crowd began stomping and clapping to the beat.

Stomp-Stomp-Clap…

Stomp-Stomp-Clap…

As our team skated back onto the ice, the crowd erupted with cheers. The color red instantly filled the arena as the crowd began waving their mini towels stamped with the red Devils' logo.

Lara and I rose to our feet.

Lara picked up her towel and started waving it around.

I smiled at her and waved my own towel.

The opposing team then made their way back onto the ice and the crowd immediately erupted with "boo's."

Together, Lara and I cupped our hands and 'booed' the Firestix at the top of our lungs.

Both teams lined up on the center line to start the overtime period.

The second the ref dropped the puck, a fight broke out between the two captains in the faceoff circle. They dropped their sticks and gloves, grabbed each other's jerseys and began spinning around throwing punches.

The crowd went even more wild. Lara grabbed the sleeve of my jersey in excitement. I looked down where she grabbed my jersey and she noticed me looking.

She immediately withdrew her hand. I must have given her a weird look. I wasn't aware of it. I was so involved with the fight on the ice that it didn't occur to me she may have been flirting with me. She had an apologetic look on her face and said, "Sorry."

Of course, I had to ruin what could have been a fun moment.

Stupid. I mentally smacked my head.

I had to do something. I couldn't let her think she did something wrong. I smiled at her and then grabbed her jersey and pretended to mimic the fight on the ice.

She started laughing at my poor fighting stance. She said, "I would kick your butt!"

I said, "I'd like to see you try…"

"You're on!" She pointed her index finger at me and squinted her eyes trying to be intimidating. It was quite cute, actually. She turned her attention back to the ice and shouted, "We're missing the fight!"

The fight ended once our captain landed the final punch to the chin to the Forsyth City's Firestix captain which made him drop to his knees.

This was the referee's cue to skate over and break apart the two opponents. They were both escorted to the penalty box and were each assessed a five-minute major for fighting. The game went on without the two captains for now. There was a bunch of back and forth passing with a few shots here and there but nothing to break the 2-2 tie. The whistle blew after the puck went out of play and the two captains had served their time. The penalty box doors opened up and they both skated back to the bench to join the rest of their teams.

About a minute later, our team captain's shift began. He hopped over the wall as a passing teammate climbed onto the bench to complete the shift change. Our captain was about to accept a pass from our defensemen when he was met with a monstrous check by the Firestix captain. The hit was so big that our captain went air born. He spun around in mid-flight and fell hard to the ice. The crowd erupted with boo's. Fans waved their hands and pointed at our captain looking for a penalty. The referees ignored it and let the teams play on as he continued lying on the ice, obviously injured.

Both Lara and I started banging on the glass and yelling at the refs. It obviously didn't make a difference, but we liked to think it did.

The Firestix captain took the puck which was intended for our captain and made his way up the ice. He bounced the puck off the wall to skate around our only defensemen. He accepted his own pass and was now on a break-a-way. He approached our goal, faked a shot on his right and made our goalie go down to block the shot. As our goalie moved one way, the Firestix captain moved to the other direction. He flicked his stick and put the puck into the upper corner of the net. The buzzer went off and the lights behind the goal started flashing. He skated around the back of the goal with his hands raised high above his head while his teammates on the ice met him there.

The rest of the Firestix team started to jump off the bench to join their winning teammates but not before the Devils began going after anyone they could get their hands on. Fights broke out between almost every player on the ice. Our captain was finally helped off the ice. That cheap shot the refs chose to ignore had cost us the game.

The crowd booed and started a "cheater" chant.

Whether it was directed toward the referees or toward the captain of the other team, it didn't matter. They both deserved it. It was a horrible ending to an amazing game and a very exciting series.

My co-workers and I parted ways once we made it to the parking lot, except for Lara and me. I walked her to her car as we discussed the unfortunate loss.

"What a game, huh? We definitely got screwed out of that one," she said.

"Yeah, we did. It was a good game though. Those refs just have it in for us. They hardly see anything the other teams do, but they always call penalties against us. It's ridiculous!"

"It's because our hockey team is so strong on the ice, and we don't take any crap from anyone. We would easily beat every team we faced if those refs didn't cheat us. They've got it out for us, for sure. We have to play harder every time to make up for those stupid refs," Lara said.

The fans of Decker City are passionate about their sports, and Lara fit right in. I definitely needed to take her to another game next season.

We made it to her car much too quickly. Lara took her keys out of her purse and started jingling them in her hand, instead of opening the car door.

I knew this sign; she was waiting for me to kiss her. It probably would have been an opportunistic time for this to happen, but I guess I didn't see our first kiss being in the middle of a dirty parking lot with thousands of drunken witnesses.

Maybe it was the butterflies in my stomach. Whatever the case may be, I didn't go through with it.

She looked at me and said, "I had a good time tonight."

"Me too," I replied as we both smiled at each other.

Before the awkward silence began, I leaned in and gave her a hug.

She wrapped her arms around me and squeezed.

It was a long hug. It was the best feeling in the world to be close to her.

Was I hugging her too long?

I pulled away first. I said, "I always enjoy those Lara bear hugs."

She smiled, but I could sense a tug of disappointment around her eyes. She started to reach for her door.

I said, "I'll see you Monday. Be careful on your way home."

She unlocked her car door and grabbed the handle. Lara opened the door and looked back at me. "You too. Enjoy the rest of your weekend."

I walked back to my car, embarrassed and mad at myself. I should have kissed her, even if it was a dirty parking lot. I had the perfect opportunity and I blew it. I could tell she wanted me to kiss her, so why didn't I?

It seemed like I walked for miles from where Lara parked to my car. When I finally made it to my car and drove toward the exit, it seemed like no one was moving. I sat there in the parking lot for what seemed like an eternity. 25,000 drunken, angry fans leaving at the same time wasn't something I planned for this evening. No one had left early. Not for the final playoff game. And that just made matters worse when it was over.

Once I finally made it out of the parking lot, I made a right down Broad Street and headed for the highway to go home.

***

I was two miles from my exit. I entered a small two lane bridge. That was my signal that I was almost home.

The houses along the river during the night were lit up with colorful lights. It had snowed earlier and the lights reflecting off the snow and ice over the water made everything sparkle.

Out of nowhere, my car jerked to the right and my back window shattered.

Someone had hit me.

My car lurched forward and spun out.

Adrenaline.

My body panicked and my mind went numb.

I tried to regain control, but my tires continued sliding to the right no matter what I did.

Black ice.

Helpless to do anything else, I kept pumping the brakes and turning the wheel.

I couldn't remember in that moment if I was supposed to turn into the skid or away from it, but it was too late anyway.

I was committed.

The brakes finally engaged. I could hear the tires of my car screeching along the pavement.

The car stopped.

My heart was pumping out of my chest. I was breathing so hard my lungs felt like they were on fire.

I patted my chest, my legs, my face. I was all right.

I turned every which way in my seat, trying to assess my situation so I could get out of there.

To my horror, I saw that I was now in the right lane, perpendicular to oncoming traffic. My car was facing the river.

Something caught my eye in the passenger side window.

Headlights.

"Do you remember anything else?" Officer Reed asked me.

I shook my head. "That's it. After that was blackness and then coughing up water."

Suddenly the officer's radio chimed to life. He grabbed it off the dirt next to him and turned it up to respond. "Reed here. Go ahead."

"Sixty seconds out. Did you find the body? Over."

The officer grabbed his radio. He turned away from me, hoping I couldn't hear the radio operator.

I heard.

"Reed? You there?"

"Yeah, I'm here," Reed said. "We have a male in his 20's needing immediate medical attention. Come prepared with warm towels and clothing if you have any. We are located below the highway next to the broken guard rail. Over."

"Wait, the victim is alive?"

The officer looked back at me again.

This was very weird. I'm a victim? And a body?

Reed glanced away. "Yes, he's alive. Hurry."

Yes, he's alive?

As if being in a car accident couldn't get any worse.

"What do you mean I'm alive? What exactly happened?" I asked.

Officer Reed looked reluctant to come forth with an explanation. He sighed and spoke in rapid fire. "I arrived a few minutes after your accident. Your story matches up with what I was told. Your vehicle was hit and it smashed through that guard rail above, tumbling down here and landing in the river in front of us. Your car submerged with you inside."

"I was still inside?"

He nodded. "Presumably unconscious after the vehicle collided with yours. I received the 9-1-1 call and arrived ten to fifteen minutes later. When I got here, people were pointing to the river and saying a car was in there with someone inside. I rushed down the hill and dove into the freezing river to fish you out of your car. When I finally found you, you were still strapped to your seatbelt. I cut it off and pulled you to the surface. I brought you to the ground here and began CPR. I figured with the amount of time you were under water I didn't have a chance. I attempted anyway."

The flashing lights from the ambulance began to reflect off the darkness of the water.

Officer Reed turned around. "Good timing."

I started shivering uncontrollably. I couldn't tell if it was because of the cold or the fear and confusion from my car accident. "How long was I under?"

Officer Reed started to wrap his arms around me because of my shaking. "Let's just say you're lucky to be alive."

"What do you mean by that?"

"Well, either you are the only person I know that can hold their breath for a long time or you have one special guardian angel watching over you. I could have pronounced you dead. You had no pulse and no signs of life. You were under that water for a long time."

I stared at him in disbelief.

He continued. "Look, there's a general consensus that the human brain cannot survive without oxygen for longer than six minutes. You seem to be doing all right after about twenty."

I couldn't believe it. I should be dead. Under water for twenty minutes? I think the longest I ever held my breath was about 30 seconds.

The shaking became worse.

The officer held me tighter.

"Hurry up! He's going into shock!" he yelled to the paramedics above.

Within seconds, someone came down the hill and wrapped a warm blanket around me.

"It's going to be okay," I heard someone say. The warm blanket helped a little. I laid my head back against the officer's shoulder.

I closed my eyes and everything went black again.

I awoke on my way to the hospital. I was strapped to a gurney on the bumpiest ride I'd ever experienced.

Don't they put shocks on ambulances?

The only good part was that I was in clean and dry clothes. I had multiple towels laid on top of me. I still felt a little cold, but the towels and dry clothes were warming me up.

Once we arrived at the hospital, the nurses treated my wounds. I had a few bumps and bruises, two bruised eyes, and whiplash. I didn't have any broken bones, but my body still really hurt.

All I wanted to do was sleep, but that wasn't happening anytime soon. I squinted at the bright fluorescent lights.

A doctor brushed past the curtains and came in the room to examine me. He began looking through my papers. "So Devin, I see here you were in quite the accident. I've got to say, I'm extremely pleased that you walked away with just a few minor injuries. Most people aren't quite as lucky as you."

20 minutes under icy water? It's more than lucky. I would call it a miracle. I nodded my head ever so slightly. "Yeah, I guess so," I replied.

"We owe your life to the heroism of Officer Reed. He's the one who pulled you out of the water," the doctor said.

Officer Reed, I don't think I ever thanked him. I'll definitely have to do that when I see him again.

The doctor then introduced himself. "I'm Dr. Andrew Kane." He reached out to shake my hand.

I reached out and took his hand. My handshake was weak, wet and fishy. "Sorry for the limp handshake. It's usually much stronger," I said.

"No worries. You're doing great to have a handshake at all at this point." He whistled while he looked through my papers.

Then he stopped whistling and looked puzzled. He studied the page in front of him. His brows furrowed deeper.

This had me worried. Doctors should know what's going on. They shouldn't look confused.

He cocked his head to the side and said, "Hmm…"

Okay, he had my attention now.

He looked up at me for a moment and then back down to his papers.

What was going on?! Was there something else wrong with me? Was I dying after all?

The loud tick of the sterile white clock on the wall kept the time as he studied that same page. It felt like an eternity.

"How are you feeling?" he asked.

"I'm in some pain, but I guess it could be worse, right?" I said.

"So you don't have any problems with any bodily functions? Walking? Talking? Breathing? Any memory issues?" he asked me.

I began thinking for a moment. I knew what day it was, I knew my birth date, I knew my address, I could remember the accident and I could think back to my early childhood memories. I even knew the name of the president…they always asked that question.

I was walking earlier, so I knew that was good. I was breathing, right? I took a deep breath in and then exhaled.

The doctor smiled.

"No, I think I'm okay," I simply said as I felt my face flush red with embarrassment.

He looked at me as if he was expecting a different answer. He pursed his lips together as if to hum something but nothing came out. "I would like to run some tests, if you don't mind."

He asked as if I had a choice.

"I would just like to do a brain scan. You experienced a traumatizing event and based on the police report with this time frame…" he paused. "Your brain was without oxygen for longer than it should have been. Technically, you should be…well…let's just say you are very lucky to be alive and fully functioning right now."

"Wait a minute. Are you telling me that there may be something wrong with me?" I asked. My heart started racing. What was wrong with me?

I didn't feel any different, besides the physical injuries. "Do I have brain damage?"

"No, I didn't say that. Based on what I've seen here and what I've read in the report, there seems to be a mistake or some confusion because this can't be right," he replied.

I must have looked at him like a deer in headlights.

"I can see you're confused. Let me explain." He sat down in the chair across from me, put his folder down on his lap and took a deep breath. "A human brain needs oxygen to survive, we all know this. When the brain lacks oxygen, it's called cerebral hypoxia. Head trauma, choking, suffocation and in your case, drowning can all create conditions that lead to cerebral hypoxia. Brain cells are extremely sensitive to oxygen deprivation. Many begin to die as early as four or five minutes. Once the cells die, they're gone. In early stages, a patient may experience memory loss, problems with basic motor functions and inattentiveness. The more serious stages include comas, seizures and death."

Dr. Kane let that sink in for a few seconds before he continued. "The reason I asked those questions earlier and why I want to have a brain scan is because from what I'm seeing in the police report, you were without oxygen for over twenty minutes. According to the report, you should have drowned."

"I thought there were people who could hold their breath for a long time?"

"Not like that. Besides, what's the longest you've ever held your breath?"

"Maybe thirty seconds. In high school swimming class."

The doctor said nothing.

He didn't need to.

"So you're saying I should be dead?" I asked.

"Technically, yes. Any other person would have died on the scene. This report should say you drowned, and in all honesty, you did. But somehow you're sitting with me here, alive and well." He grabbed the folder again and opened it up. He moved a few pages around and said, "The police report says the accident was first reported at 11:38 PM from a 9-1-1 call. We can assume the accident took place a few minutes prior to the call coming in. A police officer arrived on the scene thirteen minutes later."

Dr. Kane looked up at me and shrugged his shoulders. "Traffic."

Wonderful, I have a doctor that has a sense of humor about my near-death experience.

"He got you out of the water and had you breathing by…" He trailed off as he scrolled his finger down the page. "…11:57 PM. So, from the looks of things, you were under that water for a long time. I don't know what happened to you during that time, but I just want to make sure everything is working the way it should. You are in a rare, if not an impossible scenario so I want to take the necessary steps in this situation."

"Could I have had an air bubble in there?"

"No. The officer reports here that the car was filled with water. And the witnesses state that the car filled with water immediately."

I stared dumbly at the white curtain surrounding my bed.

Dr. Kane closed his folder, stood up and smiled. He walked over to me, patted my shoulder and said, "Just wait here and relax."

My eyes flicked to his. "Relax? Are you serious?"

Dr. Kane chuckled. "I'll come back when I get everything set up for you. In the meantime, do you have someone you would like to call to let them know where you are and what happened?"

"My, uhh…my grandfather," I stuttered.

He pulled the curtains aside and left the room only to came back a few seconds later with a portable phone from one of the offices. "Push one to dial out and then put in the phone number to call. I'll be back shortly."

He left.

The room seemed to close in around me. I was sweating. My heart was racing. I could feel it pounding in my head. Was I panicking or was this a symptom of cerebral hypoxia?

I needed to calm down.

What did the doctor say? Symptoms were memory loss, problems with basic motor functions and inattentiveness.

None of those applied to me. I'm fine. I'm really fine.

I looked at the phone, realizing I had a death grip on it.

I eased the tension in my hands and used my shirt to wipe the sweat off. I pressed one to dial out and began to dial my grandfather's phone number.

On the fourth ring, I expected the voicemail to kick in. Instead, I heard some rustling on the other end of the phone and a faint, "Uhh, hello?"

"Hi Grandpa, it's Devin. I'm sorry I had to wake you."

There was some more rustling on the phone.

It sounded like he was sitting up, trying to wake up and talk. "Oh, uhh, it's okay." He paused and then asked, "Is everything all right? It's 2:30 in the morning."

"Not really. I've had some…car trouble."

That was the appropriate way to tell someone you were in a car accident, supposedly died but came back, right?

"How soon could you get to Decker City Hospital? I've had quite an interesting night…"

CHAPTER THREE

I sat alone in the doctor's office. The white walls surrounded me in my thoughts while I waited for the results from my brain scans. Every time I closed my eyes, I saw the headlights of the vehicle that hit my car. Right before they make contact, I opened my eyes and my heart started to race.

The doctor's words echoed in my head. *Your brain was without oxygen for longer than it should have.* I kept replaying the accident over and over again, trying to piece it together. What happened to me under that water? How did I survive this ordeal?

My alone time didn't last long though as I heard my grandfather storming through the hallways.

"Devin?! Where's my grandson Devin? What did you idiots do with him? Devin?!"

If I wasn't already immune to his crazy antics, I might have been embarrassed. Instead, it was a welcomed distraction.

My grandfather was the type of person who would turn the attention on himself, rather than you. I'm not quite sure if he even knew half the time he was embarrassing himself because he didn't care what people thought of him. I really admired that. He'd do anything to make sure you were okay. Especially me. He loved to make people laugh, though some people thought he was crazy until they got to know him. The nurses out there might think he's nuts, but listening to him yell my name made me happy.

He had been there for me since the beginning. My parents died when I was only three. My mother developed breast cancer just after I was born, but a doctor misdiagnosed her illness and it went untreated for six months. By the time the doctors discovered what was really happening, the cancer had spread to her lungs and her stomach.

My father took her to specialist after specialist to get as much treatment done as they possibly could to prolong her life. From what my grandfather told me, my father loved her dearly. She was his life. They were childhood sweethearts. They first met in elementary school and were inseparable ever since. They became best friends growing up and they began dating just after they graduated high school. Once they both graduated college and found jobs, they got married. Two years later they had me.

My mother bravely tried every treatment the doctors came up with. After a while, it just made her weak, and I think she eventually gave up. She died a few days after they put her on hospice. After being inseparable with her since they were children, a week after my mother passed away, I was told my father died of a broken heart.

I suspect my grandfather was covering for my father's suicide.

I didn't blame my grandfather for not telling me. I was too young at the time to fully understand what happened.

My grandfather took me in and raised me on his own since my grandmother had passed away before I was born. He has been there for me ever since the death of my parents.

He used to own a scrap metal yard. His father owned it before him. My grandfather dropped out of high school to help his father with the family business. Once his father passed away, the business became his. He expanded and opened up two more scrap metal yards before big corporations came in and made him an offer he couldn't refuse. My grandfather has been retired since he was 45. Now, he just sits on his computer and day trades in the stock market. He's very good at it, too. I learned a lot from him, and I learned to enjoy it. That's why I now work for TruGuard, one of Decker City's best investment companies. Without my grandfather, I don't know where I would have ended up.

Whenever I tell him how grateful I am that he took me in and saved me, he tells me that I saved him, too. When I was younger, I didn't really understand what he meant. But now I see that he was left alone when my mother died. Both of us were.

"Us Shephards gotta stick together," he'd always tell me with a half-grin.

The doctor's door flew open with such force, it was like a fan began blowing air into the room.

My grandfather burst through the doorway. "There you are! It would have been nice if you answered me instead of sitting in here, smirking like an idiot. What in tarnation are you smiling at anyway? Never mind why." He came over and hugged me. "I'm glad you're okay."

"Me too," I said.

He squeezed harder and took the breath out of me.

I was gasping for air. "Too tight."

"Sorry," he said as he released his grip and took a step backwards. "So, tell me what happened." He sat beside me.

I told him about the accident, what the doctor said and that I just had a couple of different tests done. He remained quiet and expressionless. A few seconds later he broke the silence. "So my grandson is indestructible—" He began to smirk and exclaimed, "That's awesome! So tell me the truth, you had a snorkel down there with you, huh? Don't lie to me!"

I started laughing.

His face became serious. "You cheated death twice tonight. You survived a serious car accident and you survived drowning. Don't get greedy."

I shook my head to agree with him.

The door opened again and the doctor walked in. He was looking down at his folder, engrossed in whatever he saw there. "Devin, I have the results from your scans." He looked up, catching my grandfather's eye. "I'm Dr. Andrew Kane, Devin's doctor this evening." He reached out and shook my grandfather's hand.

My grandfather stood to greet him. "I'm Paul, Devin's grandfather."

They both sat down.

"I have some good news," Dr. Kane began. "I looked over the results from your scans and I don't see any damage or anything that would be a cause for concern."

Immediately, all the stress and tension melted from my body.

"But..." he continued.

I held my breath in anticipation of some bad news.

"There are some strange spots on your scan. It's very rare. I have seen cases like this before, but..." He trailed off again. Grabbing a picture out of his folder, he placed it on the table in front of me and my grandfather. He pointed to it. "This is an imaging of an average human brain through our P.E.T. scans. Do you notice the different colors on the pages?"

Both my grandfather and I nodded in agreement.

"These colors represent brain activity. The darker colors mean higher brain activity in those areas and the lighter colors represent lesser brain activity, not that lesser is a bad thing. It just means certain parts of the brain aren't stimulated or as stimulated at the moment."

I tried to understand what he was talking about. I was suddenly regretting not paying attention in human anatomy class. I furrowed my brow and leaned closer.

Dr. Kane then pulled out another sheet and placed it on the table in front of us. He looked at me and said, "Devin, this is your scan." He pointed to the shades of colors on both mine and the other human brain and said, "Do you see the differences between these two?"

I looked at both as closely as I could. "They look pretty much the same," I answered.

"Well, it's there. It's quite hard to see actually. It looks like during your... incident...neurotransmitters flooded the left side of your brain and essentially changed some of its structure." He pointed to a spot on the page and said, "Right here, there's a small color change."

I saw what he meant but I didn't understand it.

My grandfather chimed in. "Okay... So what does that mean?"

"It could mean nothing. Or it could mean something. Some of the previous cases have shown people with this occurrence experiencing hyper-specialized senses. And sometimes, it has shown nothing. I believe it is different for every individual." The doctor then looked at me. "Right now, you are one of maybe a handful of people to have this happen. This is a very special case and it's something I would like to keep a close watch on. As of now, you're fine and like I said, I don't see anything on these scans to show any sign of concern. You're a very lucky guy."

All of this information was a lot to absorb. I wasn't really sure what I was feeling. Knowing something changed in my brain set me on edge and made me nervous. However, hyper-specialized senses didn't sound awful. Did he mean enhanced eye sight or taste or smell? Would I get better vision? Maybe I could have x-ray vision like Superman. That would be interesting. Or maybe—"

"Devin," Dr. Kane said, snapping me out of my thoughts. "Are you listening?"

I was so deep in thought I had no idea my grandfather and my doctor were talking. "Yeah, I'm sorry."

"I want to see you again in two weeks. You should take it easy over the next few days. If you notice any changes, please don't hesitate to call me," Dr. Kane said. He reached in his coat pocket, pulled out a business card and handed it to me. "I'm available 24 hours a day. Any changes or any questions, please call me."

"Thank you," I replied.

My grandfather followed suit. "Thank you, Dr. Kane. I appreciate you taking care of my grandson." He stood up and reached out to shake the doctor's hand.

Dr. Kane turned his attention to me. I shook his hand and thanked him again. My grandfather and I walked out of his office and toward the elevators at the end of the hall. My grandfather reached out and pushed the down button. We stood there in silence waiting for the elevator to arrive. The elevator doors dinged and proceeded to open. We both stepped in and the doors shut. I suddenly heard my grandfather humming the song playing in the elevator. I start listening closely and notice it was an instrumental version of *Crash Test Dummies—Mmm Mmm Mmm Mmm*. How appropriate. A car crash song playing for a recent car accident victim.

"Really, Grandpa? You're going to get into this song after what I just experienced?" I asked.

He looked at me and shrugged his shoulders. "What? I like this song."

CHAPTER FOUR

On the drive home, my grandfather and I remained quiet. After my horrific accident and being awake for almost 24 hours, my body was shutting down. My grandfather must have been tired, too, after I woke him in the middle of the night. I felt awful about that, but I was thankful to have him there to help me through this.

My grandfather promised to help me look for a new car during the week. In the meantime, he told me I could drive his car as long as I didn't go sailing down the river with it.

Despite hitting every green light on the way back to my grandfather's home, the ride seemed to take longer than usual. Maybe it was just the quiet ride or maybe it was because I just wanted to get back to his house and go to sleep. The doctor's words kept echoing in my head. *Hyper-specialized senses.* It made me think about all the superhero comics my grandfather used to share with me while I was growing up.

My grandfather had boxes upon boxes of these old comics in one of his closets. He was a dedicated comic collector. I wouldn't be surprised if he had first edition volumes of many different comic series.

My grandfather used to read comics to me instead of traditional bedtime stories. I loved them. Eventually, once I learned to read, he gave me some of his collection to start sorting through and read on my own. My grandfather would always bring home new comics for us to read together. We would read for hours.

We drove by a flashy billboard advertising a car model's new year release. It jerked my mind to the present, back to my visit at the hospital. Only a handful of cases like mine had ever been noted in medical history. Some of them experienced enhanced senses.

Would I have enhanced senses? What did that even mean? Would I inherit a stronger sense of smell? That would be something I don't think I'd enjoy. There are just some smells not worth smelling. Stronger hearing would be interesting though. Maybe a healing ability? I wonder how that would work. My palms began to sweat and I felt my heart beat a little faster.

Hey, calm, down, I told myself. What were the chances of having something like this happen to me anyway? Was it even worth thinking about?

My mind wouldn't rest. I started thinking about all the superheroes and their superpowers my grandfather and I loved. There was super speed, x-ray vision, regeneration, flying–

My grandfather's car door shut with a solid metal bang. I turned to the left. His seat was empty. I panicked for a split second, but then I saw my grandfather standing outside with his arms up in the air.

"Are you coming or what?" he asked me.

I unbuckled my seatbelt, threw it back over my shoulder and grabbed the handle to exit the vehicle.

The sun was just beginning to rise as I entered my old bedroom. The sunlight radiated into the room from the open window near the corner. I walked over to the window and closed the blinds. I turned around to look at my room. It had been unchanged since I moved out a few years ago. Comic book memorabilia posters from my childhood still covered the walls, acting like colorful wallpaper. My old soccer and baseball trophies were still on the book shelf, tucked behind all the bobble heads I collected when I was younger.

It was nice being back in my old bedroom. It felt comfortable and safe and that's exactly what I needed right now.

I turned around to sit down on the bed and started untying my shoes. I was still very sore from the accident and untying my shoes proved to be a tougher task than I thought it would be.

I needed sleep.

After untying my shoe laces, I slipped my shoes off each foot. I took my cell phone out of my pocket and placed it on the night stand. It was one of the few things that actually flew out of the vehicle and remained dry before my car and I submerged under the water. The phone had definitely seen better days, but it still managed to work. I pushed myself backwards to the head of the bed and just collapsed. I slipped under the covers and let the sleep settle in.

I opened my eyes to the blurry sight of my grandfather standing over me.

"You sleep funny," he said, glaring at me with his creepy stare.

I felt his breath on my face. I blinked.

The end of his nose was only an inch from mine.

I threw my head back from the shock of him being so close to my face, except I hadn't fully realized I was on a pillow and couldn't go back any further. Pain instantly filled my neck and head. The pain from my whiplash made its comeback. "Geez, Grandpa. Must you be right up in my face?" I asked.

"Sorry, I was making sure you were still breathing on me and didn't check out last night. You just happened to wake up as I was checking."

"Oh, thanks," I said sarcastically. I eased into a sitting position and began rubbing my neck, trying to ease the pain.

"Here," my grandfather reached in his pocket and handed me three pills. "Take these. It'll help with the pain."

I grabbed them and tossed them in my mouth. I reached over to the bedside table and grabbed the bottled water my grandfather left for me. I took a drink to help wash the pills down. "Thanks. What is it?" I asked.

"Cocaine in a pill form," he said.

"What?!" I yelled. "You gave me drugs?!" I could feel my face flush red with anger.

My grandfather started cracking up with laughter.

I looked at him and once he calmed down he said, "It's ibuprofen, you dummy." He turned for the bedroom door, still laughing.

Of course. Grandpa up to his same old tricks. Where would he ever get drugs from anyway?

He got to the edge of my door, turned around with a big smile on his face and said, "You're so gullible. It was too easy." He continued out the door and his laugh echoed as he walked down the hallway.

"I just woke up!" I tried yelling out to him. "Of course I'll fall for your jokes now!" I was quiet as I listened for a response, but none came.

Oh well, he must not have heard me.

I grabbed my phone on my night table to check the time. "Wow," I said out loud to myself.

My grandfather came peeking back in the door frame. "What's wrong?"

"Oh, that you hear?" I said. "It's 4:45 in the afternoon. Why did you let me sleep this late?"

"I didn't feel like making three meals for you. I figured if I had only had one to make, I'd have less to clean up," he said.

"Thanks. I feel the love."

"See? I knew you'd understand." He turned and walked back out of my bedroom.

Once he left, I went back to my phone. I had a text message from Lara that she'd sent this morning. I hadn't even thought about looking at my phone. I opened up the text and read her message.

I had a good time at the game last night. Don't forget to watch 'When Zombies Ruled the World' tonight. See ya Monday!

Crap! I completely forgot about the zombie show tonight. *When Zombies Ruled the World* was one of our favorite shows on TV. I couldn't miss an episode and lose my chance to discuss it with her.

I wondered why she didn't ask about my car accident. Then it hit me. No one knew about it. I hadn't told anyone other than my grandfather. I picked up my phone to text her back.

I had a good time as well, except for the car accident I was involved in on my way home. Don't worry, I'm fine. I'll explain tomorrow. I'll watch our show tonight. Lunch tomorrow?

I put my phone back down on the night table and rolled the covers off of me. I threw my legs over the bed and sat there for a minute. I still felt exhausted.

My phone vibrated. It echoed off the wooden night stand which made the vibration seem much more intense then it was. I reached back onto my night table to grab my phone. It was a text from Lara.

Are you okay? What happened?!?

I typed back, *I'm fine, just a little sore and banged up. I'll tell you all about it tomorrow.*

This time I kept the phone in my hand, anticipating a response. It made me feel good knowing Lara cared about me. It gave me a little more confidence. I'd ask her out one day soon. It just worried me that I might ruin what a great friendship we already had. She was one of my closest friends. My phone began to vibrate in my hand.

Okay. I'm here to talk if you need me. Tomorrow at lunch, you owe me a good story. Feel better!

Thanks, I typed into the phone. I put the phone back on my night stand and stood up. I lifted my arms in the air and stretched everything out. It felt wonderful, but it didn't help my achy neck and head. I walked out of my bedroom to join my grandfather downstairs for dinner.

When I got to the kitchen, he was just hanging up the phone.

"Who was that?" I asked.

"The pizza man," he said.

I raised an eyebrow at him. "So much for cooking dinner, huh?"

"Of all the years you've known me, have you ever seen me cook? And I mean really cook–not making waffles, or bacon, or soup, or pasta, or the occasional stir fry, or a salad, or–"

I cut him off sticking my hand up at him. "Okay, okay. I get your point."

He looked proud of himself for a moment. "Actually, come to think of it, I can make quite a few things."

"No, no, you can't," I said, starting to laugh. "You burn the waffles, and the bacon is either not cooked enough or too crispy. The soup? You make that from either a box or a can, how can you screw that up? Same with pasta. And a salad? Really? You are the biggest carnivore I know. The only time I've ever seen you have a salad is when it comes free with your meal at a restaurant."

The way he squinted his eyes and pursed his lips, I could tell he was looking for a witty comeback.

I knew I had him beat.

He accepted defeat and said, "Touché."

I made a fist and threw my right arm in the air and exclaimed, "And a victory goes to me!" I regretted doing that as the pain in my neck shot through me again. I lowered my arm and said, "So, what is that, like 8 wins to your 850?"

"You're catching up, I'm so proud of you," he said.

The pizza arrived. In moments, we were both eating at his kitchen table. We discussed the accident, which lead to a conversation about what car I may want to get.

Per usual, he had to bring up the girl conversation. As if I didn't have enough on my mind already.

"So, have you started dating this Lara Croft character yet?" he asked.

"Her name is Lara Scarlett, Grandpa. Not the fictional video game character you seem to have a huge crush on."

He winked at me and said, "All I'm saying is that you should ask her out. I know you like her."

"I will. I looked away. "Well, I want to. I do like her, I'm just afraid I'll screw it up."

My grandfather shook his head. "Full of excuses are we? Let me tell you a little story about your parents." He stuffed the rest of his pizza in his mouth and then picked up a napkin to wipe his hands. He took a big gulp of his beer. "Your father and my daughter, your mother, were best friends growing up. You know this already. I kept asking your mother why she wasn't dating this guy. She kept saying they talked about it before and they didn't want to ruin their friendship. They had been friends for 10 years or so. But I could tell she really liked him. I found out it was him who held back. He didn't want to lose the friendship with her if they dated and something went wrong."

"How did you know?" I asked.

"Your mom eventually told me. Your father always said she was his best friend and he didn't want to lose that if something bad happened and they didn't work out. I know it's usually the other way around with the girl not wanting to risk the friendship, but your dad was a special kind of man. I knew from the moment I met him he was one of the good ones. He was an honest and caring guy. He was someone I wished my daughter would end up with." He leaned in a little closer to me. "You'll understand one day if you ever have a daughter."

His eyes began gloss over as he continued. "Anyway, he finally grew up and got over his fear and asked her out during the summer after they graduated high school. I remember your mother coming home with the biggest smile on her face. I never saw her so excited and so happy in all my life. It was like a dream come true for her. Your father took that risk and it paid off. They fell in love, if they weren't already in love during their years of friendship. And then they got married. They were the happiest couple I've ever seen."

His happiness turned sour as the smile disappeared and was replaced with a frown. "I know this story doesn't have the happiest of endings, but that was a completely unexpected tragedy." He wiped away the wetness from his eyes and continued. "Anyway, the point I was trying to make was that I know where you're coming from. I know what you're afraid of. But if you don't take that chance, you'll never know what you're going to miss out on."

I couldn't decide whether to be depressed by my grandfather's story or encouraged by it. I know he was trying to help me out, and my parent's story is a perfect example of the point he was trying to make. I knew he was right, too. I also knew how their story had ended. I nodded my head and said, "I know, Grandpa. Maybe I'll talk to her tomorrow."

"Well, you may want to wait a few days. I don't know if she wants a raccoon man asking her out," he said, mocking my two black eyes.

"Wow, thanks," I said, trying to shake off a smile. "You sure know how build up my confidence."

He stood and patted me on the back as he walked over to wrap the rest of the pizza up in foil to put in the fridge. I helped with the dishes and grabbed my stuff from my bedroom. "I'm gonna get going, Grandpa." I was recording my show back at home and wanted to watch it before I went back to sleep.

He gave me his keys to the car and hugged me. "Be careful driving home. I don't want a phone call again tonight."

"I'll be careful, don't worry," I reassured him. We parted ways and I entered his car to begin my drive home.

During the ride, I constantly searched around me, fearful of the other cars. It wasn't that I didn't trust myself behind the wheel. I was severely distrustful of everyone else on the road. I could feel my whole body tense up as I drove. This only made the pounding in my head worse.

After what seemed like an extremely long 16-minute drive, I arrived home in one piece. I parked the car in my assigned spot in my apartment complex. I turned off the engine. The languid thought that I should get out of the car crossed my mind. But I just sat there for a moment as everything that happened this weekend began to sink in.

I almost died. What if I had died? I would've missed out on ever asking Lara out. I would've missed all the exciting opportunities that I turned down because I was always too busy with work or just wanting to go home and relax. I never would have had the chance to travel. I've lived in Decker City my entire life. I've always wanted to travel, but I never have.

I needed to make sure I didn't pass up an opportunity again. I needed to make sure I didn't let life pass me by. Who knows when my time will be up?

I also needed to take my grandfather's advice. If my father didn't wait as long as he did to start dating my mother, they would have had more time together as a couple. He wasted so much time dwelling on the negative possibilities and the what-ifs rather than just living his life.

I wondered if that meant that I took after my father. I looked up at the roof of my car and said, "Thanks, Dad."

Why couldn't I find the confidence to ask Lara on a date? I know she'll say yes, so what am I waiting for?

I wasn't going to wait anymore.

I finally got out of the car feeling energized and excited about tomorrow. I made my way inside my eight story apartment building. I lived on the top floor and had to wait for the elevator to arrive in the lobby to take me to my cozy apartment.

Once I made it inside my apartment, I headed for the medicine cabinet in my bathroom to find something to help with my headache. I found some Advil and popped a few pills in my mouth. I turned on the faucet, cupped my hands with water and used that to wash them down.

After a shower, I sat down on my sofa and grabbed the remote to turn the TV on. I found *When Zombies Ruled the World* on my recordings and pushed play. I only made it halfway through the episode before I fell asleep on the couch.

CHAPTER FIVE

I arrived at work early to avoid possible confrontations with anyone who might have found out about my accident. I didn't want to talk about it. I didn't like bringing my personal business to work. I knew my injuries would give people around here a nice talking point. Gossip spreads quickly around the office and I wanted to stay out of the spotlight for as long as I could. The only one I wanted to see or speak with was Lara.

I sneaked into my office and shut my door. I walked over to my desk and sunk into my office chair. My head collapsed against its back. The springs squeaked as I reclined. I rubbed my hands through my intentionally messy hair.

Today is going to suck, I thought. I stared at the ceiling and sighed.

With an abrupt motion that made my head hurt again, I returned to a full upright position and stared at my computer screen. I reached for the keyboard and tapped the space key. My computer came to life.

My head hurt worse when I saw my inbox. I received a ton of email this weekend. The market was down big time on Friday and my clients were freaking out as if it were the end of the world. They see their portfolios go down and they panic. This didn't just apply to my clients. As I learned from my grandfather, this was most of the people who follow the stock market but don't understand it. The market goes up and down. I knew I would be writing 100 emails today, reassuring clients to hang in there and try not to worry.

As I was working on a response to one on my clients, a knock came at my door. I looked up and saw a blurred figure standing outside. Our offices had floor to ceiling decorative ice glass windows. Before I could even say anything, the door swung open.

"What happened to you?!" Tommy exclaimed as he slammed the door behind him. Tommy Gelrod was my closest friend in the office. He started here around the same time I did and we just clicked. We went through training together and pushed each other to pass all our exams. We made it a competition, but it was always in good fun. Once we established a good client base, we were promoted and were given our own offices. His office was right next to mine. This was great, except for the fact that Tommy blasted music and lifted weights during lunch. If I ended up staying in my office during that time, it was never quiet. I could have done without those noisy lunches. It paid off for him though. He was in good shape. He made me look like a twig in comparison.

"Well, won't you come in," I said while waving my hand to a chair. So much for trying to keep a low profile today.

Without missing a beat, he continued, "Seriously, don't give me your sarcasm today. Lara told me you were in a car accident after the game on Saturday. What happened? Why didn't you let me know?"

His voice was full of concern. I'd never seen this side of him before.

Wait, did he say Lara told him?

"Lara's here?" I asked.

"Don't change the subject. Tell me what happened?" Another thing about Tommy. He's always persistent and his size made him quite intimidating. I didn't have a choice at this point. He pulled up one of my two guest chairs and sat across the desk from me, anticipating my story. He waved me on. "So? Let's hear it."

I took in a deep breath and began telling him about the car accident.

"Holy crap, Dude," Tommy said after my story. He leaned back in his chair and said, "That's crazy! I mean, I'm glad you're okay and all, but seriously that's one messed up story."

"Now you know how I feel. I have to constantly relive it in my head." It was a little difficult having to relive that story all over again, but it had to be done. I didn't exactly tell him everything though. I kind of left out the part where my doctor talked about hyper-specialized senses. I didn't want Tommy thinking I was going to be some weirdo now or that something was wrong with me. Certain things you just keep to yourself.

"So how are you feeling?" he asked.

"I'm sore but other than that, I feel fine."

"You're incredibly lucky, Devin. I never expected to hear a story like this from someone I know. It sounds like something I would see on the news. And usually it involves the police pulling a dead body from the wreckage, not a live one. I don't know how you managed to walk away. You must either be indestructible or you're really a cat and you used up all your nine lives in one accident. I'd be careful if I were you."

"I'm careful," I said putting my hands up at him. "What are the chances of something like this happening to me again?"

"Seriously? Don't say that! What are you, stupid? Knock on wood or something, geez!"

I laughed at his superstitious thinking. I stood up and reached across my desk to knock on his head. "There, you happy now?"

It seemed to break the tension as a smile spread across Tommy's face.

"Come on, I've got a lot of work to do this morning."

Tommy stood up and said, "So that's basically the polite way of telling me *get out*."

"Yup."

"Come on, don't leave me now. I don't want to start working yet. I want to hang out a little longer."

I couldn't help but laugh at his whining. I started pushing on his back and assisting him out my office. "We can hang out later, I need to get to work. I haven't been near a computer all weekend and I have a lot to catch up on."

"All right, all right. Monday's suck." Tommy reached for the handle and opened the door. He stepped into the hallway and turned around and said, "Are you going to go talk to your girlfriend?"

I shook my head and rolled my eyes at him. "She's not my girlfriend."

"...Yet." Tommy smiled, winked at me and then strolled down the hallway to his office door.

I closed my door and locked it. I leaned against the glass behind me and pressed my head against the coldness of it. Today was going to be a long day. I hadn't even been here an hour yet and already I was being interrogated about my accident. I pushed myself forward off the glass door and walked back to my desk to get back to work. I sat back down in my chair and noticed my screen saver had activated due to my inactivity. I reached out and pressed a letter on the keyboard and the screen blinked back to life. I opened up an email and started typing a response.

Knock. Knock.

The noise startled me. I looked up from my computer and saw a figure at the door again. "Tommy, I said I needed to get my work done. Come back later."

Knock. Knock. Knock.

The knocking came again, more pronounced and eager this time. I was never going to get any work done today. So much for showing up early. I stood up and walked over to my door. I reached for the lock, unlocked my door and began to open it. "Tommy, seriously, I need to–"

Lara pushed the door out of the way and wrapped her arms around me. "I know you said we'd hang out at lunch, but when Tommy said he saw you, I had to come see you, too."

I winced in pain as she held her strong grip around me. "Not too tight, I'm still in some pain."

She released her bear hug on me and stood back a little. "I'm sorry, I didn't know. How are you feeling?"

"I'm all right, just going through the healing phases now."

"I'm so sorry. I feel horrible you had to go through this. I wish I would have been there with you."

"It's not your fault. I'm glad you weren't with me. Who knows what would have happened to you if you were in the car with me? I barely made it out alive. Don't worry about it though."

"I know, you're right. I just wanted to stop by and say hi. Is there anything I can do for you?"

"I'm okay. I survived and I'll heal up in a few weeks."

"Okay, I'll let you get to work. We're still on for lunch, right?" Lara asked.

"Yes, we are. I'll come get you when I'm ready. Thanks, Lara."

She smiled and said, "You're welcome." She began to walk away but then stopped and turned around. "Text me if you're bored. I can always use some entertainment."

"I will. It can be just as boring in here as it is out there, trust me. Expect a text at some point." I winked at her.

Lara turned and continued her walk down the hall and around the corner. I closed the door, once again locking it. Lara was the only interruption I wanted this morning. I walked back over to my desk and sat down. I started typing a message to one of my clients but after the first sentence, I came to a stop. I needed to get to work, but it was so hard to concentrate. I looked at the time on my computer.

8:47

I groaned and rolled my eyes back in my head. There was so much time left before lunch. I couldn't wait to finally tell Lara how I felt. I daydreamed about our lunch date. First, I'd have to tell her my accident story. I promised her that. I went back and forth in my head, wondering if I should tell her what the doctor said about my hyper-specialized senses. I didn't tell Tommy and I didn't want him to feel betrayed if I told Lara and not him. Usually I told her everything. I started to feel a little guilty at the idea of keeping something from her. Yet, I also didn't want to cause any unnecessary worry if this turned out to be nothing.

8:48

I never understood why time moves at the same speed all the time, yet at this very moment, it felt like it was moving so slow. I knew it was moving at the same speed as it was earlier and it would be moving at the same speed later. But right now, time isn't my friend.

8:49

I found myself watching the second hand tick around the clock. This wasn't helping. I shook my head to clear my thoughts and realized I only wrote one line in a matter of 3 minutes. I tried to think of what to write next.

Nothing came to mind.

The only thing I was thinking about was talking to Lara some more.

Why had I rushed her out of my office this morning?

Screw it. I pulled out my phone and scrolled through to find Lara's contact information. I tapped the text messaging app and began texting Lara.

Finally, it was lunch time. After an unproductive morning, it was time to meet up with Lara. I walked out of my office and down the hallway toward the front of the lobby.

Lara was sitting at her chair behind her large, L-shaped desk when I arrived.

"Ready to go?" I asked.

"Oh hey," she said a little startled as she looked up at me.

I must have scared her.

"Yeah, let me get my jacket." She stood up, grabbed her jacket from behind her chair and put it on.

We were heading to the office's cafeteria, but it was in the annex of our building and we had to walk outside to get there. It was only a 20 second walk outside from building to building, but it required a jacket in this cold weather. The pathway outside had a roof over it just in case of rain or snow. We were thankful we could get to where we needed without getting wet.

Once we made it downstairs, I opened the door to start our walk to the annex. A cold gust of wind welcomed us outside. A shiver ran through my body. Lara, walking to my left, wrapped her arms around my left arm and huddled close to me as we continued our walk.

I could get used to this.

We made our way to the annex and opened the door to the cafeteria. The smell of fresh chicken soup was overwhelming. We got in line and stared at the menu plastered on the wall behind the chefs preparing the food. We both stood there, staring aimlessly at the wall. Lara asked, "What are you thinking?"

"Definitely something warm." I looked up and down the menu until I found something. "The chicken soup and a hot turkey sandwich sounds good."

She nodded.

I placed my order and walked over to pay. The cafeteria food here was pretty decent, compared to cafeteria food in general.

"I'm going to go find us a seat while you get your turkey sandwich, *again*. Why don't you get something different?"

"I get what I enjoy," I told her.

"Well, while you're repeating your common lunch order, would you mind grabbing my lunch, too?" Lara asked. "I also got the chicken soup but with a salad."

"I don't mind. It seems pretty packed in here," I said as I boosted myself up on my tiptoes and looked around the cafeteria. "I hope you can find a seat."

Lara walked into the sea of people trying to find a spot for us.

Once our food was ready, I put it on a tray and walked around the cafeteria until I found Lara.

I sat down at the table.

Before I could even take a spoonful of my hot soup, Lara said, "Okay, you promised. Start talking."

"Aren't you the impatient one? I didn't even take a bite yet."

"Impatient? I have been *patiently* waiting since yesterday afternoon when you let me know what happened. And on top of that, I haven't asked you once to tell me this morning. You promised you would tell me during *lunch* today. It's now lunch time. I think I have patiently waited long enough."

I smiled at her. She was right. She hadn't beg me or harass me about it. She had waited patiently until this very moment. I had to give her credit for that. "Okay, you win. It's lunch time and you were very good."

She raised her eyebrows and tilted her head to the side with a slight smirk. A facial expression which clearly said *I told you so*. It was one of her favorite expressions; one I knew all too well.

"I was driving home from the game and next thing I know, I was clipped by someone and then my car hit a patch of ice. My car spun and finally came to a stop after what felt like an eternity slamming on the brakes trying to get my car to stop spinning. I barely had time to take a breath when my car lit up with bright headlights. The car came at me so fast, I didn't even have a split second to brace myself. The oncoming vehicle plowed into the passenger side of my car and rammed me off the road, through the guardrail and down into the icy river below."

She put her hand over her mouth in shock. She slowly removed her hands from her mouth but then lowered them toward her chin. "I can't even imagine what was going through your mind."

I shook my head. "Nothing. After the car hit me, I was knocked out. My car submerged with me still in it. A police officer arrived and dove in after me. He pulled me from the car and gave me CPR until I started breathing again. So he told me"

"Well, thankfully that officer came when he did. You might have drowned if it weren't for him. Didn't anyone else try and jump in after you?"

"From what I was told, people just stood around and watched. I don't think they knew what to do. They left before I regained consciousness. And as for the drowning part, well..." I trailed off. I didn't know if I wanted to tell her how long I was under the water for and that I should be dead. I fell right back into what my grandfather was telling me yesterday. *No more what ifs.* I was going to tell her. "Technically, I did drown. I was under the water for about 20 minutes."

"What?!" Lara shouted.

I looked around in concern. Even though the cafeteria was already noisy, she managed to draw a few glances.

She covered her mouth with her hands, noticing she was too loud. Her eyes locked on mine, and she uncovered her mouth. "Sorry. So you were under the water for 20 minutes? How is that possible?"

"Honestly, I have no idea. I ask myself that same question. When I met with the doctor after I was taken to the hospital, he was stumped as well. No one seems to have an answer for me. A medical mystery, I guess?"

She sat, stunned and silent.

I used the opportunity to take a bite of my sandwich.

Lara blinked a few more times at me in shock before breaking the silence. "How can the doctors not have an answer for you? What did they say? Did they run any tests?"

"You sure like to ask a lot of questions, don't you?" I asked. I tried to smile to lighten the mood.

"I'm worried about you. It just sounds like your doctor doesn't know what he's doing."

"I'm fine. My doctor knows what he's doing. He ran some tests and everything came back normal. There's nothing to be worried about." Except for the part where my doctor mentioned hyper-specialized senses.

I decided then not to tell her. Yet. I'd already thrown a lot at her today. If I told her about that, she would just be even more worried. "I'm fine, okay?"

"Okay," she agreed.

"Can we talk about the show last night? Or are you still fascinated by my near death experience?"

"I'm glad you think this is all one big joke," Lara said with a hint of anger and disappointment in her voice.

I reached across the table and took her hand. "Trust me, I'm okay. I don't mind joking about it because it already happened. I can't just live my life in a shell now because I almost died. I can't pretend like it didn't happen, but I've got to move on and keep going. There was a time to be serious about it and that was after it happened and when I was at the doctor's office."

Wow, I even surprised myself for a moment. I was actually taking my grandfather's advice and gaining the confidence I needed. It felt good. Now was the time to tell her how I felt.

"I know, I'm sorry. I'm just being weird. Don't mind me," Lara said.

"No, it's okay. I know you care and I know you're worried."

"I do care about you."

"I care about you, too," I said.

I could feel my heart begin to race. Nervousness took over. This was really going to happen now, wasn't it? How would this conversation go? My mouth began to dry out. I needed a drink before I said anything else or the next few words out of my mouth would sound awful.

I let go of her hand and reached out for my water bottle. It slid into my hand as if I was holding a magnet and it attracted the water. I released the grip on it. How did it end up in my hand? I slid my chair back and jumped to my feet, kicking the table in the process and making a screeching noise with the chair.

I could feel hundreds of eyes on me. Did everyone just see that? Was it just me? What just happened?

Lara looked up at me, her face registering a startled expression. "Are you okay? What's wrong?"

"Umm–" I stuttered. Did she see that?

I looked around. I was making a scene. This was bad. But the magnitude of what had happened to the water bottle gripped my mind in shock and fear. I had magically attracted a bottle of water into my hand.

Things weren't going as planned.

Maybe I was overreacting.

But I just reached my hand out and my water bottle slid across the table and into my hand. No, I was definitely not overreacting. I locked eyes with Lara. Her face was full of concern.

"I'm so sorry. I…I need to get to my office." I had to get out of there. As I turned to leave the cafeteria, I could hear her calling my name. I ignored it and didn't turn around. I needed to get back to my office. I needed privacy.

Once I left the cafeteria, I rushed down the hallways to exit the annex to get back to my building. I sprinted outside and back into my building in record time. I hit the elevator button to go to my floor. Thankfully the doors opened right away. I stepped inside the claustrophobic space and hit the number six. The elevator doors shut and started moving up.

I looked down at my hands. They were shaking. I crossed my arms and placed my hands underneath my armpits to prevent them from being noticeable. The elevator reached the sixth floor and dinged. The doors opened. I stepped out and made my way to my office.

As I entered, I turned and closed my door behind me, locking it with a reassuring click. I ran to my desk, placed my jacket on the back on my chair and sat down. I brought my hands in front of me, palms out and just stared at them.

What had just happened to me at the cafeteria? Did that really just happen? It seemed farfetched and unrealistic. I brought my hands down and tapped on my desk as I looked around for something to try and move.

A pen! I opened my desk drawer and found one. I grabbed it and placed on the center of my desk. I took a deep breath in and then out. I kept doing that until I could feel myself calm down.

Once I relaxed, I reached out for the pen. My thumb and index finger were about 2 inches apart with the rest of my fingers curled up as I tried grabbing it from about a foot away.

It didn't move.

I retracted my hand into a fist and then tried again. I reached out with my whole hand this time as if I was grabbing the bottle of water from the cafeteria.

The pen still didn't move.

Of course it didn't. It was impossible. How could I move something without touching it?

I had probably just overreacted and now Lara was probably mad at me for embarrassing her. But then again, how did the bottle find its way into my grip?

I brought my hand back again and tried one more time. Once again, nothing moved. I grabbed the pen and moved it closer, thinking maybe this would help. Why isn't this working? What was I doing wrong?

Maybe it never really happened to begin with. Maybe I just saw something that wasn't there. I reached for it again, and still nothing.

This was ridiculous! I was getting nowhere! It was all a waste of time and I completely ruined a perfectly nice time with Lara.

I waved my hand in annoyance like I was swatting a fly with the back of my hand. The pen flew off the table and slammed into the wall. I jumped out of my seat and backed up against the wall behind me. I never touched the pen. The hairs on the back of my neck were rising.

This was getting creepy. How was this happening? I ran over and picked up the pen. I grabbed my jacket of my chair and headed to Dr. Kane's office. He was the only person who would have answers for me.

CHAPTER SIX

"Hold on, calm down, Devin. You did what?" Dr. Kane said through the phone.

"I made my pen fly across my office without even touching it!" I screamed into my phone. "How many times do I have to repeat myself?" I was freaking out and Dr. Kane was as calm as could be. Was he not realizing the importance of this matter?

"That doesn't make any sense. Are you sure something else didn't make it move?"

"No, because like I told you earlier, I also moved a water bottle without touching that either. What's happening to me?"

"I don't know and I can't give you any answers until I see you. Are you on your way here?"

"Yes," I replied.

"Okay. How long until you arrive?" Dr. Kane asked, still as calm as ever.

I glanced down at the dashboard of my car and looked at the time. "I'm probably about 20 minutes away. I'll be there around 1:30."

"I'll make sure the receptionist knows you're coming and sends you back immediately. Be careful, Devin. I'll see you when you get here."

"Thanks," I said as I hung up the phone. I threw it on the passenger seat and focused on driving.

Thankfully, focusing didn't seem all that difficult. Everything seemed to slow down as I sped down the roads and weaved in and out of traffic. Everything seemed quiet. I took it all in as I closed my eyes. Things felt different. I was able to relax. It was a comfortable feeling, like the feeling you get as you're about to fall asleep.

My eyes snapped open. Horns from oncoming traffic were blaring at me as my car began to drift onto the other side of the road. I swerved back into my lane.

I needed to be more careful.

What was happening to me?

I arrived at Decker City Hospital and made my way to Dr. Kane's office. The receptionist brought me back to one of the empty rooms. She told me he would be right in and shut the door behind her. I sat down at the table and pulled out my pen. I placed it on the table in front of me and tried moving my hand, waving it, pushing it, basically any direction I could think of in order to get this pen to move again. Nothing seemed to work. I didn't understand this. Why was this working at certain times and other times I'd look like I'm crazy?

I heard a knock on the door. As I turned around in my chair, the door opened and Dr. Kane walked in.

"Hi, Devin." He shut the door behind him and sat down across from me. "So let's go over what's happening here. Let's begin from once you left this office. Tell me what you've done since we last saw each other yesterday."

"After I left early yesterday morning, my grandfather took me to his house and I slept for most of the day. We had dinner. I went back to my place and fell asleep again. I woke up this morning and went to work. That's it."

"Okay," Dr. Kane replied. He started taking notes in his folder. Afterwards, he looked up at me and said, "Is there anything else you did?

Anything minor? Take any medicines? What did you eat? Fill me in on everything. I need to know in order to try and help you."

"No, nothing else. I've been taking Advil as a pain reliever. I had a few ibuprofens yesterday. I had pizza last night and starting having soup today when everything began to happen."

He continued writing things down in his folder. "Now tell me about when you first noticed something going on."

"I was at lunch with Lara–"

I was interrupted when he asked, "Who's Lara?"

"Oh, uh, my friend from work. We were having lunch and I reached for my drink and it…it just slid it my hand all by itself."

"What were you talking about? Was anything else going on during this time?"

"We were just talking about my accident." I paused. We talked about more than that. Dr. Kane was only trying to help so I guess telling him was the best option, as uncomfortable as this was. "We, umm…also were talking about our feelings for each other. I finally built up the courage to ask her out and was going to do that during our lunch together, but I was a little distracted by a bottle suddenly sliding into my hand."

Dr. Kane looked back down at his folder and began writing more. He stopped writing and looked back up at me. "So you were nervous during this time?"

"I guess so."

"Are you sure your friend didn't slide it to you? Maybe you didn't realize you grabbed it and moved it yourself?"

"No. I swear, I know what I saw. I went to reach for my drink and it just slid into my hand. I don't know how it happened. Lara didn't slide it to me and I'm sure I didn't move it myself."

I began to feel like no one was going to believe me or take me seriously. I wasn't even sure if I could take myself seriously, so what did I expect? But I had to prove to Dr. Kane I was telling him the truth. I picked up the pen I brought from my office and held it up to his face. "This pen, I threw it against the wall in my office."

"Why did you throw your pen?"

"No, I mean the same thing that happened to me during lunch happened again when I was in my office trying to move this pen. I tried grabbing it like I did during lunch and it didn't work. I tried a few times and had no luck. I got annoyed and waved my hands and it flew off the desk into the wall."

Dr. Kane looked puzzled. I didn't think he believed my story. "Hmm…" he started to say. He went back to writing again.

"Just say it, you don't believe me," I accused him.

"That's absolutely not true, Devin. I never said I didn't believe you. I think this is a very interesting case. I'm trying to determine if there is some medical or some scientific reasoning for this. I've just never heard of this happening before."

The term he mentioned in our previous session instantly popped into my head. "Didn't you say something like hyper-specialized senses? Would this be what you pointed out on my brain scan? Is that what's happening to me?"

He looked back down at his folder and moved some papers around. As he was trying to find what he seemed to be looking for, he said, "It could be, but I've never heard of something like this. I've read studies about how others have come across their abilities. For example, there was man who was struck by lightning. He survived and one day decided he wanted to play the piano. He began playing some of the classical artists: Beethoven, Mozart, Chopin." He paused and looked up at me, stopping what he was looking for. "This individual had no training in piano. Never played in his life. Yet somehow, he was able to perform like he had been playing his whole life."

What did that have to do with me? Some guy playing the piano? Big deal. As Dr. Kane went back to looking through his folder of papers, I interrupted him by asking, "Is that what's happening to me? Am I developing some ability like that?"

"I don't know." He pulled a few papers out of his folder and placed them on the desk. "These are my notes from our last visit as well as your brain scans." He removed everything off the desk, except for a pen and his notes on my visits. He placed the pen on top of the papers as a paper weight and said, "I want you to remove everything on this desk without touching it. I need to see this for myself before we can move forward."

"How am I supposed to do this?" I asked Dr. Kane. "I can't do this at will. It seems random or accidental. I don't know how this even works."

"I want you to try," Dr. Kane replied.

I shook my head in annoyance and decided to focus on the papers he laid out. I waved my hand and the edges of the papers moved slightly by the air passing under my hand.

I took a deep breath and tried again.

Nothing.

"Try again," Dr. Kane said.

I shook my head again, trying to wash the frustration away and said, "This isn't going to work. I don't know what I'm doing."

"Just try again," Dr. Kane reiterated.

I focused once again on the pen and papers. I stared hard at them as if I was using some crazy make-believe mind tricks. I wanted them to move so badly now. I needed them to move. I needed to prove I wasn't crazy. I needed to show Dr. Kane what was going on with me.

I picked up my hand and tried waving them off the table.

Once again, nothing moved.

"Try again," Dr. Kane said again.

"I am trying! I don't know why I can't do it now." I was getting frustrated. I waved my hand again at the papers. And again. And again.

I couldn't move them.

Dr. Kane looked at me and said, "I don't know if I'm going to be able to do anything for you if you can't prove this to me. Try again."

I moved my hand once again and still nothing.

"If you wanted me to think you're making this up, I think you're proving your point."

I looked at him with anger now.

"Again," he said.

I waved my hand one more time, and the pen flew in the air and bounced off the cabinet to our left. The papers drifted up to our left and floated down to the ground like a bunch of leaves. His notes were scattered all over the office now.

Dr. Kane looked at me in disbelief.

We stared at each other in silence for a moment.

"Well…that was interesting," he said. He reached toward the floor and scooped up all the papers and placed them back on the table. He turned around and pointed to the plastic container full of q-tips. "Knock that off the table."

"How? I barely made the pen move."

"Do it again," Dr. Kane said. "Prove to me that wasn't a trick."

A trick? Was he really going to tell me this was only a trick? I wasn't some magician that could pull a rabbit out of a hat or make someone's card appear in their pocket. This was really happening to me. This wasn't some kind of trick. I didn't know what was happening to me and all my doctor could do was anger me and tell me I was faking it.

I rolled my eyes at him and turned toward the q-tip container. I reached out with my right hand and swung it toward the wall, which would have knocked the container off the table, if my "trick" would have worked.

"Again," Dr. Kane said.

I wanted to scream at him. He wasn't helping me at all. He was irritating me. I wanted to just leave his office and curse him, but doing that wouldn't get me the help I needed or find the answers I was looking for. It wouldn't help me figure out what's happening to me. I turned back at the container and screamed as I swung my hand again from a distance. The container fell off the table and bounced off the carpeted floor.

I turned back to him and said, "Happy now?"

He looked at me wide-eyed. I didn't know whether he was surprised or scared. "Very interesting," he said.

I sat down in the chair across from him. "What was with the attitude? Why were you talking to me like that?"

"Emotion." He stood up and walked over to the container and picked it back up. He examined it as if he was expecting to see a string attached to it or something that would have moved it.

"Emotion? What do you mean?" I asked him.

Satisfied, he put the container back on the counter and walked back to his seat. "I egged you on to put you in a heightened state of emotion. You told me you first noticed it when you were at lunch with your friend. You were in a heightened state of emotion then. You were talking about the accident which I'm sure brought up some memories and feelings during that time. You also said you were telling this girl how you felt about her. You mentioned you were nervous. Strong emotions were flowing through you. This led to your movement of the water bottle you experienced."

It made sense. I was amazed at how he was able to pull all this together so quickly and how he could do this under such a bizarre and an impossible scenario. "You mentioned others with similar abilities. Is this how they, you know, used their ability...or whatever this is?" I asked.

"I'm not sure," Dr. Kane replied. "I've only read summary reports about those people. I don't know the details. But as for you, it seems emotion leads to your enhancement of this feature of yours. You had it during lunch and once again back at your office where, as you said, you became annoyed. That is why I angered you during this session. I was testing my hypothesis. I believed emotion led to unlocking your ability. So my thought on this was that any emotion that becomes strong enough to fuel you, for example, fear, love, nervousness, sadness, and for this scenario, anger, would enable your ability. And with time, and probably a lot of practice and patience, I'm confident you could have full control over this."

"So, am I okay? Is this normal? What do I do now?" Questions just kept popping up in my head. I had so much trust in Dr. Kane now that if he couldn't help me, I wouldn't know who to turn to.

"Yes, Devin, according to all those tests we did the other day, you're fine. I would, however, like to do more testing once you're feeling up to it. I would like to document this project and determine the extent of this ability. For now, I would suggest keeping this to yourself. I wouldn't tell anyone about this."

"Why not?"

"This ability, what you can do, is not normal. It's something people wish they can do. It's something magicians make others believe is real. And up until this point, I believed it wasn't real and that it was only a trick. The reason I ask for your discretion is because you don't know who's out there who will attack you because of this. You don't know who could hurt you, or even come after you. Some people may be scared of you. Some people may want to use you and take advantage of you. I'm just trying to protect you. As exciting as this is, it's also very dangerous. For now, I ask you keep this between us. Will you agree to that?"

Who would hurt me? I'm 28 and live a very average life. I don't have any enemies, at least none that I'm currently aware of.

I thought back to all the comics I used to read. The public was always scared of the new superhero at first. They thought of him or her as an enemy, someone who would cause panic and chaos. It wasn't until later the public would come around and learn the true intentions of the superhero. The hero was there to save the day and protect everyone.

But that was storytelling. That wasn't real. What I was experiencing was very real. Still, maybe Dr. Kane was right.

"I won't say anything to anyone," I said.

CHAPTER SEVEN

A dull feeling filled the pit of my stomach on my drive home. How was I supposed to keep this a secret? Especially from my grandfather. Yet this ability was definitely not something I wanted to flaunt.

Dr. Kane was right; coming forward with what I could do could put me in harm's way. People would surely fear my power. And it would only be a matter of time until the whole city came together and came after me. I would be the outcast.

Goosebumps appeared down my arms. I wasn't about to tell the world what I could do.

I arrived back home and was able to get into more comfortable clothes. I sat on the sofa and held my cellphone in my hand. I kept turning the cellphone screen on and off while I debated whether or not to tell my grandfather.

I should probably listen to my doctor, but I couldn't keep this entirely to myself. My grandfather had been there for me my entire life. If I kept the biggest thing that had happened in my life from him, he would feel betrayed. He had done so much for me and loved me like no one else. I knew I could trust him. Plus, who else was I going to be able to talk to about this?

I pulled up my grandfather's contact info and hit the dial button.

Ring...

Ring...

Ring...

Of course he wasn't going to pick up. The one time I actually need to talk to him, he wasn't going to answer. The phone rang one more time and his voicemail picked up.

"Hello. Paul Shephard's answering machine is broken. This is his refrigerator. Please speak *very* slowly, and I'll stick your message to myself with one of these magnets," my grandfather's recorded voice said. The message must have been at least 15 years old. He thought it was the funniest message back then, and to this day he still thinks so.

The recorded message was followed by a *beep*. "Hey, Grandpa, it's Devin. Give me a call when you get this. I need to talk to you. And please change your answering machine message. I was a teenager when you recorded that. It's about time I heard something new. Anyway, call me back."

I hung up and put the phone next to me on the sofa. I sunk into it, leaned my head back on the cushions behind me and lifted my feet up on the coffee table.

What a day it had been. A sense of dread and guilt overwhelmed me as I thought about all the work I hadn't done that I should've done today. I missed half the day freaking out, and the other half of the day I was so distracted I barely got anything done.

Maybe I needed to take the day off tomorrow and collect my thoughts. I could just relax and maybe just return some emails from home tomorrow. I wouldn't have any interruptions if I worked from home so I'd be able to be more productive. I would also be able to avoid everyone and not have to go into my accident story anymore. Tommy wouldn't be able to barge into my office and ask me about my accident and talk to me about Lara.

Lara!

I groaned into my hands. She must hate me after what I did this afternoon. She told me she cared about me and I got up and left her. I had to call her and apologize.

I picked up my phone again and scrolled through to find Lara's contact info. The phone began ringing on the other end.

On the first ring, my heart leapt into my throat. A million questions entered my mind. What should I say? What if she doesn't pick up? Should I leave a message? Is she going to be mad at me? I probably should have prepared something to say before I called.

"Hello?" Lara's soft voice made me feel hopeful even though I was worried she might be mad at me.

"Hi, Lara, it's Devin." I braced myself for her reaction.

"Hey, I was actually about to call you."

"You were?" I asked.

"Yeah, I wanted to find out what happened today at lunch. You kind of freaked out and ran off. I didn't know if I did something or said something wrong, but it worried me. I went to your office, too, and you weren't there. I thought something happened."

Relief flooded my whole body. She wasn't mad. She actually sounded more concerned than anything.

"Lara, I am so so so sorry. I...it had something to do with my accident, a side effect would be the best possible explanation. I don't really want to go into it right now but trust me, you did nothing wrong. I'm sorry I freaked out and ran off."

"It's okay. I just didn't know what happened and it had me worried. I mean, I said I cared about you and then you just jumped out of your seat and ran off. I thought maybe I stepped over our friendship line...or something," Lara explained.

"No, no. It had nothing to do with that. Just something from my accident came about and it freaked me out. I went to my doctor after that and I'm fine. I just need to relax and get better."

"Well, if you want to talk about it, I'm here to listen," she reassured me.

"Thanks, Lara." I was taken aback by how well she was taking this. I guess there was no better time than now to continue what I had been promising myself I would do. "So I kind of wanted to talk about this whole caring business we started getting into before I made my quick getaway."

Her quiet giggle on the other end of the phone was adorable.

I continued. "What are you doing this Friday night?"

"I don't think I'm doing anything. Why?" Lara asked.

I finally managed to say, "I...uhh...I wanted to ask you out to dinner this Friday night."

"On a date?"

I hesitated for a moment. My words seemed trapped in my throat before I finally answered, "Yes."

It was quiet on the other end with what seemed like minutes that ticked by.

My heart started to pound. My palms were even sweaty. I put everything on the line asking her out. It was against everything I would have done prior to my accident. But since then and the talk with my grandfather, I needed a change.

Lara's voice finally came through on the other end of my phone. The elation in her voice was overwhelming as she said, "I thought you'd never ask."

CHAPTER EIGHT

I woke up the next morning feeling excited for the week to end. I had a date with Lara on Friday.

My clock read 7:01 A.M. I had the day to sleep in and this is when I wake up? Unbelievable.

I rolled out of bed and headed into my kitchen to make some coffee when my phone started ringing. I ran back into my bedroom to grab my cell. It was my grandfather. "Hey," I greeted him.

"You rang?" he responded.

"Yeah, I did but I didn't expect you to be calling me back at seven in the morning."

"Well, shouldn't you be up and getting ready for work?"

"I decided to take the day off today. I had an incident at work yesterday."

"An incident?" my grandfather asked me. "What do you mean? What happened?"

"That's what I was calling you about last night. Are you going to be home later today?" I asked him.

"Yeah, you coming over?"

"I'd like to. I'll tell you what happened when I get there. I'll be there after lunch. I want to get some work done here before I head over."

"Okay, that's fine. I'll see you when you get here."

We both hung up after we said our goodbyes and I walked back into the kitchen to make my coffee. I opened up my cabinet, grabbed a mug and placed it on the counter in front of me. I went to reach behind me for the container of coffee beans but stopped myself.

Could I grab it without touching it?

I reached out for it and nothing happened. I rubbed my hands together, as if doing that would make a difference. Maybe some static electricity would help? Reaching back out for the container another time still accomplished nothing. I needed to learn how to control this ability.

One more time. This has to work.

Again, nothing.

Defeated, I reached out for the container and placed it on the counter. Maybe I just needed more practice.

<hr/>

"So let me get this straight, you can move things with your mind?" my grandfather asked.

"I don't know how it works. All I know is what I told you so far."

"Look, Devin, I know you went through a lot the past few days. But you can't make up stories like this. It's been proven that this...thing, whatever you say you can do, doesn't exist. People have made claims that they can make things move with their mind, basically claiming they harness the ability of telekinesis. And all those people have been proven to be a fraud. No one can honestly do what you claim you can."

My own grandfather was doubting me. I stood up from his kitchen table and walked over to the counter. I opened his drawer and found a pen. This seemed to be my go-to item. I brought it over to the table and placed it about a foot in front of me.

"What are you doing?" he asked. "You don't have to prove anything to me. I believe that you believe you can do it."

Disappointment. The perfect emotion to get this rolling. I reached out to grab it and the pen instantly flew into my grip. That seemed too easy. I guess I was finally getting the hang of this.

"What the–" My grandfather reached across the table and took the pen from my hand. He began spinning it around, closely examining every inch of his pen. His eyes were fixated on it. He finally leaned back in his chair, still holding the pen. "Okay, I get it. It's a magic trick. You're just messing with me, right?"

"No, Grandpa. I'm not messing with you. This is what's happening to me."

My grandfather, still not convinced, pulled his wallet out from his pants pocket. He opened it up and grabbed a $20 bill. He held it up above his head. "Grab this from me. If you really can do what you claim, you'll have no problem taking this from my–"

He was interrupted when I reached up and snatched it from his grip. The bill quickly zipped across the table from his hand to mine.

"–hand," he said. His face showed utter bewilderment. He lowered his hand from above his head and folded his arms. "Let's say you can do what you claim you can. How does it work? I mean, how can you do this? It's impossible. I don't understand it."

"Neither do I. All I know is what the doctor told me. Apparently, it's tied to emotion. The more I feel, the easier it is to do what I can. Dr. Kane told me with some time and a lot of practice, I could learn to control it with ease."

"Then you need to get practicing." My grandfather stood up and said, "Follow me." He began walking out of the kitchen and down the hallway. I stood up and followed. Once I caught up, he opened the garage door and we both stepped into his messy garage. There was stuff everywhere. This must be where he puts all his junk and other crap that he couldn't find a home for in his house. Granted, some of this junk was my junk that I had as a child or other stuff I left behind when I moved out.

"So what are we doing out here?" I asked.

"I've been waiting for the right time to start cleaning up this stuff. You need practice and I need a clean garage."

I glared back at him. This was supposed to be my day off and he wants me to clean his garage using this new ability?

All he could do was smile and say, "Let me go get a chair and some popcorn. I can't wait to watch this!"

CHAPTER NINE

Robberies Running Rampant in Decker City
By Kate Phillips

The Decker City Police Department has asked that citizens be made aware of a recent wave of robberies. To date, many of the crimes have been against local businesses although citizens have reported being robbed as well. The most recent robbery was a local pharmacy, Howard's RX. Official reports indicate that two men brutally attacked owner Howard Woodman, 47, and left him unconscious. Woodman was taken to Decker City Hospital where he was treated for bruised ribs, a concussion and a broken arm. Police said the two men stole approximately $2,000 in cash and multiple prescription medications worth thousands on the street.

In a similar incident three days ago, Booster Electronics was robbed. According to the police, two men approached the owner Sean Golloway and held him at gunpoint while he was closing his store. Golloway pulled out a gun in what appeared to be in self-defense and shots were fired. Sean Golloway, 35, was pronounced dead at the scene from a gunshot wound to the chest.

Police chief William Conway said the department has reason to believe that the recent robberies are connected.

The police are concerned that this crime spree could signal a drastic rise in violent crime in the city. Conway said the increase may be related to a growing gang presence in the city.

When asked about whether this should be a concern for the public, he responded, "We want everyone to continue living their lives and going about their day. But if you suspect any dangerous or suspicious activity, we advise you find a safe place and call the police immediately."

CHAPTER TEN

The next few days seemed to fly by. Since I had taken a few more days off from work to recover, I spent my time researching everything I could get my hands on. I tried studying and understanding what was happening to me. The study of psychokinesis dated all the way back to the mid 1800's. Many others have claimed to share the psychokinetic ability throughout history. Unfortunately, everyone who was studied had been labeled a fraud. I guess finding someone with experience was now out of the question.

I must have read every page on the internet regarding the topic. What I found most interesting was all the forums where people claimed to have this ability and gave instructions, teaching others how to adopt it. It was quite humorous. Some people gave step by step instructions on what to do and how to practice it. It was incredible how gullible some people were and how many of those websites provided this kind of information.

During my time off, I passed along some work to Tommy. We worked together with most of our clients to make life easier if one of us needed time off. I told him I would be back on Friday.

When I was growing up, if I was ever sick, my grandfather always told me if I felt good enough to go out and play, I was good enough to go to school. When I got older, I applied the same theory to work. I knew if I wanted to see Lara tonight, I needed to go to work.

Friday morning, I opened the door to my office and walked inside. My desk chair slowly spun around and Tommy was sitting in it. He had it facing the window so I couldn't see him at first. It was like what those bad guys do in movies when they are waiting for someone to walk in a room. He had his right leg crossed, resting on his left leg when he turned. He had his hands folded across his chest when he looked at me and said, "What's up, Stud?"

"Stud?" I asked.

"That's right. I heard you asked out Lara."

"You heard that from who?" I liked keeping things private, but within a few days, my personal business was flowing around the office like a dirty little secret.

"Lara told me. Why? Is that a problem?"

A sense of relief came over me. "No, not a problem. I just wanted to make sure this wasn't being spread around the office. Please don't tell anyone."

Tommy had a puzzled look on his face. He switched his crossed legs and leaned back in my chair, unfolding his arms and placing them behind his head. "Why not? She's hot. Why wouldn't you brag about that? You're taking the hottest girl in our office out on a date. I think that calls for some bragging rights," he said.

"I don't want to brag about it. I just want to do the right thing and not have this be the big office romance everyone talks about. I'm sure if you asked her, she wouldn't want this news going around either."

"Actually," Tommy began saying as he brought the chair back to a standard upright position, "she did say something along those lines, too."

"Then why do you want to tell everyone when both of us said not to?" I asked.

Tommy started looking up at the ceiling, as if the answer he was looking for was up there somewhere. Then turned his head back to face me and shrugged his shoulders. "I don't know. I guess I'm just excited for you guys and I want to talk about it."

"Well, when you have news that's *your* news, you can tell the entire office. In the meantime, leave *my* news alone."

Tommy put his hands up in retreat. "Okay, okay, you got a deal." He stood up from my chair as I approached. "Where are you taking her tonight?"

I slid my jacket off and rested it behind my chair. "I haven't decided yet. Probably to one of the restaurants in the city."

"The city?!? Didn't you see the paper this morning," Tommy asked. His voice was raised, higher and more excited than usual. There was something I didn't know yet.

"No, I didn't see the paper, I just got in. Why? What's wrong with the city?"

"Hold on," Tommy said as he turned for the door. "I'll be right back!"

Tommy stormed out. He seemed more concerned about my date than I was. Why was he so worried? His heavy feet were thumping as he ran down the hallway, making his way to his office and back.

"Here." Tommy dumped the paper on my desk in front of me.

"What's this have to do with my date?" I asked.

"What do you mean?"

I spun the newspaper around to show him. The article was titled "Cats vs Dogs: Who's Human's Best Friend?"

"What? No. Give me that." Tommy ripped the paper out of my hand and flipped it over. He then tossed it back to me. "This!" The article he wanted me to read was circled in red pen. "Now do you see the right article?"

"How could I miss it?" I said sarcastically.

The article was titled "Robberies Running Rampant in Decker City." I only managed to read the first sentence before Tommy interrupted. So much for reading.

"There was a guy who was shot and another who was beaten unconscious. The police said a gang may be forming in the city that is responsible for the recent crime sprees. There's a lot of crazy stuff going on down there recently. Just be extra careful if you're still going down there tonight."

"I will, Tommy. Thanks for the heads up."

"No problem. If you'd like," Tommy began to say as he started flexing his bulky muscles, "I can be a hired bodyguard for you guys. My rates are conveniently affordable." He kept flexing, raising his arms above his shoulders showing off his well-toned biceps and triceps as they appeared to bulge through his white buttoned down shirt.

I just shook my head at him. "You're an idiot." I pointed to the door and said, "Get out of my office. I've got work to do."

Tommy brought his arms down to his side and started laughing. He turned around and walked out of my office. I held the paper in my hands, skimming the article. Tommy was right, there were a lot of bad things going on in the city. After finishing the article, I placed it on my desk in front of me. Maybe I shouldn't take Lara to the city for dinner if there was so much crime downtown.

But there's crime everywhere. Lara and I were only going to a restaurant for dinner and then coming back home. We weren't going to be spending a lot of time walking around.

Everything would be fine.

CHAPTER ELEVEN

I hadn't been on a real date in a few years. That's not to say I hadn't spent time with any women. I'd gone out and had dinner or drinks with other women in the past, but they never turned into anything. Maybe my heart was in a different place then.

My last date was a nightmare. One day I had worked up the nerve to ask out a girl I saw at a coffee shop every morning. She was nice and seemed interesting, but we had nothing in common. Literally nothing. She was a beauty advisor at a major woman's makeup outlet. She watched girly shows and all those scripted reality shows. She hated sports and liked all the music I couldn't stand to listen to. It was just one awkward silence after another. We both couldn't find an interesting topic to stay on and keep an interesting conversation going. Now I avoided that coffee place as if it were some contagious disease.

Getting ready for tonight had me as nervous as I'd ever been. Maybe it was excitement. I wasn't quite sure. Either way, I didn't want this to go as badly as my coffee shop date. Nothing I chose to wear looked quite right. I kept changing restaurant locations every five minutes, thinking the next one would be better. I even had a mental list of conversation topics lined up.

I heard my grandfather's voice in my head, "Stop overanalyzing everything!" I sighed in one explosive breath and glared at myself in the mirror.

"Stop overanalyzing," I told my reflection.

I arrived at Lara's home at 6:30 PM. Lara lived in her grandparent's house. After her grandfather died, her grandmother had to move into an elderly care facility. Her grandmother didn't want to sell the house because of the sentimental value and because she wanted to keep it within the family. Since Lara began working in Decker City when her grandmother had to move, she just let Lara buy it for what she paid for it 60 years ago–$35,000. Lara got very lucky in this arrangement.

I made my way up to her house when the front door opened and Lara walked outside. She was wearing a beautiful long black skirt that had a slit on the left side. Her jacket and scarf were lying on top of her darkened gray sweater, which was still visible under her unbutton jacket. Her hair was curled, which was not how I'm used to seeing her. It looked better like this.

"Hi," Lara said as she approached my car. Her heels clicked with each step she took.

"Wow," I uttered, unable to string together anything more coherent. "You look beautiful," I managed to say.

"Really? I'm wearing a coat. The same coat you see me wear to work all the time. It's taken you now two years to say I look beautiful in this coat?"

She completely caught me off guard. "I...uhh...your dress. I mean..." I choked and sweat began to pour from my palms.

She broke out in laughter.

I stood there stunned, unsure how to react. My heart sunk into my stomach.

Lara shook her head and glanced at me. She was wearing more mascara than usual, too. Her beautiful eyes were even more breathtaking. "I'm just messing with you, Devin. I just wanted to lighten the mood a little."

My heart returned to its rightful place in my chest. "I thought you were serious. You totally freaked me out." I smiled as I opened the car door for her and started our journey into the city.

I parallel parked on the street about four blocks away from the restaurant. I wanted to take her to this place called The Italian Grill, which was the tenth place I had considered. It was a nicer restaurant than all the chains and the quick in and out places that had popped up all over Decker City. I made sure to reserve a table before I left, and it was a good thing I did. When we walked into the restaurant, there were at least 12 other couples and families waiting to be seated. Thankfully, we were able to be seated right away.

As we settled into our seats, the hostess handed us our menus. She walked away, and it occurred to me that tonight's dinner date had officially begun. I smiled and opened my menu. I glanced at everything on the page even though I already knew what I wanted. Chicken Parmigiana. It's kind of plain and unoriginal, but it's my favorite Italian dish. I put my menu down and looked across the table at Lara. "What are you getting?" I asked.

"Umm..." she started saying as she was looking through the menu. "I think I'll get the Chicken Parmigiana."

I tilted my head and squinted my eyes a little bit. "That's what I'm getting, you can't copy me!" I said.

"Oh, on the contrary, I believe I said I was getting that first. So, it's actually you," she then pointed to me, "who is copying me." She finished that sentence by flipping her hand to point to herself.

She had a big smirk on her face, to the point where she was really about to burst out laughing from trying to hold it in. "Are you messing with me again?" I asked.

Lara put her hands to her mouth to cover her laughter. She dropped her head toward the table and her shoulders bounced up and down. She finally picked her head back up, her face now flushed red. She took in deep breath and said, "I'm sorry, it's just too easy with you."

"I get that a lot," I replied, thinking about how my grandfather teases me the same way.

"Come on, Devin, you always order the same things wherever we go. You're so predictable."

"How did you know I'd order this though? We never had Italian before."

"Really? Where did we go for our company's annual meeting?"

A few months ago we had our annual meeting at the city's top hotel. They have an Italian restaurant on the bottom floor inside. In fact, we went there every year for our company's annual meeting and I always ordered the same thing. "But how did you remember what I ate there?"

"And what about the time we all went out for happy hour at the Italian restaurant around the corner from our building. What did you get there?"

I felt embarrassed. She had me pegged. She knew what I was going to eat before we even walked into the restaurant. "Okay, you got me. I got the chicken parmigiana. So? I like to eat what I enjoy. There's nothing wrong with that."

"Absolutely nothing wrong with that," Lara replied, agreeing with me. "I just find it funny and cute."

"Cute, huh? Is the beautiful Lara Scarlett hitting on me?"

"I could ask you the same thing."

Our waiter came over just as Lara finished looking over the menu. He introduced himself and took our order. Lara ended up ordering mussels pomodoro.

My nervousness lifted as we continued our conversation. We were laughing and having fun. We talked about our TV shows, people from work and work-related stories. We talked about how our sports teams will never win a championship because they always choke during the playoffs and can't win a game when it counts. It was almost as if we were already a couple.

"So our dinner should be out any minute and I wanted to ask you something first," Lara began saying. "Why did it take over two years to finally get here? Why did you wait so long to ask me out? I mean, when you said you wanted to ask me something, I honestly didn't know what to expect. I kind of thought you would be asking me something personal or embarrassing or quite possibly setting me up for another joke."

I paused to look at her. I couldn't believe I was finally sitting down to dinner on a date with Lara. "I really don't know why it took this long. I guess I was nervous. I thought I might lose what a great friend you've become. I know it's a lame excuse. I've liked you since we first started talking to one another."

I paused to reflect and take a sip of water.

Lara waited, her eyes soft and thoughtful.

I continued, staring into the distance over her shoulder. "I think I got into the same predicament my parents got into. I never realized how much I'm like my father. I obviously didn't know him considering he died when I was a baby. But my grandfather told me about how he and my mom were basically like you and me. My father and my mother were great friends growing up and they both liked each other but my dad never wanted to ask out my mom. He thought he might lose his best friend if they ever broke up. Which is exactly how I felt about this situation.

My eyes moved to catch hers. "You've been great to talk with at the office and we have a lot of fun together. It doesn't hurt you're incredibly attractive as well."

Lara rolled her eyes.

"You are. I didn't ask you out because…I was looking at the worst case scenario so I never got to enjoy any case scenario." I sighed and looked down. "As you can tell, I overanalyze everything and thought about this way too much."

Lara reached across the table and took my hand. "I never knew that about your parents."

I looked up. "Yeah, my grandfather just told me about it after my accident. I didn't really know about it either."

"It's a sweet story. I had no idea you felt that way about me," Lara said.

"Is that a bad thing?" I asked.

"Are you kidding me? Not at all. I thought I was the one who felt that way. I didn't want to lose you as a friend as well. I couldn't help how I felt though. Every time you would come hang out with me at my desk, I always imagined you asking me out. And when you never did, I guess I just assumed you didn't feel the same way."

I squeezed her hand and smiled.

"Oh, and thanks for the incredibly attractive compliment. You're not too bad yourself." She smiled and winked at me, withdrawing her hand and settling it in her lap.

A few minutes later our food was served.

After we finished dessert, I paid the bill and we walked out of the restaurant. As we began our walk back to my car, she reached out and grabbed my hand. As corny as this sounded, I couldn't have been more into this girl.

"How was your dinner?" I asked.

"It was very good. I've never been there before. Thank you for taking me," Lara replied.

"You're welcome. I'm glad you enjoyed it."

"Me too. So what's the plan now? Are you taking me home or do we still have more of the night to enjoy?"

Lara sounded like she didn't want to go home yet. I didn't want the evening to end yet either. Of course, I didn't make plans for anything past dinner.

"We can do something. Do you have anything in mind?" I asked her.

We approached a crosswalk and had the red light. We stopped and she turned to face me. "Well, there's this bar a few blocks past where you parked. I go there from time to time with a few of my girlfriends. You want to grab a few drinks there?"

Before I had the chance to respond, someone ran into Lara and knocked her to the ground. She pulled me down with her when she lost her balance and didn't let go of my hand. I braced for the impact with my one remaining hand.

As I knelt in the street, I started to brush off all the rocks and debris off my hands. We both looked up and saw someone running down the street away from us, the person who knocked us down.

"HEY!" Lara yelled. She tried standing back up as quickly as possible, using my shoulders as support, but her heels prevented her from doing so. "He took my purse!"

I quickly looked at her naked arm. "Stay here, I'll be back." I leapt to my feet and began my pursuit of the thief. I took off without even thinking about it and wasn't even sure what I was going to do when or if I caught the guy.

My adrenaline was pumping through my body. The arches of my feet rocked back and forth with each step I took. The guy was quick, but I was gaining on him.

We ran about a block before he turned down a side street. I was maybe thirty feet behind him at this point. I turned the corner after him. He looked back at me as he kept running. As he did so, I gained a step on him. He started grabbing things on the street and knocking them over to try and slow me down. I jumped over the trash can he threw down, and I ran around the boxes he knocked over. Maybe twenty feet now. I was closing in.

Every few steps he took, he continued to look over his shoulder. With each glance he took, his speed decreased. I was closing on him. He ran past another pile of boxes and knocked into them to try and slow me down. The boxes scattered in front of me. An easy jump here, a quick step there, and I was through the next obstacle.

I felt like a contender on American Gladiators. I guess if my career didn't pan out, it was nice to know I had options. Except my lungs were burning and my legs were beginning to feel like lead. And I realized I was going to have to get back to Lara after this was over.

He turned a corner down an alley and I followed. As I made my turn, the air left my stomach and my feet went air born. The thief plowed into me with his shoulder as I ran full speed around the corner. He threw me to the ground, turned and kept running down the alley. It was a small alley, possibly about the width of two cars. I sat up and tried catching my breath, coughing. He was getting away. Every moment I stayed on the ground was another step he had on me. Two steps…three steps…five steps…ten steps. I sat there catching my breath as he sprinted away.

Doors were littered on both sides of the alley. Back doors from the store fronts on the main streets which leads to the dumpsters out back. The thief was now weaving his way between the dumpsters as he ran toward the end of the alley.

I wasn't going to let him escape.

It was then something came over me. I don't know what happened or how I knew what to do next, but it all came together so smoothly. As the thief ran full speed past the one dumpster on the right side of the alley, there was a door on the left. Whether he saw it or not, I'll never know, nor do I care. When he was past the dumpster, I reached out to that door from at least forty or fifty feet away and imagined grabbing the handle and pulling the door open as hard as I could. I pulled my arm backwards with a jolt. The door flew open with such force, I thought it came off its hinge. The thief ran straight into the door at full speed with a loud CRACK. If I didn't break the door when I opened it, he certainly broke something by running into it. He bounced off the door like a ragdoll and fell to the ground.

Once I got back to my feet and caught my breath, I jogged over to him and saw him lying on the ground, unconscious. I bent down to pick up Lara's purse and took a close look at this idiot who tried to rob Lara. Blood was starting to ooze out of his nose. Probably broken. I reached in my pocket and took out my cell phone. I texted Lara and let her know I got her purse and everything was fine. I then dialed 9-1-1 and was connected to an emergency operator.

CHAPTER TWELVE

"With all the recent crime and bad news coming out of Decker City, we have a heroic story that took place last night. With this exciting story we turn to our man on the streets, Alan Haven. Alan?"

"Thanks, Bill. Over the past few weeks, crime in this city has been on the rise. There has been a growing presence of gang violence that the police just can't seem to control. But for Lara Scarlett, she was thankful to have her boyfriend Devin Shephard with her when she was mugged.

"The couple were walking down 2nd street, crossing over Pavilion Drive, when the mugger, Benjamin Perma, ran up to Lara and Devin, knocking them to the ground. He snatched Lara's purse and ran down a nearby alley. Devin chased him for a few blocks, and found Benjamin unconscious. Devin was able to retrieve Lara's purse and contact the authorities. Investigation is underway as to how Benjamin was found unconscious and bloody with a broken nose but the police have said Devin was clear of any foul play or wrongdoing. It seems as if it was just good luck for Devin. Both Lara and Devin were both unavailable to comment.

"The police have said they do not suggest or encourage any citizen to chase a mugger because of the threat to their own safety. At the same time, they are thankful for how the outcome turned out. I'm sure Lara is thankful as well. The police have told me if other people are caught in this situation they should contact the authorities instead of engaging the criminals as they may be armed and dangerous. Back to you, Bill."

"Thank you, Alan. Heroic story indeed. We will have more on this story as details further develop. In other news–"

I muted the TV and pointed at it. "Did you see that? I was on the news!"

I went to my grandfather's house for brunch almost every Saturday afternoon. It was the usual spread: bagels, waffles or pancakes, bacon, eggs, and real maple syrup. We ate with the TV on.

It was usually just background noise, but not today. The news story brought back the events of last night. Once I called the police, everything happened quickly. Lara met up with me in the alley a few minutes after I texted her my location and what happened. As she showed up, so did the police. The mugger, or Benjamin as I knew him now, was arrested. Lara and I were only at the scene for a few minutes while the police questioned us and asked for a statement. I guess the news picked up the story from the police scanners and from the public police report. Now that I think about it, I wish I wasn't on the news. So much for keeping a low profile.

I turned to look at my grandfather and he didn't look too excited. "You did this?"

"Yeah," I replied, nodding my head.

His eyes lowered and eyebrows curved downward as his forehead scrunched together, showing all the wrinkles. He looked angry. "What were you thinking?"

This caught me off guard. I would have thought he would have been proud of me. "What do you mean? I didn't ask for this news story. You know me, I don't like the attention."

"That's not what I'm talking about. I mean what were you seriously thinking? What if he had a knife, or worse, a gun? How would you have defended yourself against a weapon?"

That never even occurred to me. It never even crossed my mind. What if he did have a gun? I could have been shot. Even killed. What if it was a knife that slammed into my stomach, rather than his shoulder? My grandfather was right.

"I don't know. I just saw the guy take her purse and my instincts kicked in. I really don't know what came over me. I just chased him down and got her purse back. That's all."

His angry face turned worrisome. He took a deep breath and let it out like a sigh. "Look, I know you were just trying to do the right thing. But it's dangerous out there and before you act, you need to think first. He could have killed you." He paused for a moment. His expression changed. "Wait a minute, you're dating her? *And* you didn't tell me about this?! "

I winced. I didn't think about telling anyone. Lara and I just wanted to keep what happened to ourselves. I'm sure the mugging was embarrassing for her, possibly even terrifying. And with my grandfather knowing what I can do now, this would give him even more reason to freak out. I used my...power or ability or whatever I wanted to call it. And I used it out in the open.

"I didn't want to make a big deal about it. You know me, I keep to myself," I said.

"Yeah, but this is big! You took down a criminal on the streets and helped the police apprehend him. You were a hero last night. A dumb one, but still a hero. I'm proud of you for doing what you did, but you need to be more careful and better prepared next time."

"I know, I shouldn't have just chased–" I stopped for a moment. "Wait, did you say next time?"

"I did," my grandfather said. "I'm going to assume you..." he started waving his hands around in the air, "...did your thing and stopped this guy, right?

"Yeeaaaah." I said, stretching it out, not knowing where he was going with this. "Why?"

"Tell me what happened," he asked with anticipation.

"I chased the guy down the street into an alleyway where he knocked the wind out of me. I was on the ground while he was running away. I was so angry. Lara and I were having a nice evening and this guy had to ruin it by snatching her purse. I had to protect her and get it back. I guess I just used that anger.

"As he was passing one of the back doors to the buildings in the alley, I reached out and opened the door with my mind. At least I think that's how I do it. I don't really know exactly how it works yet. Anyway, I opened it into his path. He went face first into it and was knocked out."

I paused. It actually sounded kind of silly and stupid when I said it out loud. What a lame way to take a criminal down.

I continued, "I called the police and then they came and arrested him. That's all that happened."

My grandfather stood so quickly that his chair skidded across the tiled kitchen floor. "Do you know what you've become?"

It must have been a rhetorical question because before I could even respond, he threw both his arms out toward me like he was introducing me. "A superhero!"

"Huh?" First my grandfather was angry at me for doing what I did and now he was standing up, cheering me on and calling me a superhero. This made no sense. "Okay, Grandpa, calm down. I'm not a superhero. I just got Lara's purse back. I just did what anyone else would have done."

"First of all, not many people would have done what you did. Many people fear confrontation. You ran into it. Also, people tend to fear for their own lives. You risked yours just to get back a purse. *A purse!* You chased this guy and used your, now here's the best part, your superpowers to stop him and retrieve the purse." His face glowed with excitement.

I couldn't help but feel excited as well. It was a little weird and kind of insane, but for the time being he made me feel excited, too.

"So let's recap," my grandfather continued. "You, Devin Shephard, in the face of danger, risked your own life to help rescue someone's stolen property and in the process you brought down the criminal behind the crime by using a unique ability of yours, a superpower if you will. What would you call someone who does that?"

When he said it like that, it didn't sound lame at all. It sounded pretty cool.

But I wasn't a superhero. I did one thing for someone and that was it. Although, if I could do it once, who's to say I couldn't do it again?

Great, now he has me thinking and believing in this crazy tale. I couldn't be who my grandfather wanted me to be.

I've been in one fight in my entire life, and I got my butt kicked. I was just over six feet tall and about 185 pounds, who was I intimidating? The only thing I had going for me was this ability, and that wasn't enough.

I shrugged. "A police officer. Not me."

He shook his head and said, "They have training and weapons. If you have training, you won't need weapons."

"Training? What are you talking about?" I asked.

"To fight. Don't think I don't remember about that kid in high school. What was his name? Mark? Mike?"

"Mitchell. Mitchell Quinn," I said, not liking the fact he was bringing up a depressing time of my life. This kid all throughout middle school and high school teased me about my parents. About how my mom was sick because she probably deserved it and how my dad killed himself. Kids can be cruel, but this one in particular was downright despicable. He bullied everyone but he seemed to focus on me most of the time. I eventually got sick and tired of it. One day after so many years of him doing what he did to me, I snapped and took a swing at him. I don't know what came over me because my grandfather raised me to not fight. *Just ignore him and he'll stop,* he always said. But Mitchell never stopped.

My punch landed on the left side of his jaw and brought him to his knees. I thought that would have stopped him, but I was wrong. He faced the ground and spit out blood, followed by a tooth. He slowly stood back up and simply told me I was a dead man. He attacked me and threw me to the ground. His friends and other classmates closed in and started chanting *fight fight fight!*

The fight ended when a teacher came to the rescue. I ended up with a broken arm and a beaten face full of bumps and bruises. He landed most of the attacks. I had one punch to the face, the only hit I had on him. Mitchell and I both got suspended from school for fighting. I came back to school after two days while he had a week suspension.

Upon his return the following week, I heard rumors he brought a knife with him and was going to use it on me during lunch. I didn't believe it until a few of my friends convinced me to tell the school office about this planned attack of Mitchell's. I don't rat on people or get anyone in trouble, but in this case, I was happy I did what I did. They called in an officer to search Mitchell and his belongings. They found a knife stuffed in his backpack. They took him out of the school in handcuffs and I never saw him again. After graduation, I heard he got into drugs and crime. I wouldn't be surprised if he's currently in jail or has at least seen the inside of a jail cell at some point of his life.

"Yeah, Mitchell," my grandfather said. "I know I taught you not to fight, but right now you may need it to defend yourself when something like this happens again."

"Whoa there, again? I don't plan on doing anything like what happened last night again. That was a rare circumstance. It was a one-time thing. I'm not getting involved with this."

"Why not!? You have this amazing gift! Why not use it for good? What if Lara gets in trouble again? Why not help the police clean up this city? They used to do their job well. I can't say the same recently. There's just too much crime for them to keep up with," he said.

"Because…"

I realized that I really didn't have a good answer. Besides the fact that it might be wrong to fight this way, outside of the law.

That was a good enough answer for me, but not for my grandfather. He had an obsession with comics and superheroes. I think he saw an opportunity for me to become this vigilante and clean up the city by taking the law into my own hands. He wanted me to be like the characters in the comic books he read to me as a child. As exciting as that could be with my new gift, it could get me injured or killed.

"Because it's dangerous and I could get killed. You had no trouble throwing that in my face earlier. Why the sudden shift in decisions?"

"I said what I said because you just did what you did without thinking. Of course if you just went out there and tried replicating what you did last night, something horrible could happen to you. You're unprepared. You're untrained. You don't know how to defend yourself. Think about it like this, if you went into your job with no training and completely unprepared, how do you think you'd do? How would you work with your clients? Would you be able to serve them financially or give them the right advice or the right products? Would you be able to–"

I interrupted him, "Okay, I get it."

"So you're on board then?"

My grandfather's face was lit up like a Christmas tree, he was so excited. I fed off his excitement and was seriously considering being on board with him. But doubts kept floating around in my head. What if I got injured? What if I got arrested? What if I was killed?

I realized I was falling into that same old thought pattern of what if's. That had to change.

I had made a promise to myself to start living every day to the fullest after my car accident. I needed to start experiencing life as it came to me. I already began that adventure with Lara by finally asking her out after years of hiding.

It was time to stop hiding. It was time to start living this adventure. It was time to–

"Ouch," I said as my grandfather smacked my face.

"Oh, you're such a baby, I barely touched you. I had to bring you back somehow. It looked like you fell asleep standing up."

A small chuckle emerged. "I was thinking."

"So, are you in?" he asked again.

The more I thought about it, the more excited I became. I liked the idea of using my ability to help the people of this city. It made me feel good knowing I stopped that guy who tried to rob Lara. I wanted to make sure she would be protected. I wanted to make sure that couldn't happen to anyone else. This ability gave me the confidence I needed to change and help make a difference.

I didn't know what kind of training my grandfather had in mind for me but I think I was going to look forward to it. "Yeah," I said. "I'm in."

CHAPTER THIRTEEN

O ut of nowhere, a fist flew toward my face. I ducked, reached forward with my right arm and pulled my elbow back into the man's head. I grabbed the back of his shirt and tossed him to the ground. The man landed with a loud *umph*.

As he attempted to get back up, I threw my right arm down, slamming him back into the ground. With my arms dangling by my side above the man with my palms facing out, I used my ability by moving my arms forward and slid the guy into a pile of boxes. The mountain of boxes came tumbling down on top of him as he slid into them. He became lost underneath the flood of brown cardboard.

Another man to my left began to flee the scene. I started my pursuit after him. He turned down a side street to try and elude me. As I approached the corner, I threw my back against the wall. My heart pumped in my chest as I turned my head around the corner to check for any attacks. It was clear. There was an open door in the distance. I sprung away from the wall, ran down the side street and continued the chase.

I approached the open door and made my way inside. It led to the back entrance to an apartment building. I found my way into a hallway which came to a four-way intersection. Each hallway led toward a new set of hallways. I was nowhere nearer to finding the fleeing man.

"Hey!" someone said in the distance. It came from the hallway to the left. I began running toward that direction.

After about four or five hotel room doors, the hallway angled right. I started to run around the bend when I saw someone sitting against the wall. They were holding their head in their hands.

"Which way did he go?" I asked.

The woman looked up and pointed to a door about 20 feet away. "Up the stairs."

I turned toward the door and sprinted. I opened the door with such force that the cheap decorative glass on the door cracked. I jumped up the stairs, taking two at a time. Pounding came above me. It was the footsteps of someone thumping his way up the stairs. I knew I was close.

The pounding stopped and I heard a door open. I leaned over the railing and looked up to see a door swinging shut. He was on the sixth floor.

Once I made my way to the top, I opened the door and stepped out onto the floor. I turned to my right and then my left. A man peeked out from behind a corner and quickly disappeared. I ran down the hallway at full speed.

I arrived at the corner and came to a complete stop. The man I was chasing now held a gun in his right hand and had it pointed at me. Wrapped up in his left arm, he held a woman as close as he could, using her as a shield.

I raised my arms just a little and said, "Okay, I'm backing off. Let the girl go."

He took the gun off me and pointed it at his hostage's head. "I won't let her go until you leave this building!" He took a step back with his hostage.

"I can't do that," I said. "She has nothing to do with this. Let her go and we can talk this through."

"I don't trust you! How do I know you won't do to me what you did to Chris?" he asked, followed by taking another step back.

Chris? That must be the guy I took down earlier. "Chris attacked me. I had to defend myself. You and I aren't fighting. If you let the girl go and put the gun down, we can avoid anyone else getting hurt." I took a step closer to him.

"Stop!" he yelled. "Don't come closer or I'll shoot her." He took two steps back this time. He kept looking around for something, possibly an escape.

I held my hands out toward him, "Okay, okay. I'm sorry. I won't come any closer." He kept stepping backwards and if I kept letting him, he would eventually get to the window behind him. His only escape was down, and if that meant taking the hostage with him, this was now turning into a possibly deadly situation.

I wanted to remove the gun from his hand but not while it was pointed at the woman's head. I didn't know whether grabbing it from him would make him pull the trigger out of instinct or fear. I needed to wait for the right moment.

I had a better chance of rescuing the hostage if he had the gun pointed at me and not at her. I put my hands down and stood straight up. I locked eyes with him. I took one step forward. Then another.

"Stop!" he yelled again, taking another step back.

I took another step. This man wasn't a killer. He wasn't going to kill her. If he wanted to, he could have shot me when I came around the corner. He could have easily killed me moments ago. But he didn't. Once I took the next step toward him, he whipped the gun past his hostage's head and pointed it at me.

"I SAID STOP!"

In that moment, I threw my right hand up in the air as if I was grabbing his gun from him. The gun left his hand and was thrown in the air toward me. He looked completely stunned. It must have been out of shock, but once the gun left his hand without me touching him, his grip loosened on the woman and she was able to run free. The man turned to his right and pulled the red fire alarm. The siren pierced my eardrums. I winced.

Weeeooo-Weeeooo

I turned my head downward for a split second to adjust to the noise. When I looked back up again, the man was gone. There was nowhere for him to go. He couldn't have just vanished. The end of the hallway was a floor-to-ceiling glass window and he couldn't have gotten out in that split second. The window was not broken and it was still shut. All the doors were shut as well. There was no one behind me either.

Weeeooo-Weeeooo

Where did the woman go? She was just right here. Why did everyone disappear? What was happening?

Weeeooo-Weeeooo

CHAPTER FOURTEEN

eeeooo-Weeeooo

W My eyes bolted open. I rolled over in bed and grabbed my phone off my night stand and shut off my alarm. It was just a dream. But it was an amazing dream. I groaned. "Grandpa, this is your fault" I muttered to myself. It wasn't bad enough I actually agreed to play the superhero role he wanted me to play, but now I was dreaming about it. At least the dream was exciting.

I wanted to go back to sleep to see what happened next. Unfortunately, I didn't have time for that as I had to get ready to go to work.

Monday mornings always sucked. I loved my job, but I loved my free time more.

I groaned as the elevator crept to my office's floor. I was running a little late, but it didn't matter. I was given the freedom to manage my own schedule as long as I didn't abuse the privilege.

The elevator doors opened and I was greeted by half the office in the front lobby. They started clapping the moment I walked off the elevator.

Why were they clapping? Was this for me? Did I miss something?

As I walked by my co-workers, completely unaware of what was happening, one by one they all started congratulating me.

...Good work Devin...

...That was awesome what you did...

...You're a hero...

...Great job...

And then it hit me. They saw the news report and it had spread around the office. So much for keeping things private. Everyone was all smiles, high fiving me and patting me on the back.

Once I got through some of the crowd, I saw Lara at her desk. She shrugged her shoulders and mouthed "Sorry." Suddenly, an arm flew around my neck. Tommy was standing on my right, smiling with his arm around me.

"Everyone," Tommy began, "may I have your attention." The lobby started to quiet down, all but for a few whispers here and there. "This is a special day. We have a hero in our office today. It's this man right here, Devin Shephard."

The crowd broke out in an applause. I nodded awkwardly. This was embarrassing. It was nice to be recognized but I didn't want all this attention on me. However, I couldn't help but smile at the appreciation everyone was giving me. I could feel my face flush.

Tommy continued, "If anyone doesn't know what happened this weekend, you guys seriously need to pick up a newspaper or turn on the news once in a while."

A few laughs came throughout the lobby.

"Devin here was a hero this past Friday night. These two love birds," Tommy said as he kept his grip on me and pointed to Lara still seated behind her desk, "were on a date. Not only was it just a date, it was their *first* date."

The crowd began to fill the noise with "aww's."

"Anyway, after dinner as they were walking around Decker City, a mugger came out of the shadows and ripped Lara's purse from her hands. I tried to warn Devin about the dangers and criminal activity going on in the city, but he didn't listen." Tommy threw up his hands to emphasize his point. "I tried to tell him to be careful. And what happened? Lara was robbed. A heartless *criminal*, stole our loving, hardworking receptionist's purse. So what would you guys do in this instance? Well, I'll tell you what not to do." Tommy turned and looked at me, "Chase him." He turned back to the crowd and continued. "But that's exactly what Devin did. Our calm, shy and 'keeps to himself' Devin decided to chase this guy down. And in the danger of it all, he remained unharmed, got Lara's purse back, and brought down the criminal who robbed her."

The clapping and roar of the office began again.

Tommy then held his fist up to his mouth as if he was holding a microphone. "So Devin, while you were chasing this guy down, what was going through your head?" He moved his pretend microphone from his mouth to mine and held it there waiting for a response.

"I...uhh..."

He brought the microphone back to his mouth. "He's a little shy, guys. Let's give him a round of applause again. Show him you guys care."

There was more clapping, followed by his hand in front of my mouth again.

I shot him a look. It was a look that said 'why are you doing this to me?'

He just smiled and continued holding his pretend microphone waiting for me to respond.

I stammered into the pretend microphone. I don't know if it was the absurdity of talking into a fake microphone like a ten-year-old or if it was authentic embarrassment at all the attention that made me feel so awkward. "I don't know really. I watched the guy take her purse and I decided to chase him down and get it back. It was my immediate reaction." I shrugged for emphasis.

Now he changed his voice to imitate a news reporter. "Immediate reaction? Many would say it was an act of stupidity and that you should have just called the police. But there are many others who are calling it an act of bravery. How did you manage to stop the mugger?"

I couldn't tell them the truth. But I couldn't keep quiet either. I had to tell them something. I had to tread carefully on what I said next. "I guess I can't take full responsibility for catching him. I chased him down an alley and found him lying on the ground. The police think someone opened a door into his path and he ran into it, knocking himself out."

"Well, there you have it folks. One man's stupidity is another man's heroism. Until next time, this is Tommy Gelrod reporting from TruGuard news. Have a wonderful day!" He released me and began applauding.

The rest of the crowd in the lobby followed his lead.

"Why did you do that?" I asked Tommy as we walked into my office.

"Dude, you're a hero. That story was amazing. What an incredible first date you had. I mean I would have kicked the guy's ass for stealing my girl's purse, but that's me. I had to tell the office. It's exciting. Especially for a Monday. What a way to kick off the work week."

I had to give it to him, he did just make the morning a bit exciting. I walked over to my chair and sat down. "Shut the door," I asked.

Tommy turned around and shut my door. He quickly made his way over to my chair as if he was expecting me to tell him something exciting.

"I may need your help."

"With what?" Tommy asked.

"I need to get in shape. I need to bulk up a little bit. Obviously not like you, but I want to be stronger."

"Yeah, man, I can help you out. What made you decide this all the sudden? Was it the hero stuff? Was it because of what happened on Friday?"

"I want to make sure if something were to happen again, I can defend myself if I must. Or possibly someone else."

"Someone else?" Tommy asked.

Oh no, did I let that slip? Does he think I took down that criminal and plan on doing it again? "Like Lara?"

A wave of relief came over me. "Yes." I paused. "Yes, Lara."

He couldn't find out about my ability. I was becoming paranoid that I might let it slip. Keeping this to myself was tougher than I thought.

"Well, I can definitely help you out with that. It's going to take some time, but not as much as you'd think. You have very little to no fat on that skinny body of yours. You'll see and feel a difference in a much shorter amount of time than most others."

"Thank you, Tommy. When can we get started?"

"Tomorrow morning work for you? We can use the gym on the first floor. It even has a shower which you can use afterwards."

"Yeah, that's fine. Thank you."

Tommy began to stand up but stopped himself. "So what really happened in the alley? Between you and me."

I almost laughed. "Nothing ever stays between you and me."

"Yeah, yeah," he said waving a hand at me. "I have problems keeping secrets, we all know that. So what really happened?"

"Nothing. I ran down the alley and he was already unconscious. I grabbed Lara's purse and called the police. I'm sorry I'm not the hero you think I am."

"You're more of a hero than any one of us. Between you and me, knowing that I know you keep better secrets than me, I wouldn't have done what you did. You definitely have some balls on you. Running after a criminal unprotected like that. Especially with all that crime in the city. He could have led you into a trap. He could have killed you. And just letting you know, all the muscle in the world won't stop a bullet." With that, he got up and walked to the door.

Before Tommy could get to the door, it began to open. Lara peeked her head inside.

"Lara!" Tommy said. "Come on in."

"Oh, I didn't mean to interrupt you guys," Lara said.

"You're not interrupting anything," I responded.

"Don't worry, I was just leaving anyway," Tommy said as he walked by Lara. "You two love birds can have the room."

Lara gave Tommy a friendly shove as he walked by.

"You couldn't move me if you tried," Tommy said.

"One swift kick to your groin ought to do it," Lara responded.

"You win," Tommy conceded as he left the doorway covering himself and headed into his office.

Lara turned and closed my office door. "I wanted to thank you for the other night. I know things were kind of hectic and we didn't get a chance to talk much afterwards."

"It's all right. I know you were visiting your parents and I didn't want to bother you this weekend," I responded.

"Ugh, it would have been welcomed if you bothered me. All they could do was pester me about why I moved so far away and why I don't come visit more. I don't think they understand I have a life here now. My family moved to Mapleton when I was a child. I never left until college. They think I should have found a job back home and stayed close. Anyway, enough about my weekend, sorry about that."

I laughed and said, "Don't worry about it. And you're welcome for the other night. I had a good time. Except for when that guy tried to rob you, obviously."

She started to smile and said, "Yeah, he tried ruining a good night for us. Thank you for getting my purse back for me. I'm incredibly impressed."

"I really wasn't trying to impress you. It just kind of happened."

"Well, you did a good job. So, I know you told the police you found the guy the way you did, but I was thinking about it and it doesn't make sense."

"What do you mean it doesn't make sense?" I asked. Nervous energy arose in my body. I didn't want to start this relationship out by lying to her. Plus, if it didn't make sense to her, what do the police think?

"If he ran into the door, wouldn't you think he would have seen it? How does someone just run into a door?" Lara asked me.

I rattled my brain trying to come up with a response as quickly as possible. "The police think someone opened a door while he was running by. Maybe he was looking back at me trying to see how far away I was."

"But if someone opened the door which he ran into, where's that person? Why didn't they come forward? Wouldn't they have seen it happen? Or heard it or felt him hitting the door they just opened?"

She had me stumped. If she was coming up with these questions, I knew the police must have their suspicions too. "I honestly don't know. Maybe they didn't know what happened."

"I don't know. It still doesn't make sense. Whatever, it's done with. I'm just glad you're okay."

"More importantly, you're okay."

She walked a little closer to me. We were now about a foot apart from one another. "I know you're fine. And I'm glad I got my purse back. But you've got to stop scaring me with these accidents and dangerous situations you're getting yourself into. You've been my best friend since I got here and I guess now I can consider you my boyfriend after going on that unique date with you. I'm not ready to lose you just yet."

"Don't worry," I said as I reached out to hug her. "I'm not going anywhere."

She wrapped her arms around me and squeezed, giving me one of her famous Lara bear hugs. As she did, I felt my back cracked in a few spots. It made a popping noise each time. She quickly released after feeling the cracking.

"Oh, I'm sorry. Did I hurt you?"

Now my brain said.

What are you waiting for?

Do it!

What was I waiting for? This was my chance. "You didn't hurt me enough to do this." I leaned in toward her and kissed her. Our lips locked. She was kissing me back. This was it, this was the moment I've been waiting for since I met her. A few seconds went by.

She pulled away and looked up at me with those enormous blue eyes. "It's about time," Lara said.

CHAPTER FIFTEEN

C ar horns blared as the man jetted across the street. One car slammed on their brakes and a screeching noise echoed off the pavement. A man crashed into the car's windshield.

I burst through the door of Best Tech's store at full speed after him. I exited just in time to see him bounce off the windshield. He rolled off the vehicle and ran down an alley, leaving shards of glass from the windshield in his wake. Shocked pedestrians watched in horror as he continued his escape. He landed on his feet and continued running across the street. I noted he was not running as fast as before and that he had a noticeable limp. I began my pursuit.

Over the past three months, I had trained almost every day. Tommy had put me on a specific diet and workout routine. The guy really knew his stuff. For the first time in my life, I had abs. I mean I had real abs, six pack abs. I was in the best shape of my life. My grandfather had also helped by setting me up with a local martial arts expert who was often hired by the police department. He trained me to fight and defend myself. Every day after work, I went to my grandfather's house and trained with this expert.

I had also worked on my ability. I practiced every moment I had. I started with smaller objects like pens, utensils and books. Once I mastered that, I moved onto larger objects like chairs, heavy boxes and people. I found I couldn't move objects heavier than I could physically lift. I also realized that it tired me when I used it often. But practice made me stronger.

With all of this training, I pursued the man with confidence. He turned down Francis Road. I made a pathway through the pedestrians on the sidewalk by moving my hands apart, as if I was parting the Red Sea. They never knew what was happening.

I had tried this on Grandpa. He had said that it just felt like a slight force, as if they were moved by a strong gust of wind.

I was gaining on the thief.

I turned the corner of Francis Road and he was on the right trying to pry open a door. When he saw me, he dropped his tool and ran.

"Stop!" I yelled.

He turned and yelled something. The words were lost in the wind.

"You can either stop, or I will make you stop!"

He paid no attention.

I was within distance now. Although I didn't want to hurt him, I knew it was unavoidable.

I threw both of my arms to the right. The man flew to his right and fell into a pile of metal trash cans. The lids flew off and trash flowed out of the fallen cans. His impact dented a few of the cans. The man turned over and pulled out a switchblade as I approached and faced him. He stood as the knife *clicked* into place.

"Back off, man. Stay away from me," the man said. "I'll cut you if you try that on me again."

I wore a dark gray hood over my head so people had a hard time seeing my face. He couldn't see it. Otherwise he'd see me holding back laughter.

I took a step toward him. He swung forward with his knife wielding hand. I lifted up my left hand. Before he could reach me, the knife left his hand and flew into the air. I lifted my right hand in front of me and swatted it in midair. The knife flew against the wall and the blade broke off. The man stopped. He looked at me in complete astonishment.

Without waiting for him to recover, I threw my right arm into his stomach, knocking the wind out of him. He bent over, grabbing his gut.

Before he could react, I shoved him against the wall. His legs crashed through the trash cans and his back hit the wall with a thud. He landed in a pile of trash. I reached in my back pocket and grabbed zip ties. I pulled one of his arms up and locked his wrist against the drain pipe on the wall.

Sirens. The sound was distant but becoming louder by the second.

As the man realized what was happening, he began pulling at his wrist. I made this easy for the police. He still had all the cash he stole from the store sticking out of his pockets, his fingerprints are all over the crime scene and I had caught the guy for them.

"What is this? Let me go!" he yelled as he started to understand his fate. He kept pulling on the pipe which wouldn't budge. The sirens grew even louder.

Without answering, I started to run down the street.

The man yelled after me, "No! Stop! Come back! Don't leave me here!"

I turned down an alley. Climbing the fire escape and hiding behind a lawn chair perched on the landing, I watched as the police arrived and arrested the man.

CHAPTER SIXTEEN

Vigilante Strikes Again in Decker City
By Kate Phillips

Last night, Best Tech Store was robbed as a knife-wielding man took a cashier hostage and demanded cash. The manager turned over the cash and the man released the hostage, fleeing the store. The man has since been identified as Henry Feldman. After crossing traffic and getting hit by a passing car, witnesses indicate that Feldman disappeared down an alley with a man in a gray hood in pursuit. A few minutes later, Feldman was found attached to a pipe behind a building near Francis Road. The police noted he was found alone and the man in the gray hood was nowhere to be seen.

Although no one witnessed the capture, citizens at the scene believe it was the man the gray hood who caught Feldman.

"It was like magic," eyewitness Kim McCann said. Kim reported that she was walking down the street where the chase between Henry and the man in the gray hood occurred. "People parted in front of him like they were all on a movie

set. If I didn't know better, I'd say he was moving those people with some kind of magical power."

Over the past few days, the man in gray, or The Gray Hood as many are now calling him, has been seen throughout Decker City, taking out the criminals who have been plaguing the city. Some officials worry that he might be part of the criminal network, but to date he has only targeted criminals.

Police chief William Conway said this during a press conference, "We believe this man has the right intentions, but we please ask this individual to cease their actions. It's dangerous, it's irresponsible and it's a disruption to the police force and the community. We ask for your assistance and respect in this matter and hope you leave this work to the police department."

When asked about the rumors of the man's magic, police chief William Conway said, "There is no such thing as magic."

CHAPTER SEVENTEEN

There was a knock at my office door.

"Come in," I said.

"Hey, Devin," Lara said as she opened the door and walked in. "Tommy's been annoying me at my desk again. Can you take him back to your office, please? He won't leave me alone."

I stood up. "What's he bugging you about now?"

"Ugh, everything," she responded while having her head fall to her chest. She picked her head back up and said, "He's fun to be around, I love the guy, but I want to kill him sometimes."

I walked over to her and wrapped my arms around her. "What's he doing this time?" I asked. I released one arm and kept the other around her as we walked into the hallway toward her desk.

"He keeps talking about that vigilante, The Gray Hood. I think he was waiting for you to come in but found me instead. He just kept going on and on about him. I've got a lot of work to do and personally, I don't see the fascination in this guy."

She doesn't like the vigilante? No, wait, she doesn't like me? I thought of the five criminals I had taken down so far. My mind flashed to last night. Grandpa and I rode around listening to the police scanner, waiting for our next opportunity. It was awesome.

But Lara doesn't like him? Me?

Am I going to alienate the people I care about the most? The thought turned my guts inside out. I shoved the thought from my mind. I couldn't go there. Not now, it was too early. I couldn't stop now – there was too much at stake. And I knew I had to use my power for good. I couldn't just let it become some party trick, especially with my own city suffering like it was. No way.

"So if he kept going on and on, how did you manage to get away?"

"I told him I was on my period and needed to go to the bathroom. He said 'ew' and then took a step away from my desk."

I laughed and shook my head.

"What?" Lara asked. "It worked, didn't it?"

The hallway opened into the lobby.

Tommy was waiting by Lara's desk. "Oh, you brought reinforcements or something?"

I removed my arm from Lara's shoulder as she walked back over to her desk. "Come on, Tommy, leave Lara alone and talk to me about this vigilante." I felt a little thrill, knowing we'd be talking about me.

Tommy looked at Lara as she walked by him and said, "Tattletale."

She replied by scrunching up her face and sticking her tongue out at him.

Tommy and I walked to my office and sat across each another at my desk.

I started the conversation. "Okay, so tell me about this guy in the hood."

"Dude, he's incredible! He's been taking out guys left and right. I don't think he's part of the police force because they don't want him doing what he's doing–they said it in the paper. But I think it's ridiculous. He's helping the city. How could the police not want him helping?"

"I don't kn–"

"I'll tell you why," Tommy continued.

I smiled. Evidently, it was a rhetorical question. Tommy was on a roll.

"It's because the police are being out policed! This vigilante, The Gray Hood or whatever they are calling him, is doing the police's job and they don't like it. They feel belittled, threatened and incapable of doing their job because this guy can do it better. That's why."

"Well, maybe they–"

"Oh and another thing! This guy has magical powers or something. They say he can move things without touching them…"

Lara was right; he just kept going on and on. I turned my chair to face the window behind me and looked outside while Tommy continued talking. I wonder how long she had to listen to this before she came and got me? I turned around to focus on Tommy.

"They say he's a hero. It's amazing!" Tommy paused. "Are you listening to me?"

"Who're they?" I asked.

"What?" Tommy replied.

"Who're they? You keep saying, 'they say.' So, who are they?"

Tommy shrugged his shoulders. "I don't know? They."

I shook my head back and forth. "Do you believe everything you read?" I had to play devil's advocate. I knew he had no idea it was me under the hood, but I still had to make sure he didn't have any suspicions.

"I'm telling you the truth. It's true," he said.

My office phone began to ring, thankfully interrupting Tommy's endless conversation. "Hello, this is Devin…" I answered.

"Devin, its Lara."

"Hey, what's up?"

"There's a gentleman here to see you. He said he doesn't have an appointment. Do you have a moment to meet with him?"

This was odd. This was the first time someone came in and asked to meet with me. I was usually the one tracking people down. I would love it if the business worked this way, but it rarely did.

"Sure. Send him into the conference room and I'll be there shortly. Thanks, Lara." I hung up and paused, catching Tommy's eye.

Tommy furrowed his brow. "What is it?"

"I don't know yet. Somebody wants to talk to me. Asked for me personally."

"Weird."

"Yeah. Would you work with me on this one?"

"Of course." Tommy rose and headed out the door. "I'll get my portfolio and meet you in the conference room."

I stood and walked over to my bookcase, grabbing a binder off the shelf. I mentally prepared myself for the meeting, knowing the roles Tommy and I would take. I usually did the intro, fact finders and technical stuff and passed the closing to Tommy. We both knew our stuff, but we made a good team when we built on each other's strengths. I was smooth and easy with the facts, and Tommy had a way of making clients feel comfortable in moving forward.

A blur of movement outside my door drew my eye. It was Tommy running by my office. I shook my head and smiled. I swore the guy never stood still. I grabbed a pad of paper and tucked everything under my arm and walked out of my office, shutting the door behind me. I made my way into the lobby.

Lara was ready for me. "Hi, Devin." She pointed to the room across from her desk and said, "he's in there."

"Thanks," I said.

As I approached the room, I could hear Tommy already introducing himself and beginning his endless conversations. He was the social butterfly. He could strike up a conversation with anyone about anything–a gift I wish I had. He made it seem so easy.

I walked through the doorway and closed the door behind me.

"Hey, Devin," Tommy began.

I turned and smiled, ready to greet our prospective client.

I blinked. My smile faded and my heart sunk. It couldn't be.

The man and I locked eyes and the worst parts of my childhood flashed back to me.

Tommy hadn't noticed my reaction yet. He smiled and waved his hand in a broad, welcoming arc. "This is–"

Anger rose in my chest, displacing the shock. I interrupted Tommy, finishing his sentence. "Mitchell Quinn."

CHAPTER EIGHTEEN

What was he doing here? Last I knew this guy was in prison. Right where he belonged, as far as I was concerned. I'm usually a forgiving guy, but this was one person I would never forgive nor forget what he did to me.

Yet here he stood, looking like he just popped off the pages of some men's model magazine. His attire and appearance screamed expensive. He wore a slim black suit with a white button-up shirt underneath and a royal blue tie. He had a matching blue handkerchief in his suit jacket's chest pocket and shiny cuff links that sparkled with the sunlight that was shining through the windows. His head wasn't shaved like it was back in school. He grew his hair out. It was a messy gelled-look like mine, except his looked professionally done. Mine looked like I had just rolled out of bed a few minutes ago. His cologne radiated off him and gave the room a fresh scent.

I felt like a bumbling fool next to him.

Just like I always had.

Six years of daily beatings, putdowns, and humiliation. And now he just waltzed into my office and wanted to meet with me? Knowing how he had treated me and seeing him show up like this, it seemed like he was still the narcissistic idiot he had always been.

Tommy looked confused. "I take it you two know each other?"

Mitchell smiled as he reached out with his right hand. "You could say that." I couldn't tell if his smile was friendly or devilish.

He wanted to shake my hand? I'd rather pet a snake. But I had to treat him like any other client. This was, after all, a business setting. I had to look past our previous issues and find out why he was here. I kept my eyes locked on him and slowly reached out and shook his hand. He had a tight grip, confident in his hand shake. Mitchell continued to smile. My face was a stony mask.

Mitchell's smile finally faded.

We released our grip.

Tommy chimed in. "Well...that wasn't awkward or anything. Care to fill me in on this history lesson?"

We both turned to Tommy. His look went from mine to Mitchell's and back to mine. He asked the question to both of us, seeing who would respond first.

I swallowed hard, trying to keep my voice even. "We knew each other back in grade school."

Mitchell continued where I left off. "I was–" His eyes looked up toward the ceiling as if he was trying to find the rest of his sentence up there somewhere. "...kind of a jerk to Devin back then."

"That's putting it lightly," I said.

Tommy stuck his chest out a little, showing off the size of his muscles. "I hate being the third wheel here. May I ask what happened? I know it's probably not my business, but you two seem to have a history with each other and I want to make sure this meeting doesn't end up in a fight," Tommy said.

I don't know if he meant a fight between Mitchell and him or Mitchell and me. Either way, I was thankful to have Tommy in there with me.

Mitchell ignored Tommy and said, "Devin, I was a jerk. I was wrong to treat you that way. No one should ever have to suffer through that kind of punishment and torment. I was an immature bully and I'm sorry."

He's apologizing? He sounded sincere. . . but was he for real? I wondered if it was even possible for someone to change so completely. Either this wasn't the guy I knew all those years ago or he was putting on a good act.

I decided to play along with Mitchell's apology. For now. It was in everyone's best interests, and I wanted to know why he was here. I nodded to Mitchell and said, "It's fine. It was a long time ago. We're good."

Mitchell's broad smile reappeared. "Thank you for accepting my apology. It means a lot. I've grown up a lot since then. I had my problems and issues. It was my fault and my actions that caused my problems. I got the help I needed and turned my life around."

"Good. I'm glad everything worked out for you," I replied. I realized that I had actually meant it. Still, I knew I needed to proceed with caution. Sociopathic serial killers tortured animals as children. So what did that say about children who tortured other children? Don't get complacent, I told myself.

"Uhh, okay? Being ignored isn't something I feel very strongly about," Tommy muttered.

I shook my head at Tommy's persistence. We all sat down and Mitchell and I went back and forth explaining our history–the teasing, the threats, the drugs, the jail time.

Mitchell finished the story with another display of humility. "I ended up in jail. On more than one occasion. I realized I was ruining my life and I needed a big change. I wanted to do something more with myself–something big. I started reading up on buying a business. I decided I wanted to own my own business and work for myself since it was very hard to find employment. Of course, finding a loan with my history was extremely difficult as well. People have a very hard time trusting you when you have a history like I do. Just as I'm sure you're having a hard time trusting me now." He made a point to look me in the eye.

His gaze made me feel insecure, just like it always had. I brushed it aside. I wasn't that little kid anymore.

"Eventually, after what I believed was the ultimate failure trying to secure some funds to purchase a business, I found a lender. Then I bought my first business. It was a small, going out of business arcade." He put his hands up in defense and said, "I know, an arcade, right? Who goes to those places anymore? Well, I bought it and made some upgrades. I built a concert stage, added a bar, and expanded to add some more machines and a few pool tables. I turned the place into a twenty-one and over bar and club. In the end, I had a profitable business. Besides having to pay back my debt, I wasn't operating in the red.

"I was making money, good money, and I wanted more. I found a broker to help find me another business to buy. A year later, I acquired another business. And then another. And another."

"So it sounds like you're doing well then," Tommy said.

"Yes. Over the past six years, I've acquired eight different businesses. I'm always looking for the next opportunity. Which brings me here," Mitchell said, pointing down at the table. "I've been watching the news and noticed all the crime happening in Decker City. It's awful what's happening."

"Yeah, it is," Tommy said. "Ask Devin, even he had an experience a few months ago."

I immediately glared at Tommy. Did he have to bring that up? Really?

"Seriously, Devin?" Mitchell asked. "What happened, if you don't mind me asking?"

I leaned back in my chair, cursing at Tommy in my head. He knows how much I don't like sharing my personal life. "Well," I started to say.

"He was on a date with Lara–" Tommy interrupted, clearly seeing my hesitation.

I cut him off. "Tommy...please." I spoke in the sharpest tone I had ever used with him.

His face went from excitement to sadness.

I'd have to apologize for that. "I'm sorry. It's my story, let me tell it."

I saw Tommy cheer up a little, but I could sense that sadness was still there.

"I was on a date, and some guy came out of nowhere and stole her purse. I chased him down and got it back. That's it."

Mitchell started pointing at me. "You know, I remember hearing that story on the news a few months ago. I had no idea that was you. I think you...uhh...something like you found him on the street or in an alley knocked out. Right?"

"Yeah," I responded.

"That's right, I remember that." Mitchell nodded his head. "Okay, back to the point as to why I'm here. I've been following what's happening here in the city. I've done some research and found property values are dropping. People are afraid and want to leave. Businesses aren't worth as much anymore. Land values aren't worth as much as they used to be. As troubling as the issues are right now, it's a business opportunity for me. I came back home to Decker City to build an empire. I am hoping I can rebuild and revitalize the city."

I had to admit, it sounded good. An investor with a passion for rebuilding the city was just what we needed. Still, I was struggling to trust his intentions. And I had to admit I was jealous of all the money he was making.

But it wasn't just about jealousy. It was about justice. It didn't seem right. Why him? Why was he able to find this kind of success? Knowing the kind of person he had been, why was he rewarded? My grandfather always told me I had to work hard for my success. It seemed like success had just fallen into Mitchell's lap. Who gets an investor for a business like that? I would never be able to pull that off.

Yet he seemed genuine. Maybe it was just me who couldn't let go of the past. Maybe I was bitter because of how he previously treated me. Did I want to be that person?

He'd been nothing but nice and respectful to me since he arrived here. I had to honor that by returning the favor.

Mitchell placed his hands on his folder. "And this is where you guys come in." He pointed to both of us. "Coming back to Decker City and wanting to make it my home again, I wanted to bring my investment portfolio here. I want to have a local investment adviser. I looked into what companies were around here and I saw TruGuard was number one in Decker City. What surprised me was you, Devin. You worked here. I saw it as an opportunity to make amends and hopefully have you and your partner here manage my portfolio. Think of it as an extension of trust. I'm trusting you with my money, and hopefully I can begin to earn your trust."

I thought of my own binder that lay on the table. I usually pitched new clients, but it sounded more like Mitchell was pitching me. And it was surely an interesting offer.

Mitchell added, "I heard this place was the best and I want to work with the best. I currently have a ten-million-dollar portfolio. I'll have millions more coming in once I begin my work here in Decker City. What do you guys think? Do we have a deal?"

I looked at Tommy and saw his eyes widen. I knew what he was thinking. Tommy had dollar signs in his eyes. Ten million dollars is a lot of money. Most of the clients we worked with had assets ranging anywhere from five hundred thousand to one million dollars. Mitchell was offering ten million of investable assets, with the added bonus of more on the way. This would be a big payday for us.

I just hated the fact it had to be Mitchell Quinn.

This was the proverbial offer I couldn't refuse. No matter how much I wanted to. Tommy would be furious if I refused. My superiors would be furious. I'd probably get fired, if I was truthful with myself. I had to push my emotions and feelings aside and do my job.

I knew that I didn't trust Mitchell and I never would. No matter how shiny his suit or how sweet his words. At least I could keep a close eye on him if I took his deal. Keep your friends close and your enemies closer. And I could profit from him, too. A bit of a payback, perhaps.

If someone had told me this morning when I woke up that at the end of the day, I'd be partnering with Mitchell Quinn, I'd have thought they were crazy. Yet, here I was.

"Yes, Mitchell," I responded. "We have a deal."

I could see Tommy's face light up with a huge smile. If he could have expressed his true self, he would have jumped up and down and screamed for joy. He would have leapt out of his chair and hugged the crap out of me. Thankfully, he somehow managed to keep it all inside. For the moment.

"Great! I'll send over all my account information in the morning. Do what you have to do and let me know what you need from me to get started. I look forward to working with you guys." Mitchell stood up and began walking to the door.

Tommy and I followed.

We all met at the door and shook hands. Mitchell opened the door, said his goodbyes and left. I looked at the clock. It had been just twenty minutes since we'd entered the conference room.

Life can change in an instant.

I turned to Tommy and was about to speak, but I never got the chance as he attacked me with his huge arms in a crushing bear hug. He wrapped his arms around me and lifted me off the ground. "Victory! Thank you! Thank you! Thank You! You just made us a lot of money! Woo hoooo!" He kept bouncing me up and down in his arms.

I laughed. I couldn't take away his excitement. Even Lara saw us in the doorway and couldn't help but laugh.

CHAPTER NINETEEN

Tonight was a good night to go out and blow off some steam. Whatever emotions I kept in check during today's meeting with Mitchell needed to come out. There had to be a crime happening somewhere in the city; it was almost commonplace for Decker City nowadays.

My grandfather and I went on these crime-fighting excursions together, so all of my stuff was at his place. Tonight, we were driving around town, waiting for a call.

And we'd gotten on the topic of Mitchell Quinn.

My grandfather kept his eyes forward, staring out the windshield and said, "Hmmm..." A few seconds later he turned to face me. "Sounds like he's doing well for himself."

"I don't know," I said, hesitating to agree.

"Do you trust him?"

"That's funny you mention trust. He didn't think I trusted him either. He said he wanted to bury the hatchet between us and that by handing over his assets to me, he was trying to earn my trust. He apologized for how he treated me in school and said he's done a lot of growing up. He sounded sincere."

"So it sounded like you had a good meeting," my grandfather said. "What's the problem?"

"My problem is I had to deal with his torture, his bullying, his name calling and physical abuse for six years of my life. He tormented me throughout school. You made me work part-time to help pay for my college while I worked really hard to get my degree. I had to sacrifice many hours to study in order to pass exam after exam. I went on interview after interview to finally land the job I have now. I had to work hard to get to where I am today. My problem is he was a bully. He physically and mentally abused many people growing up. Who knows, maybe he still is. He dropped out of school. He got involved with drugs and crime. He went to jail. And now he's a successful business owner with multiple businesses and has millions of dollars to show for it. How is that fair? How can he just flip a switch and be 'Mister Nice Guy' now and suddenly he finds success and money? It makes no sense!"

"First of all, you need to calm down. Second, you're right, it makes no sense. But that's life. Bad things happen to good people, and good things happen to bad people. Sure, he was a bad person to you in school. And yes, he probably doesn't deserve the success he's found. But he's just as human as you and me. He found success. You have success, too. Maybe not like him, but at least you're not suffering. Maybe he is being sincere with you. Maybe he's telling the truth. Maybe he's grown up. And I hate to say it, but you need to learn to deal with it."

"Deal with it? How could you say that after everything he's done to me? You experienced it with me. You know what he did and tried to do. You saw what it did to me during my school years."

"Devin, relax. I'm on your side."

Static from the radio interrupted our argument. "...all units...robbery in progress..." More static. "Corner of 5th and Main."

That was two blocks from me. Finally, some action! I reached for the door and pushed it open but something held me back. I turned and saw my grandfather holding onto my sleeve.

"Devin, wait–"

I pulled my sleeve free and got out of the car.

"Devin, stop!"

I slammed the door shut. I pulled the hood over my head and ran to the streets.

I turned the corner of the side street and headed down Main Street toward 5th avenue. I felt angrier as I ran. The rage built up inside of me. I could use it tonight. This was going to be fun. It would be easy. I needed to take my anger and aggression out on something, or someone, especially after how my grandfather defended Mitchell. How could he do that to me?

I crossed over 6th avenue and could see the corner ahead of me. There was a white pickup truck sitting by the corner. I moved toward the side of the buildings as I ran over there. I tried to stay out of sight. A man came rushing out of the store holding a barrel of something I couldn't see. I moved to the right into a store entrance. Looking around the corner, I watched as he placed the barrel in the truck bed and darted back into the store. I crept out of the walkway and kept to the side of the buildings.

I heard a loud bang. I found another entrance to hide in. Rolling out of the store came another barrel. A man came running after it. He picked it up and dumped it in the truck bed. He turned and made his way back into the store's dark entrance.

Once the man went back into the store, I left my hiding spot, this time sprinting toward the store. I crossed the street and threw myself against the wall of the building. With my back planted against the brick wall, there were some footsteps coming from inside the store.

I waited.

The footsteps got louder.

I peeked around the corner and saw him with some containers of liquids. He dumped them in the truck bed and ran back inside.

It was time to get this party started. I turned the corner and stood at the entrance of the store. The lights were off inside but the store was lit up with a large tactical flashlight which was stationed on the front counter. It pointed into the depths of the hardware store.

This was a well-organized hit.

I saw the shadow of the man scrummaging through some electronic devices. He was pulling them off the display shelves, tossing the ones he didn't want onto the floor.

"Hey!" I yelled, startling him in the process. He bolted upright and turned toward me. He looked like a deer in headlights.

He was still about 30 feet away from me. No problem. Before he could make another move, I pushed my arms forward, palms out, as if I was physically pushing him.

His entire body flew into the shelves behind him, knocking everything over.

I ran over to where he fell. He was pushing all the merchandise off him and kicking to help crawl backwards away from me. He started to reach in his jacket pocket. Before he could, I jumped down on top of him and pulled his arm out. He now held a knife in his hand. Disarming him would be easy.

I leaped off him to keep my distance and to avoid being sliced or stabbed. He made his way to his feet. He tried swatting at me with the knife but with a quick side step, I grabbed his arm and slammed it into the shelves next to us. One time, two times. By third time, the knife fell from his hand and dropped to the floor.

Having him distracted and stunned, I used my right hand and motioned by lifting my hand up in the air, to lift a computer monitor a few feet from us. I brought my hand toward the direction of the man standing in front of me, waiving it. The monitor flew toward him and hit him in the head. Both the man and the computer monitor fell to the ground. The monitor shattered.

I jumped on top of him and I held his right arm extended while reaching in my back pocket for my zip ties.

"Help!" the man struggled to say through his thick beard. It was hard to tell that his mouth was even moving.

I paused. He was going to call for help? He's robbing a store and then asks for help while being caught? What's wrong with this guy?

"Help!" he exclaimed again.

I pulled out the zip tie from my back pocket and was about to tie his hands to the vent grate behind him when I heard a loud pop. The noise was followed by an unseen force that pushed me forward on top of the man.

Extreme pain radiated down my left arm to my fingertips and up into my shoulder.

The man pushed me off of him and I rolled onto my back as he stood up. He started running across the store.

I laid there as a sharp and shooting pain rushed through my left arm. My breath became jagged and labored. What happened? Was I shot? It hurt to move. I lifted my head a little bit to look down.

Blood.

A lot of it.

Dizziness took over. I was weak. How did this happen? Where did the bullet come from?

Voices. Two of them. The man was talking to someone else. There were two people. I never even saw the other guy.

"Leave him," I heard one guy say.

"But he–" The guy I attacked started to say.

"I said leave him." They both ran out of the store.

I heard the truck's doors slammed shut as the engine kick to life. The tires screeched across the pavement as they hit the gas and made their getaway.

I used my right arm and pushed myself to a sitting position. I backed myself against the wall.

"Devin? Are you there?!" My grandfather said over the ear piece. "I heard a gunshot. What's happening?!"

I raised my right hand and activated the talk back feature. "Help."

It was the only thing I managed to say before I slid down the wall and everything turned to black.

CHAPTER TWENTY

P ain jolted me awake. I blinked into the darkness. Bright pinpoints of
light moved past me one after another.

Where was I? I had been in the hardware store.

But I was moving now. I was in a car. How did I get here? Who was
driving?

I tried to move. I groaned in pain. "What's happening?" I asked the
unknown driver.

"Devin, relax! Lay still. We are almost there." The voice sounded far
away and garbled. I tried to lift my head to see who was talking to me, but
I couldn't see anything. Darkness consumed me once again.

"Devin...Devin...can you hear me?"

I opened my eyes. I squinted into blinding lights.

"Hi, Devin. Welcome back."

I turned my head toward the voice. It sounded familiar. I blinked as
my eyes adjusted.

"Dr. Kane," I croaked.

"Yes, Devin, it's Dr. Kane. I want you to remain calm and lie still. How do you feel?"

"My left arm hurts. Not like before though." I felt weak. Something tugged at my arm. I glanced down. I had an IV. I went to move my arm as I spoke but winced in pain and decided to keep it still, just like the doctor asked. "What happened?"

"You were shot," Dr. Kane said. "Your grandfather over here," he turned behind him and pointed to my grandfather sitting on a chair, "drove you here. Luckily for you, the bullet lodged in your left arm and was easily extracted. You probably passed out from shock. But don't worry, you're going to be fine. I cleaned your wound and stitched you up. You should be good to go in a few minutes. You've got an IV drip of antibiotics, morphine, and fluids. You're going to need to continue taking the antibiotics. You'll also need to change the bandage and let me know if any redness, swelling or unusual bleeding occur in the next few days."

I've been shot, but don't worry? It made no sense to my clouded mind. "Thank you," I managed. I wondered how I would know if the bleeding was unusual since I'd never been shot before.

As Dr. Kane was beginning to put his tools away, he turned back to me and said, "So...you want to tell me how this happened?"

I was hesitant to speak. Did my grandfather tell him what we have been doing? Dr. Kane said not to use this ability in public. He wanted me to keep this to myself. Of course I did the complete opposite.

"Look," Dr. Kane began to say. "I'm not an idiot. I know it's you out there doing what you're doing. You're the only one I know of that can do what you do. I watch the news. I read the papers." He raised his hand in the air as if mimicking a headline, forcing his hand to extend with each word. "Hooded vigilante, able to move objects without touching them." He lowered his hand and stared back at me again. "You really think I wouldn't know that was you? What did I tell you about doing these things in the public? You're endangering yourself." Dr. Kane looked at my wound and pointed to it. "Obviously," he added.

"I know," I replied. "I just got carried away with it. It just seemed like the right thing to do, I guess."

"It's my fault," my grandfather interrupted. "I put him up to it. He was doing it to please me."

"Grandpa, that's not true. I wanted to do this just as much—"

"Wait a minute," Dr. Kane said putting both hands up in a stop motion. He looked at both of us. "I'm not putting blame on anyone here. And Devin, I'm not mad or disappointed that you went ahead and have started this vigilantism. Honestly, I'm impressed and I have to admit, partially jealous."

"Why?" I asked.

"Devin, when we discovered what you could do, I could only imagine what trouble you would be causing by having this unique ability. You have the power to move objects without physically touching them. You could have pickpocketed people and they'd have no idea. You could have stolen money from banks and casinos. You could have just started pushing people over and no one would ever suspect you. You could have used this ability for such negative things. Evil things. But you didn't. You saw what was going on in our city and you acted on it. You've used your ability for good. And not only that, but from what I've been seeing in the news, you've been pretty successful at it."

I used my right arm to point at my wounded left shoulder, "Obviously not *that* successful."

Dr. Kane chuckled. "That right there is nothing to be concerned about. That wound will heal in due time."

"Easy for you to say, Doc. You weren't the one who was shot," my grandfather added to the conversation.

"He will be fine. I promise you," Dr. Kane said to my grandfather. He turned to me, smiling. "And as for you, Mr. Hood, or whatever they're calling you, take it easy for the next few weeks while this heals. Stay off the streets for now. Let this heal. If you're going to continue doing what you're doing, you need to be at one hundred percent. So with that being said, anytime you need medical attention, I want you to see me immediately. I hope you never come back here again. But if you need my help, I will patch you up and make you good as new. I want to help you with this crusade. I want to see you succeed."

"Why are you on my side, too? Shouldn't you be the one who's telling me I'm going to get myself killed and it's dangerous?"

"Are you familiar with the name Howard Woodman? He owns one of the main pharmacies I work with to prescribe my patients' medications. When this crime wave started to kick into gear a few months ago, he was robbed. And they didn't just rob him. They gave him a few broken bones and beat him unconscious. They stole a few thousand dollars and took a lot of medication. Howard is a good friend of mine. He didn't deserve what happened to him. He's never hurt anyone.

"There are incidents like this happening all over the city and the victims don't deserve it. If you're trying to prevent another attack like what happened to my friend, then I'm on your side. You have an advantage over these criminals, and every day I look forward to reading about what you do in the paper," Dr. Kane said.

"Thank you, Dr. Kane," I said. I grinned at him. "Welcome to the party."

Dr. Kane laughed. "Now I think that's the morphine kicking in." He finished putting his equipment away and walked back over to the table I was laying on to help me up. "I don't want to see you for a while, maybe never. Nothing personal."

"Yeah, I get it." I was still grinning like an idiot. "Hey, Gramps, ready to take me home?" I started singing some old country song that my grandfather used to play.

My grandfather shook his head. "Oh, it's going to be a fun night tonight!"

Dr. Kane became more serious. "Listen, Devin. I want you to be careful out there. It's dangerous."

Once I was upright, he placed a cotton swab on top of the needle in my arm and took out the IV. "This will be wearing off in a few hours so I want you to take these," he said while handing me a bottle of pills. "These will help with the pain. In a few days you won't need them, but until then, take them as needed."

I reached out to take the bottle.

My grandfather snatched them out of my hands. "I'll take those."

I frowned at my grandfather, but then turned back to Dr. Kane. "Thank you for everything."

"Anytime." He put his arm under my right shoulder and helped me off the table.

My grandfather helped me into the passenger seat of his car and shut the door. I heard him shuffle around to the driver's side. He sat heavily in his seat and rubbed his face before turning on the engine.

Once we started driving, I said, "Look, I want to apologize for earlier. I was a jerk. I know you were trying to—"

My grandfather interrupted and said, "Seriously, don't worry about it. I'm just glad you're okay. When I heard that gunshot…" He shook his head.

"Yeah, I was angry and upset and wasn't thinking. I just walked in and didn't even look around. I only saw one person."

"Did you see who shot you? Anything at all that may help us find these guys."

I was embarrassed. Since I started going out at night, I was lucky enough to be as successful as I was. And what kind of moron enters a robbery in progress and doesn't even check to see if there's more than one person in the place? I felt like a failure.

Maybe I shouldn't be doing this. I didn't have the training for it. I should leave it to the professionals.

"Don't be ridiculous! You heard what Dr. Kane said."

I raised my eyebrows and frowned in alarm. Was my grandfather reading my mind?

My grandfather looked at me and turned away, still shaking his head. "What do you mean, reading your mind? You're talking out loud! Man, you are a major airhead on that dope. Do me a favor – don't ever become a druggie. You wouldn't make a good one."

"Well, I guess you're right. About continuing, not the druggie thing. Well, both, but…anyway…I just need to be calm and rational, not acting on impulse and anger."

"Good idea."

I sighed in frustration. "But what now? I'm out of commission for a few weeks. Who knows what will happen now that I can't get out there and help?!"

"Did you see the guy that shot you?"

"No. I didn't see him. I was only involved with the one guy."

My grandfather's face lit up. "Okay, good. So describe this guy. What did he look like? What was he wearing? Did he have any distinguishing features? Did you see them driving a car? Anything at all?"

My brain started rattling around for answers. "It was dark," I started to say. "There was a light, but it didn't light up the store enough to get a good look at him. He was about my height, short hair, umm…he had a beard. I don't really know what else."

A wave of disappointment rushed through me. I was awful at this. How could I have thought I would make a great superhero? I can't even remember tiny details about what happened to me. And then it hit me like a ton of bricks.

"A white truck! They were driving a white truck!" I blurted out, excited that I finally seemed to have some answers.

"Okay, good. This is a start. Did you catch their license plate?" my grandfather replied.

As quickly as that excitement came over me, it was washed away with failure again. I didn't know the license plate. Why didn't I think to look at it and memorize it? I was so stupid!

"No, I didn't get it. I'm so stupid. I don't see a second guy in the store who shoots me, and the only piece of evidence I may have, I don't remember or didn't think to look at. And all I know is that there's a white truck. Gee, that really narrows it down."

"It's okay, Devin, we will find out who did this. And for the record, you aren't stupid. You are one of the bravest people I know."

I glowered out the window.

"Hey. Look at me."

I wouldn't.

"You know I'm trying to tell you something here."

I rolled my eyes and turned toward him.

"How many people do you know of that would go out hunting bad guys at night?! Dr. Kane is right. Most guys would use their ability for their own selfish gain. You, on the other hand, have stopped some dangerous people out there and the public has you to thank for that. I'm really proud of you, Devin."

He rarely told me he was proud of me. I felt like a million bucks.

"Thanks, Grandpa. I…I really appreciate that. It means a lot, especially, you know…from you."

"Yeah, well, you're welcome. But you're still one dumb idiot for allowing yourself to be shot at. We'll have to give you a third eye or something in the back of your head. You got a pain in your arm, but you're a pain in my behind."

I smiled. It didn't take long for Grandpa to return to his normal gruff self.

"Also, I think it's time we update this hooded outfit of yours. If you're going to be getting shot at, maybe we find something to make it more bulletproof. Oh, and another thing. You need a name."

"Why do I need a name?" I asked.

"Why?! Seriously?! Every hero has a name. Maybe I'll just call you the Hooded Idiot."

I started laughing. "Okay, I get it. I need a name. How about...umm... Hoodini?"

"Really? You're going to name yourself after a crazy magician who killed himself accidentally inside a box? Come on, Devin, let's have some originality."

I really had no idea for a name.

My grandfather started throwing out one name after another. I hated all of them.

Our bickering went back and forth the whole ride home as we drove into the blinding light of the sunrise.

CHAPTER TWENTY-ONE

I shot out of bed. There was a rumbling coming from my grandfather's backyard. It sounded like construction machines were battling to the death outside my window.

I turned to get out of bed and the pain from my attack last night shot down through my arm. I grabbed my injured arm and winced as I walked to the window.

An excavator was digging a large hole in my grandfather's backyard. Seven or eight burly construction workers surrounded the machine. Three had shovels and were digging some of the dirt the excavator left behind. Two were moving the dirt into a front loader with wheelbarrows.

I groaned. What was he up to now? And why so early in the morning?

I headed for the kitchen. My grandfather was sitting at the kitchen table, drinking coffee and watching the news as if nothing unusual were happening.

I walked to the glass doors and pointed to the construction. "What are you doing to your backyard?"

He put his coffee down and said, "What do you mean?" He turned to look outside. "Holy crap! What are they doing to my backyard?!"

"Really, Grandpa? I'm not falling for it this time."

He laughed and sat back. "I'm putting in a pool."

I turned to him. "A pool?" I looked back outside and saw the large hole. "It seems kind of big for a pool."

He looked back out the window again at all the construction. "It's a large pool. Olympic size."

"Why are you putting in a pool?"

"What is this, twenty questions? Summer is coming up and I want to go swimming. Do you have any more brain-busting questions for me, or can I go back to drinking my coffee?"

"Sure, Grandpa, you can continue drinking your coffee." I pulled a chair out and sat with him.

"Good. It's too early for questions," he replied.

We sat and watched the news as a report came on about the incident last night.

"A robbery turned violent last night as the crime wave heats up. Our reporter on the streets, Alan Haven, is on the scene and has the story."

"Thanks, Bill. Late last night, a gunshot was heard inside the store of Hardware Boutique on the corner of 5th and Main. Police found blood at the scene and are on the lookout for someone who may have been the victim of a gunshot wound. The store was found trashed. Police aren't saying yet whether it was a robbery. So far, police only know that there was a struggle and that struggle led to gunfire. The police don't have anyone in custody or have any suspects at this time. If anyone has any information regarding this incident, they are being advised to contact the authorities."

"Okay, Alan, thank you for that story. We will check back with you later as more develops."

My grandfather caught my eye. "I wouldn't suggest going around telling people you were shot." He looked at my arm. "How are you feeling, by the way?"

"It still hurts, but I'll live. And I'm not telling anyone."

And then it hit me.

"Crap," I blurted out loud.

"What?" my grandfather asked.

"I'm supposed to go over to Lara's tomorrow night. How am I going to explain this?" I said, raising my arm a few inches.

"Just tell her you tripped over your untied shoelace. I'm sure she'll believe you."

"Way to try and make me look bad. I'm not clumsy."

My grandfather stared at me. He had this look like he was deep in thought. It was an unusual posture for him.

After a long pause, he said, "You're right. You're not clumsy." He stood up. "Follow me." He walked to the back door.

I stood up and followed him, wondering what we were going to do now.

He opened the door and I squinted my eyes at the bright sun light. I looked up at the sky as I blocked out the sun with my hand. There wasn't a cloud in the sky. The machine's noises screamed louder once we stepped out into the fresh air. We walked to his shed as he opened the door. The sunlight found its way inside and bounced around the walls, casting prisms of light and color onto the walls. It was a stark contrast to the screeching of the machines just a few feet away.

"I was going to wait to give this to you," my grandfather yelled.

I followed him into the shed. "Give me what?" I yelled back. I closed the shed doors behind me. The noise died down to a low rumble. He moved out of the way.

"A motorcycle?" I asked in disbelief. It was a jet black motorcycle. Everything was black—the seat, the handlebars, the wheels, the body.

My jaw dropped. I don't know what my grandfather was thinking buying me this. After my car accident, he thinks I'll be safe on one of these?

"I figured this would help you get around a little quicker when you are doing your…you know…hero stuff," my grandfather said.

I couldn't wrap my head around it. It just seemed like my life was getting more dangerous by the day. First the car accident, then becoming this vigilante at night, being shot, and now a motorcycle? I couldn't decide which activity was the most dangerous.

I never thought in a million years I'd be throwing myself into this much danger. Yet here I was. And when I really thought about it, I was loving every minute of this. The bike in front of me looked incredibly cool.

"You don't like it?"

"Are you kidding me?" My face broke into a smile. "I love it! Only problem is I've never ridden one before."

"And that's exactly where your excuse for your arm will come in. You fell off and injured your arm."

It made sense. And at least I wouldn't be lying about not having a motorcycle. Except–

"Except if people knew I had a motorcycle and see me riding this, then see the…well, me in my hood riding the same bike, wouldn't my identity be known?" I still didn't know what to call myself so it seemed weird saying something other than me.

"Don't worry about that. It'll only be used by you on your adventures and there won't be a license plate or any other identifying markings on it to be traced back to you or me. Plus, I don't see you using it anytime soon. You need to fix that arm of yours first."

I nodded. I'd never ridden a motorcycle before, but I was about to learn.

I winced as a jolt of pain shot through my shoulder as if entering the conversation. Being honest with myself, I had to admit that I might have avoided getting shot if I wasn't such a hot head last night. The conversation about Mitchell between my grandfather and me set me off.

My grandfather was right. I needed to get over it. It was close to 15 years ago. I still didn't trust him, but that didn't mean I had to take out my frustration on my grandfather. I owed him an apology.

"I really appreciate everything you're doing for me. You didn't have to get this bike for me. Especially after the way I treated you yesterday. And you were right. I have to let go of this grudge against Mitchell."

"You don't have to apologize to me." A smile then appeared on his face. "But now that you did, I don't feel as bad anymore giving this bike to a *jerk*."

I shook my head. He always knew how make light of any moment. "I'm serious, Grandpa, I almost got myself killed."

"I know you're serious. I am too. You don't have to apologize to me. I'm not going to tell you what you want to hear. I'm going to tell you how it is. And it may make you angry. I won't sugarcoat anything for you."

I nodded. "I know. I wouldn't have it any other way. Even when you do make me mad." I glared at my grandfather in mock anger.

He snorted. "Speaking of sugar," he added, "my coffee is getting cold." We closed the shed and walked back inside his house.

CHAPTER TWENTY-TWO

"Oh no, what happened to you?" Lara asked after opening her front door.

"I…uhh–" I started to say. Lying to her really bothered me. All I wanted to do was tell her everything. I promised myself that one day soon I would. Just not today.

"My grandfather convinced me to try a motorcycle." I raised my arm while nodding to the sling. "This is what happened." Grandpa really had given me a motorcycle, so it wasn't a complete lie.

"And I guess you fell off?" she asked.

"How'd you guess?"

I walked inside and she shut the door behind me. "Are you okay?"

"Yeah, I'll be all right. It just hurts."

"You poor thing. You must have some bad luck following you around. First the car accident and now this? I think you should stay away from vehicles altogether and just walk everywhere from now on."

I nodded in agreement. "You're probably right." As I made my way further into her house, I was hit with a smoky barbecue smell coming from her kitchen. "What are you making? It smells delicious."

Her face lit up with excitement. "I hope you like it! I'm making barbecue pork ribs. I've been cooking them for a few hours. They should be done any minute."

"Yum," I said. I loved barbecue food. It always reminded me of how badly my grandfather would screw up cooking the easiest of foods and how frustrated he would get. How hard is it to cook hamburgers and hot dogs? Most of the time, after waiting for him to make dinner, he would throw it out because he overcooked it. After multiple attempts, he would just throw his hands up in the air and tell me to get my jacket because we were going out.

As I followed her into the kitchen, she started asking me about my meeting with Tommy and our new client. I sat down at her kitchen table while she finished making dinner and explained my history with Mitchell.

"Sounds like a nice guy," she said.

"Oh yeah. He was a real pleasure to be around back then." I shrugged. "Now, he seems all right, I guess."

"You sound like you still hold a grudge against him."

"How did you know that?"

"Come on, seriously? I've known you for a few years now. I can tell by your voice. The way you described your history between you two, you just had such resentment in your voice."

She picked up on it easily. And I know my grandfather did. I wonder if Mitchell had?

I shrugged it off as she brought over a full plate of ribs and placed it in the center of the table.

"Dig in," Lara said.

After dinner, we made our way to the couch to watch television. We ended up watching a marathon of reality storage locker shows. People bid on storage lockers that have been abandoned and whoever wins gets to keep what's inside. Lara and I made bets with one another to which lockers would be worth the most. After two shows, we were each tied.

The third show started and once we got a glimpse of what was inside, we made our bets.

"I can't believe you picked that one!?" Lara interjected. "It was full of junk! You just lost this match."

"Just wait for it. They will open that trunk and something expensive will be sitting there underneath a blanket or something," I replied.

"Well, it looks like you'll be cooking dinner the next time since you're definitely not winning this."

"I didn't have the best teacher," referring to my grandfather's horrible cooking, "so I doubt I could be able to top tonight's dinner. Wait a minute, I haven't lost yet."

Without missing a beat, Lara responded, "Exactly, haven't lost. *Yet.*"

I walked into that one. "Oh really?" I began to say. "I can easily win this battle." I reached toward her with my right hand and grabbed her left side. I squeezed it slightly and she burst into laughter and started kicking her legs all over the place. She was extremely ticklish on her sides. She slumped to her side and laid across the couch, trying to protect herself. I climbed on top of her as she couldn't control herself while I kept tickling her.

Suddenly, the room lit up by a bright light followed by a rumbling and what sounded like an explosion. Both Lara and I jumped off the couch and ran toward the front door. Lara made it to the front door before I did and she yanked it open. "Do you see that?!" she exclaimed as she placed her hands over her mouth. A large mushroom cloud of smoke was billowing up from about a mile or two away. I couldn't tell exactly where the explosion was but it was a little too close for comfort. "Was that an explosion?" Lara added.

"I don't know," I said as I put my right arm around her in an attempt to comfort her. All I wanted to do was run toward the smoke and help whoever was in need. This sling on my left arm made me feel helpless.

Lara ran out from under my arm and went back inside. I stood there for a moment as the smoke cloud rose higher in the air and began to dissipate.

"Devin, come in here!" Lara yelled from her living room. I turned toward the door and made my way back inside. She was standing by the TV with the remote in her hand. The news was turned on.

"...the north side of Decker City. Smoke can be seen high above the city. If you are just tuning in, there was an explosion at Harley's Paper Mill

Factory. We don't know what caused the explosion as of yet and we don't know if there are any casualties as a result."

"Do you think it was a terrorist attack?" Lara asked me in a panicked voice. "Like we need that on top of all this crime!"

All I wanted to do was tell her it would be all right. But that might be a lie.

"I have no idea," I said. The news wasn't giving us much to go on. Whether this was terrorism or more evidence of the growing violence in the city, it meant someone was taking things to the next level.

"We have reports beginning to come in," the news anchor interrupted, pressing against his ear listening to the incoming information. "We have just heard from our sources that the authorities are already suspecting foul play. Unconfirmed reports are saying that it might have been a bomb. We are still unsure about causalities or injuries, but we will keep you updated as the information comes in."

Lara just fell backwards onto the couch behind her. She just sunk into it as if she was sinking in quicksand. "I can't believe it," she said. "Who could do something like this?"

"I have no idea," I responded.

"I mean, I don't condone it, but I get the robberies and thefts. That's typical everywhere. But this?" Lara lifted her hands, palm up toward the television. "I don't understand this. Why would someone do *this*?"

"I don't know."

I sat down next to Lara and put my arm back around her. "Everything will be all right. The police are probably there by now and everything should be under control."

She turned to look at me. "Do you think that vigilante is involved?"

How did she come to that conclusion? After everything I've tried to do for this city, how could Lara possibly think that? I had to defend that image. I didn't want my girlfriend thinking the vigilante was a villain. "I don't think so. Why would he do something like that? The papers have been saying he's been helping, not hurting us."

She turned to face the television again. "I guess you're right." She fell silent as she stared back at the TV. She was glued to the screen, watching everything that was happening.

Reporters were discussing the same details over and over again. An explosion at Harley's Paper Mill Factory, I get it. Eyewitnesses are saying it was a bomb. I wanted to hear something new.

Lara finally spoke. "If the vigilante is here to help, do you think he's there now? Do you think he's trying to help?"

I wished I could be doing something to help. It was frustrating and disappointing not being able to help. "I'm sure the vigilante is doing what he can," I told her.

"I hope so," she replied, not taking her eyes off the screen. There was a shot from the news chopper that overlooked the destruction. We could see smoke billowing out from the building which was engulfed in flames. "I hope no one was in there."

Sirens rang in the distance as they approached the scene. We could hear them coming from all directions. I stood up and walked to the front door which I left open. I stepped outside as a fire truck came racing by, sirens blaring. Out in the distance toward the city, the area was lit up by the fire.

My phone started to ring. It was my grandfather.

"Hello?" I answered.

"Devin! Are you okay?"

"Yeah, I'm fine. Lara and I are maybe two miles away."

"Okay, good. I just wanted to make sure you guys were okay. I can't believe what they are telling us...a bomb? In Decker City?"

"I know, it's crazy." I turned around to check on Lara inside. She was still glued to the television listening to the news. I stepped further outside and spoke quieter into the phone. "All I want to do is go there and find out what's going on. After everything we've been doing, it's so difficult to stay put and watch this from the sidelines."

"I know, Devin. But this is definitely not safe right now. Staying put is the best option. We'll get back out there again when you're healed up."

As I was about to respond, Lara came walking outside. "Who's that?" she asked.

I stuck my index finger up in the air, indicating *hold on one second*. "I know," I said responding to my grandfather. "I'm going to go so I can get back to the news with Lara."

"Okay. Be careful, Devin. Talk to you later."

"It was my grandfather," I told Lara as I put the phone back in my pocket. "He just wanted to make sure we were okay."

"Oh, okay. Some new footage is coming in from the bombing if you want to watch," Lara said. We walked back inside and sat back down in front of the television.

"...some footage coming in from people on the streets who recorded what happened. Keep in mind, this is footage taken from cell phones and sent in directly to us. Some of it may be graphic in nature. If you have young children, you may want to have them leave the room," the news anchor stated. Following her warning, the screen turned into shaky camera footage.

A loud engine roared to life on the screen followed by some people talking in the background. I couldn't make out what they were saying.

It wasn't just any bomb. This was deliberate. It was intentional. The explosion was caused by a car bomb.

Lara and I watched as the vehicle sped down the street as someone recorded from a top story window. The vehicle ran directly into the front of the building and exploded with such force, the person holding the camera was blown backwards as the window he was standing in front of came shattering down. The news station rewound the footage and played it again, showing the vehicle as it approached the building and exploded.

The vehicle carrying the bomb was a white truck; the same white truck that was used by the person who shot me.

CHAPTER TWENTY-THREE

I stayed the night at Lara's place. I couldn't leave after what happened. She was terrified and I didn't blame her. The explosion was about two miles away from her house, but the massive smoke cloud made it look like it was right around the corner. She had shut down after that incident, glued to the television. We both fell asleep on her sofa watching the news reports flood in.

When we awoke, Lara told me she wanted me to drive her to work. I agreed and she started to get ready.

The water began running in her shower as I reached for the remote for the television. I turned it on to find the news coverage still on about the bombing. They were showing footage of police and firefighters starting to remove debris from the site. The news anchor still didn't know whether there were any casualties from the explosion and said they wouldn't know until the authorities cleaned up the area. There were multiple injuries, but nothing too serious.

It seemed like it was my fault. I should have stopped those guys who were robbing that store. If I did, this attack wouldn't have happened.

A few minutes went by and Lara turned the shower turn off. I glanced at the clock. 7:47. We still needed to get to my place so I could change and head into work. I had some leeway on lateness, but Lara needed to be at work and at her desk by 9:00 AM.

I continued watching the news waiting for Lara. I turned to look at the clock again-7:59. She was going to be late if she didn't hurry. I stood up and turned the TV off as I made my way to her bedroom door. "Lara, we need to hurry or else we will…" I trailed off as she came walking out of her bedroom. She wore a white collar, buttoned, long sleeve shirt. Her black skirt came down to her knees with a slit down the back. Her black heels, which must have added two or three inches to her height, clicked as she stepped off her carpeted bedroom and walked onto her wooded hallway floor. Even in the face of terror, she still looked amazing.

"Ready?" she asked. I couldn't stop staring at her. She was beautiful as always. I couldn't believe after all this time I was finally with Lara Scarlette.

"What?" she said.

I shook the thought away and smiled. "Nothing. Come on, we're going to be late." I grabbed her hand and we walked out the door.

There were very few cars on the road. It was weird. Almost apocalyptic.

We made it back to my apartment in record time and I ran inside to change. Lara waited for me in my car so I skipped the shower. I was probably less than five minutes, even with my injury.

In what should have been about a thirty-minute drive to work from my apartment, was completed in about half the time. As we pulled up to the building, we saw Tommy getting out of his car. He waved as we passed him looking for a parking spot. We parked about ten cars away. As we got out, he was already walking over toward us.

"Hey guys!" he began to say. "Look at these two love birds driving to work together."

I shook my head at him and widened my eyes, hoping he would get my message. *Don't start this now, she's not in the mood.*

He wiped the smile off his face and calmed down. He understood.

"So," he began to say. "It's crazy out there, isn't it?" He didn't address the question to either of us. It was just left out there for one of us to answer. With how Lara was feeling, I doubt it would be her.

"Yeah, it is," I replied.

Tommy did a double take of my arm, not noticing it before. "What happened to you?"

"My grandfather took me out looking at some off road vehicles for his house. He saw a motorcycle and wanted me to try. I took it for a ride. Obviously, I didn't fare that well."

"Dude, that sucks. I hope you feel better."

"Thanks, man."

As we rounded the corner to the front of the building, Tommy spoke up again. "I heard on the radio on my way here, the truck that crashed into the building was unmanned."

Unmanned? How could that be? As curious as I was now, I knew Lara didn't want to talk about it.

He unfortunately continued. "They said it was probably rigged to a device so someone can control it. Like James Bond style."

"Except James Bond wouldn't blow up a building, Tommy..." Lara butted in.

Tommy looked at me, his eyes peering at me, asking for an explanation.

I shook my head again. Lara didn't see any of this as she walked in front of us. I'd tell Tommy once we made it to my office.

We walked inside. Lara reached the elevator first. She pushed the up button. Immediately, the elevator doors opened. The three of us stepped inside. The doors began to shut when an arm reached through the doors and stopped them. The elevator doors slowly reopened. Standing in front of us was Mitchell Quinn.

He stood there in a gray suit with a blue and white colored gingham shirt. The two top buttons were unbuttoned. No tie this time. I wish I could pull off wearing that. I felt ridiculous in comparison.

"Oh, hey guys," he said stepping into the elevator with us. "Just the people I wanted to see."

"Hi, Mr. Quinn," Tommy said.

What a suck up.

I nodded at him, acting more friendly than professional. "Hey, Mitchell. What's up?"

Before he could respond, I saw him look Lara up and down. If I already didn't like him, this gave me a reason to hate him.

"Hey there," he spoke to Lara. "Sitting at your desk the last time we met, I really didn't get a good look at you. But you are absolutely gorgeous."

I may have hit him if I wasn't already injured.

"Thank you," Lara simply responded, not even turning to look at him.

Tommy elbowed me and whispered, "He's hittin' on your girl."

Mitchell turned to face us, then returned his gaze to Lara. "So this is Lara. You're one lucky man, Devin."

The elevator felt very crowded. After what seemed like twice the normal time, the doors opened. Lara walked ahead of us and went into the office.

Before Tommy and I could follow, Mitchell turned to face us. "So I needed to speak to…" He trailed off. He looked at my arm. "What happened there?"

I didn't want to explain my embarrassing cover story of falling off a motorcycle so I said, "Long story."

"Oh, okay then. I hope everything is all right. Anyway, I need to speak to you two if you have a couple of minutes."

"Of course," Tommy was quick to reply. "Give us a minute and we'll meet you in the conference room."

"Thank you," Mitchell said.

Mitchell stepped out of the way so Tommy could reach forward to open our office door. He held it open for me as I walked through, followed by Mitchell. Tommy and I proceeded straight down the hallway as Mitchell entered the conference room to the right.

Lara was seated on our left. I smiled as I walked by. She returned the smile in my direction.

Once we were clear, he said, "Dude, I think she hates me."

We walked into my office and I shut the door. "She doesn't hate you, Tommy. She's just shaken up about the bombing last night. She doesn't live far from where it happened. Her place rumbled like an earthquake when the explosion went off. She's just scared. She'll be back to herself soon."

"Oh, man. I had no idea. I should apologize to her."

"You don't have to. Don't worry about it. Just ease off the joking around for a few days. Try to calm down around her."

"Calm down?" He seemed to ponder the phrase. "You're asking a lot of me, you know that right?"

"You'll be fine." I took off my jacket and placed it over my chair behind my desk. I reached forward onto my desk and grabbed Mitchell's folder with all of his papers in it. It was just where I left it, considering we just met three days ago.

What could he possibly want to meet about so soon? We had all his paperwork in order and ready to be submitted. Maybe he wanted to back out of the deal we made? That wouldn't go over so well with Tommy. My feelings were more mixed. Sure, I would be disappointed over the lost commission we would have made, but at least I wouldn't have to work with Mitchell. Scratch that – work *for* Mitchell.

"You ready?" I asked Tommy.

"Yup," he replied.

I opened my office door and we started walking down the hall to the conference room. We walked by Lara's desk at the front and Tommy whispered, "I'm sorry" as he walked by. She was on the phone but was a great multi-tasker. She smiled slightly and nodded at him. As I passed her desk, Lara looked at me and let her head fall to the side, followed by having her tongue hang out.

A small smile emerged on my face at her lack of liveliness this morning. Maybe by lunch time she won't feel the need to look like a hanging corpse talking on the phone.

Tommy opened the door to the conference room and we entered. Mitchell was sitting down, staring out our window wall. He turned and stood up to greet us again. Once the exchange was over, we all took our seats.

I placed the folder down in front of me. "So Mitchell, what did you want to talk about?" I asked.

"Thank you gentlemen for meeting with me on such short notice." He looked down at the folder I placed in front of me. "Is that our paperwork from Friday?"

I guess he really was pulling out of the deal. "Yes, it is. Why? Is there something wrong?"

"No, not at all. I actually needed to make some changes."

"Anything you need, Mr. Quinn," Tommy said.

Tommy's attitude irritated me, even though it was the same attitude he always had with clients.

"What do you need to change?" I asked him.

"The amount of funds going into the account."

Tommy jumped in. "Mr. Quinn, we have many different options and products for your funds. We could easily move some money around if you feel uncomfortable with this large amount you're bringing over."

If this wasn't in a meeting setting, I would have begun laughing. This was too much. Tommy seemed so worried about this large amount of money.

Mitchell started to laugh for me. He shook his head. "I like you, Tommy. You're funny. When did I ever say I was moving money out? Don't worry, your fees or commission or whatever you're bound to make from this deal is still intact. In fact, it may grow. Much larger I would imagine. I want to move a substantial amount of money *in*."

Tommy's face flushed red in embarrassment.

Mitchell had called him out on wanting that commission. He still had a talent for making people feel small and stupid.

"How much more are we talking about?" I asked.

"Multiply my original value by five."

"Fifty million?"

"Probably a little above that, but yes, around fifty million. Possibly closer to sixty. I don't have an exact figure yet. I'm selling the remaining businesses and property I have back home and moving all of my funds here."

That was a lot of money. How did he make all of that from just his businesses? If Tommy wasn't salivating from the original commission, I know he's jumping for joy now. Out of my peripheral vision, I could see him holding his best poker face, possibly still embarrassed by Mitchell's comment.

"May I ask why?" I asked.

"This may come off as inappropriate," Mitchell began. "But there's a business opportunity to be had in Decker City from the bombing last night. I want to help this city. It's suffering right now from the violence and

Decker City needs someone to be their hero. Not this vigilante idiot who's running around in a hood, but someone they can see. Someone they can look up to. Someone who has the money to rebuild. And someone who can say this is their home, where they grew up."

"You sound like you're running for mayor or something," I said.

Mitchell laughed. "No, I'm not running for mayor. I wouldn't be good in office. You saw me in school, I usually lead by getting people to do things for me, not by doing them myself."

He looked over at Tommy who fell silent after his comment earlier. "What happened? Dollar signs got your tongue? You thinking about that large commission coming your way?"

He wasn't going to let Tommy live that down. Same old Mitchell. Deep down, I suspected nothing had changed.

"No sir," Tommy cleared his throat. "I'm just taking it all in. Fifty million is a lot of money. Are you sure you want to transfer it in just this one account? Wouldn't you like to spread out the risk?"

"Don't worry about that. The money won't be in there long enough to be that exposed to the market risk you're suggesting. I plan on purchasing the building that was bombed. Well, actually the land."

Mitchell was going to buy it? Why? It would require major repairs. Why would he invest all that money in something like this?

"I hate to keep asking the same question," I began to say. "But why?"

Without missing a beat, he responded. "Why not? It's in the heart of the downtown district. It's a perfect location for a thriving business to grow. Millions of people pass by there by car or bus or by simply walking. The foot traffic itself is tens of thousands daily. And as unfortunate as it is, it's not worth as much anymore. Especially after last night."

He had done his research. Could he have been responsible? I pushed the thought away. That was too much, even for him. He was guilty of drugs and some petty crimes, but not this.

"It is unfortunate," Tommy said. "I haven't heard much from it yet. I don't even think they have a suspect."

"I've been wondering the same thing. I intend to ask the police chief that very question when I meet with him this afternoon. Conway, I believe his name is?" Mitchell said.

"Yes, that's his name," I told him. I tried to sound friendly and curious. "What are you meeting with him about?"

"Just the usual. How I can help. I'm thinking a sizable donation for the police department may help with that, wouldn't you say?"

I fought to control the edge in my voice. He was just showing off at this point. "I think they will need all the help they can get, and I'm sure they will appreciate your donation."

Mitchell glanced down at his watch. "Oh! I don't mean to cut this short, but my meeting with Mr. Conway is at 10 AM." He stood up.

Both Tommy and I stood up with him.

"Thank you for meeting with me. I'll have my accountant email all the information over to you about the new funds coming in." He reached across the table and shook Tommy's hand, followed by mine.

"Thank you," I said.

Mitchell walked toward the door as Tommy opened it for him.

Lara gave him a friendly smile as he left. "Have a nice day."

Tommy shut the door and his face lit up. "Fifty million dollars!? Are you kidding me?! You are the greatest guy ever. Do you have any more rich friends like him?"

Friend? Mitchell wasn't a friend. He was far from that. Could he be trusted? Was I just jealous and holding a grudge?

Time would tell.

CHAPTER TWENTY-FOUR

Explosion Rocks the Streets of Decker City
While Local Hero Comes to the Rescue
By Kate Phillips

A large mushroom cloud hung over Decker City after a car bomb went off on Sunday night. The vehicle was a white pickup truck carrying explosives. It struck a building in the heart of downtown. The bomb resulted in seventeen injuries, two of which are in critical condition. The other fifteen injured citizens have been released from the hospital. There has only been one reported death.

The truck was driven by remote control. Police Chief William Conway acknowledged this is a highly advanced piece of technology. He held a press conference on Monday afternoon to discuss the situation.

"Terrorism like this will not be tolerated! We will find who is responsible. We will hunt them down, each and every last one of them. We will make sure they are brought to justice for their actions," the police chief said.

During this time, he brought out a local businessman on stage to accompany him. He introduced Mitchell Quinn as a homegrown local who turned his life around for the better and became a multimillionaire, almost overnight. In his younger years, Mitchell Quinn was arrested multiple times for criminal activity, including theft, assault, grand theft auto and numerous drug-related incidents. He was placed in a rehab facility and released soon after on good behavior. He moved to Forsyth City and began working for himself by owning and operating his first business. With his newfound success, he purchased more businesses and soon became a business mogul.

"I grew up in this city," Mitchell Quinn said during the press conference. "I refuse to let it die like this. I know I was part of the problem in my childhood, but I've changed. I've grown up. I got the help I needed and I've bettered myself. I've risen from the bottom and made my way to the top. If I can do it, these criminals can do the same as well. They need help. This city needs help. The police department needs help."

Mitchell Quinn donated a large sum of money to the police department to help catch and rehabilitate these criminals.

"This $250,000 donation to the department is exactly what we need to get this city back on track," Police Chief William Conway said, holding up a large check. "I look forward to a great relationship."

Mitchell Quinn also plans to pay for the clean-up and repair work to the area hit by the bombing. He stated he plans to come back home and bring the businesses and jobs back to Decker City which have left due to the increased criminal activity.

It is exciting to see a real hero emerging from the darkness that has clouded our city in recent months. I, for one, look forward to a future of new beginnings, led by our own caring citizens like Mitchell Quinn.

CHAPTER TWENTY-FIVE

It had been an excruciatingly long month since my meeting with Mitchell and my incident with a bullet. Despite Mitchell's grandiose announcement about saving the city and his huge donation to the police, crime continued to dominate the city.

My grandfather and I sat in his car around the corner of a convenience store that had been robbed three times in the past ten days. Something was bound to happen again and if something happened tonight, I would make sure that store wouldn't get robbed a fourth time.

I wondered why this store kept getting hit. My mind whirled with possibilities and with the first surge of anticipation for tonight's events.

It was good to be back.

While we listened to the police scanner and watched the streets from the car, we had on the AM radio listening to the news. "It's been one month since the horrific act of terrorism when that car bomb struck this building here behind me," the news reporter on the radio said. "Mr. Quinn has kept his word and has moved things along quite quickly, already beginning construction of his new commercial shopping center and entertainment area. He plans to have it partially open within six to eight months and will feature a concert hall, a bowling alley, multiple restaurants, places for shopping and much more. This area he's developing is a much needed change from the warehouses and run down store fronts plaguing this district. Speaking with Mitchell Quinn earlier, he had this to say."

"I look forward to having a beautiful place for families to congregate and have a good time. I'm bringing the experience and expertise from my accomplished businesses in Forsyth City to Decker City. Because of the terrible attack on this city, all the workers who lost their jobs because of the destruction of their business have been offered a job at my facility. I also have employees and contractors working around the clock to complete this construction in record time. I have faith and confidence that with all the hard work being done, we will be opening at least portions of this facility before my six-month time frame."

My grandfather reached forward and turned down the volume on the radio. "Nice guy. Seems like people are going to have a new place to visit soon."

"Yeah, I guess so," I responded. "I've driven by a few times and these guys are quick. I've never seen a new construction go up like that."

"It's pretty impressive," my grandfather replied.

"I'll also note Mitchell took no time to clean up the destruction site to make room for *his* new construction." The media was praising the guy. It was like he was the savior they needed. I felt like the time I spent recovering, everyone forgot about me. I wasn't important anymore because *Mitchell Quinn* was making this city a better place.

"You still have a problem with him, don't you?" my grandfather asked.

"I don't necessarily have a problem with him, I–"

"Liar," my grandfather said, interrupting me.

Was I that easy to read? "Look, Grandpa, I have a history with him. A bad history. I guess I just can't get past it. It bothers me that he's where he is today just by being a jerk and a bully his whole life."

"Do you want my opinion on this whole thing?"

"I'm not sure if I can validate that as a question, because I know you're just going to tell me your opinion anyway," I replied.

"Get over it. Move on. Who cares that he's rich and famous around town now? What makes him better than you? Money? He's on TV? No.

None of those things matter. He has to live with the pain he caused everyone growing up. He has to remember what he's done to people and if he's still doing it now, well, then you'll eventually see his downfall. He will lose it all if he's still the same person."

My grandfather was right, yet again.

"And," my grandfather continued. "If he's not the same person, if he's seriously changed and grown up, then good for him. So if he can move on, why can't you?"

And there it was. He was guilting me into feeling better. And it was working. I threw my head back against the head rest and sighed. "All right, you win. Again. I'll work on letting it go."

"That's my boy."

A man walked across the street and began walking toward the convenience store. He reached the front door and placed his hand on handle. Before he entered, he swung his head to the left and right multiple times before finally heading inside. It seemed suspicious, almost like he was making sure the surroundings were clear.

"Do you think that's him?" I asked.

My grandfather was already getting ready to open the door. "Only one way to find out." He opened the door and stepped outside, shutting the car door behind him. Our plan was for my grandfather to go inside and act like he's shopping. If the guy that we saw was robbing the place, he'd let me know over our ear pieces and I would come rushing in.

My grandfather was carrying out the first part of the plan. I waited, staring out the car window. The door swung open and a man walked out. I leaned forward to get a better view. It wasn't my grandfather or the man that went in earlier. My grandfather was in there for at least a minute by now. I was getting antsy.

Finally, the door opened again. The suspicious man we'd seen go in earlier came walking out. That was disappointing. I was kind of hoping he was going to rob the place. At least I would be able to do something again. A few seconds later the door opened again and my grandfather came walking out holding two cups. He must have bought some coffee while he was in there.

Before he took two steps away from the store, someone came running across the street. I only saw him in my peripheral vision for a split second before he jumped on the sidewalk and ran into my grandfather, knocking him to the curb. My grandfather went down hard and the drinks went splashing all over the sidewalk. I leapt out of the car and sprinted toward the convenience store. I threw my hood over my head and knelt down to my grandfather. "Are you okay?"

"I'm fine. Go get him!" he said while turning over onto his back and clenching in pain.

I turned and pulled open the door. The man who sprinted across the street and knocked down my grandfather stood by the front counter holding a gun at the cashier. As the door shut behind me, the small bells at the top of the door rattled together making a jingling noise.

The man with the gun turned. He swung his gun around, but I lifted my left arm up in the air, knocking the gun away from his hand. The gun disappeared from his hand and fell on the floor a few feet away from him. He looked shocked and confused. I took advantage of his hesitation and charged toward him. I hit him in his stomach with my shoulder and lifted him off the ground. I drove him into a fixture that stood behind him, knocking down the neatly displayed cereal boxes. I stood, but he took out my feet with a swift side kick. I fell flat out my back, knocking the wind out of me. This allowed him ample time to get back up and rush to get his gun. Just as he reached for it, I rolled over onto my stomach and threw my arm forward, pushing it, motioning for the gun to slide across the floor toward the back of the aisle. The man turned to look back at me as I was beginning to stand up. I moved both arms to my right and the man tumbled into the aisle. He fell down to the ground but not before knocking a few things off the shelf as he flailed his arms to keep his balance.

I ran over to him while he was on all fours, trying to climb back to his feet. I kicked him in his stomach. He lifted a few inches in the air and then fell to the ground. The man let out a few coughs as he tried to catch his breath while making his way to his feet again. I turned to the cashier and said, "Call the police."

I grabbed the guy by his hair and brought him to his feet. I reached around him and grabbed his left arm but before I could get a good grip, he blindsided me with a quick hook from his right arm. The punch caught me off guard and he landed it between my left cheek and chin. It was so sudden and quick, it brought me to my knees and I released my grip on the man.

He ran down the aisle toward his gun. I shook my head and realized what he was going for. I reached out and pulled the gun toward me. As the man went running one direction for the gun, it flew past him going the other way and landed in my hands. He turned and hesitated in his next move.

I had the gun pointed at him. "Don't make me do it," I threatened him. He either didn't want to listen or called my bluff. He turned and headed for the end of the aisle out of my line of sight. I jumped to my feet, dropped the gun and pursued him.

When I made it to the end of the aisle, I saw him double back down the next aisle and head back toward the front of the store. He was heading for the exit. I spun around and sprinted after him. I heard the jingling of the door as he pushed it open. I turned out of the aisle, but he was already outside. I pushed open the door and stood at the entrance looking both to my right and left for any sign of him.

"That way," my grandfather said, pointing to his left. He was tucked up against the side of the window clutching his right knee.

I began my pursuit.

The run was invigorating. I was getting involved again. It felt amazing to be back out here. The adrenaline was pumping through my body and allowing me more control over my ability.

The man turned down an alley in between the streets.

I approached but slowed down as I found the corner. I had learned my lesson.

I peeked around the corner and the man swung at me with a pipe. I ducked and grabbed the pipe with my right hand, trying to pry it from his grip. He spun me around the corner and shoved me up against the brick wall behind me. I kept my grip on the pipe and threw a punch into his gut with my left hand. He hunched over but kept his grip. With the strength he had left, he spun me back around and the momentum threw me to the ground. I lost my grip of the pipe. He walked over to me and raised the pipe high in the air but before he could come down with it, I shoved both my arms forward and he went tumbling backwards into the trash bags piled up behind him. He tried to brace his fall by letting go of the pipe. This was my opportunity.

I rose to my feet and ran over to him before he could get back up. "Stay down," I said. Just like everyone else, he didn't listen. Their egos were too big. He thought he could fight back. He tried making his way back to his feet. I pushed both arms forward and he went flying back down into the bags of trash. A grunt left his mouth as he seemed to ache in pain. I grabbed a zip tie from my back pocket and had it ready this time.

I reached down and grabbed his hair again, attempting to pull him to his feet. He made his way up and hunched over. I guided him a few feet from the alley out onto the main road. There was a lamp post in front of us. I spun him around and he had his back facing the lamp post. I grabbed both arms and held them behind it. I used the zip tie to hold him in place. His arms were wrapped around the lamp post and he wasn't going anywhere, at least not until the police came.

"You have no idea who you're messing with," the man managed to say as I was getting ready to walk away.

I turned to face him. "What do you mean?" This was the first time I had a chance to look at him. His color was off. He was pale. His eyes were red and droopy. Was he on drugs? I never really took the time to notice anyone I've caught before. For some reason, he caught me off guard with his comment.

He began to laugh while I searched his pockets. While reaching in his sweatshirt pocket, I found a bag of clear circular pills. I had no idea what they were. I held the bag up to his face. "What are these?" I never found drugs on anyone else. Thinking back, I never really searched anyone before. I never had or felt the need to. I usually just left this step to the police but tonight seemed different.

"That's my stash! Get off that! I'll kill you! I'm supposed to do this!"

He was definitely on drugs. "What are you supposed to do?"

"Rob that store. I'm supposed to do it."

"Why?" I asked.

"Because I'm supposed to! Give me back my stuff!" the man yelled.

"I'll give them back to you if you tell me where you got them."

He fell silent. He shook his head back and forth. "No. No man. I ain't tellin' you nothin'."

I held the bag up to his face. "You sure you won't tell me?"

He continued shaking his head. "The boss man will kill me if I say anything. I'm not supposed to tell."

"The boss man? Who's that?"

"What aren't you understanding? I ain't no snitch."

"Okay. Then I have no choice to leave you here for the cops. They are on their way." I spun around and began to walk away.

"No! Wait, come back!" the man shouted.

I turned back around and said, "If you don't give me anything then I'm walking."

"Will you let me go if I tell you? I can't go back to jail."

"Tell me what you know and I'll think about it. It's your only option."

He tapped his feet and began to twitch as he contemplated his decision. "Okay. Look, I don't know who the boss man is. I don't know his name. All I know is that this guy who works with the boss man, he gave those pills to me and said they will be free if I held up that convenience store. I did what I was told and he came back and said he'd give me more if I did it again. And again. So I did what I was told. Then the dude came back for the fourth time and told me to rob the store and the pills were mine, free of charge again. Then you showed up. Now let me go."

The sirens became audible in the distance. He began shaking his arms, trying to pull free from the lamp post that his arms were tied to. The post rattled back and forth with the man's efforts but he wasn't going anywhere. "I'm supposed to knock over that store. I have to go. You said you'd let me go if I talked," the man said. He was really trying to pull away from the lamp post. He rocked it back and forth furiously.

I leaned forward and tucked the pills back in his pocket. "I'll give you your pills back for being forthcoming with me. So, here they are. And by the way, the police may be very interested in these."

"Wait, what?" the man said clearly confused as I turned away from him and started back toward the convenience store.

"I said I'd think about letting you go. I never said I would." Did he really think I'd let him go? I felt bad for tricking him, but he deserves to be in jail. He needs help from those drugs he was on. I can't let someone like him run loose on the streets. Especially someone who's carrying around those drugs. Where did he get those? Our city hasn't had a problem with drugs before. Sure, the violence was a major concern but not drugs. I needed to figure out where those pills came from and fast, before they spread the same way the violence did.

CHAPTER TWENTY-SIX

made my way back to my grandfather's house later that night. It took some time to get there but a little bit of public transportation never really hurt anybody.

My grandfather and I had worked out an arrangement in the event we ever got split up. I would leave the scene, no matter what. I couldn't risk getting caught.

My grandfather would be okay. He could talk his way out of anything, and it helped he knew a few people on the police force. And if that didn't work, he had the money to pay his way out of anything.

I figured he would have beaten me home, but I guess he was worse off than I thought. His car wasn't in the garage and all the lights were off when I arrived at his house. I pulled my phone out of my pocket and decided to call him. It rang and rang. His voicemail picked up. I hung up. I hope he was all right. He was clutching his knee when I saw him outside the store. Maybe the paramedics were working on him. Maybe he was being questioned by the police.

It was 12:47.

I walked into the living room and sat on the sofa. I grabbed the remote and turned on the television. I flipped through the channels until I saw something pertaining to news. Maybe something will be on the news about tonight. Maybe I'll see my grandfather in the background of a report, possibly even being interviewed. At least I'd know he'd be okay.

After scrolling through hundreds of channels on the guide, I found nothing about tonight. I even checked the local news stations and there was no report.

I turned the television off and stood up. I needed to get out of these clothes. I walked upstairs to my room to change when the front door squeaked. I paused in my steps, listening for any noise to follow.

Nothing.

Quiet.

"Hello?" I said.

Silence.

I crept toward my bedroom door and stuck my head out into the hallway to listen. Once again, I asked, "Hello?"

Nothing.

Panic flooded every cell of my body. I walked out of my room and tip toed down the hallway toward the stairs. Once I got to the staircase, I leaned over the banister to peak down to the first floor.

The lights were still off. It was hard to see. I didn't want to risk turning the lights on and scaring whoever was in the house. Maybe it was my grandfather or maybe it was someone who followed me back here.

I crept down the stairs. "Hello?"

I heard a chair fall over in the kitchen and a thump.

"Dang it."

I ran downstairs, into the kitchen and turned on the lights. I laughed.

It was one of those moments when I should have done something else rather than laugh. But I couldn't help it.

My grandfather was lying on the kitchen floor with a chair on top of him.

"Well, don't just stand there laughing like the hooded idiot that you are. Come help me up."

I made my way over, picked up the chair off him and moved it to the side. I reached down and grabbed his hand and helped him up.

"What happened? Are you okay?" I asked, trying to hold back my laughter.

"What does it look like, you moron? I'm fine. Thanks for laughing at my pain and suffering."

"You would have done the same to me, except you probably would have been worse about it than I was."

"Touché," he said.

I helped him sit down in a chair at the kitchen table. His knee was bandaged up. "What happened to your knee?"

"That dumb idiot came running past me and knocked me down. I'm tough, but when you get to be my age and you get knocked to the ground, it hurts. It's harder to get back up. I fell on my knee and couldn't stand back up right away. I crawled back against the wall of the store which is when I saw you run up. The police eventually came..." he rolled his eyes. "Lousy police. Can't even stop a criminal from robbing the same store multiple times in a week. We show up once and it gets taken care of. Unbelievable–"

"Stay on topic, Grandpa."

"Okay, okay. So, the police came. They arrested the guy that *you* stopped. The paramedics arrived soon after and looked at my knee. They said it's fine and they wrapped it up and told me to stay off it for a few days while it heals."

"Well, I'm glad you're okay," I said.

"Yeah, I'm fine. Now, on to you," my grandfather said. "You tell me what happened."

"Well, I obviously caught the guy."

"I gathered that, Captain Obvious. Anything else?"

"I talked to him after I tied him up to the lamp post. He seemed...off. I found drugs on him."

"What kind of drugs?"

"I don't know. Pills of some sort."

"What did they look like?"

"Small, round, clear pills. I put them back in his pocket and I'm sure the police are investigating that now."

My grandfather nodded his head up and down. "I'll look into it, too."

"And how are you going to look into it?" I asked.

"I'm home all day. What else do I have to do?"

He had a point. He could help me figure out what this drug was and hopefully where it was coming from. And since he was injured, this at least gave him something to do without going out.

"All right," I replied. "Look into it then. He also mentioned something about his boss. Called him the 'boss man.' He said they'd kill him if he said anything to me."

"And? Did you find out who he is?"

"He didn't know who he was. But he said he worked with someone who worked under the boss. He said he would keep giving him those drugs if he kept robbing the place."

"So he kept robbing the convenience store because someone gave him the drugs and told him to do so?"

"Pretty much. He said the guy kept giving him pills and telling him to rob the store."

We fell silent.

"Why the same store though?" I asked. "Why not change it up?"

"Maybe it was a planned to see how long it would take the police to catch on? Testing them? Timing them? Or maybe to see how many times they can get away with it? Or maybe–"

"It was to figure out when I would show up," I interrupted him. "Maybe it was all just a set up. Maybe it was to get me out in the open again. Maybe it was to try and discover my identity." This started to scare me. "What if they followed me?" All this time, I had been trying to protect my identity. Dr. Kane warned me of the repercussions if people knew what I could do. This was not good.

"Devin, calm down," my grandfather said. "There was no one here when I got home. Did you see anyone following you?"

"No," I replied.

"Then you're acting paranoid. And how would they know who you are anyway? Your face is covered…" he paused to look at my hood on my sweatshirt. "Well, it's kind of covered up. Maybe we should do something about that. But I don't think your identity is compromised. What would robbing the same place have to do with you?"

He made sense, but I was still worried it was a ruse to draw me out.

Still, maybe I was imagining things. Too many criminals, too many bad people.

Maybe I needed sleep. It was after one in the morning.

"Maybe you're right," I said. "In the meantime, I need to get to bed. I've got work in the morning. Do you need help getting upstairs, old crippled man?"

"Ha…ha…very funny," my grandfather replied. "But thank you, I'll be fine. Goodnight, Devin."

"Goodnight, Grandpa,"

CHAPTER TWENTY-SEVEN

Beep…Beep…Beep…Beep

I opened my eyes and glared at the ceiling. It was one of Grandpa's stupid construction machines again. I grabbed my phone to check the time. It was only 6:27 AM. Wasn't there a law against doing this type of work this early in the morning? I had close to another 30 minutes before my alarm went off and I felt like I had just gone to sleep. I was exhausted, but I knew I wouldn't be able to get any more sleep. Resigned, I threw my feet out from under the covers and got out of bed.

I went to the window. The sun was just breaking over the horizon and a cement truck has found its way into my grandfather's backyard.

"I need to stop sleeping here," I grumbled to myself. "I have a perfectly good apartment with no crazy construction going on at 6:30 in the morning."

I got dressed and went downstairs. I walked through the foyer and saw my grandfather sleeping on the sofa in the living room. I guess he was too proud to ask me for help getting upstairs. At least he didn't injure himself further by trying. And how was he sleeping through all the noise?

I walked into the kitchen and made a pot of coffee. I turned on the TV. Something had to be on the news about last night.

Once the coffee brewed, I poured a cup and sat down at the kitchen table.

"In other news, the vigilante has struck again."

"Here we go," I said,

"It seems like he's come back from wherever he was hiding to put another man behind bars. Here's Alan with more on that story."

"Thanks, Bill. Last night around 10:45, this convenience store behind me had its fourth robbery attempt in the past few days. Except the man who attempted to rob the store wasn't expecting company. The vigilante, the Gray Hood as people are calling him, came out of hiding last night after missing for about a month and thwarted the robbery attempt, making a mess inside the store as a struggle took place. Lisa, the cashier at the time of the attempted robbery told me she was fearful of her life but was thankful that the vigilante came to the rescue. She also said during the fight, items were moving without either the Gray Hood or the robber touching them. She said the vigilante moved his arms and made the man fall into the shelves in the middle of one of the aisles. The fight then made its way outside as the criminal tried making a getaway. The Gray Hood pursued. From witness reports, it seems that the vigilante caught up to him and tied his hands to a lamp post a block down the street.

"The man who was arrested also had the drug on him that has begun sweeping across the city by storm. The new drug is known as Crystal Clear. Our sources say that it looks like a small, clear, circular pill. Its new drug-based formula has police and others stumped. It's almost impossible to detect with a drug test so it's hard to prove who's been using it. From what I was told, when someone is under its effects, people may be unable to feel pain and unable to realize what they are doing. This can cause users to carelessly engage in dangerous actions and situations. The police chief has yet to officially comment on this new drug.

"But one good thing to take away from this is that the Gray Hood has come back, and it seems like he's come back at the right time. He saved Lisa at the convenience store and has helped the police put another criminal behind bars. The police may not like or agree with him, but I sure appreciate what he does. Back to you Bill."

So now I knew what the drug was and what it did, but now I needed to know where it came from. And, more importantly, who was behind its introduction into our city.

I finished up my coffee, turned off the TV and headed off to work early.

⁂

"What are you doing here this early?" Lara said. She was already at her desk, hunched over her work and typing as fast as she could.

"I should ask you the same thing," I replied.

Lara was the last person I expected to see in the office at 7:45 in the morning.

She stopped and gestured casually at the computer. "Just something I'm working on."

I walked around the desk to peek at her computer screen. "What are you working on?"

She turned the monitor away and turned off the screen. "I'm kind of embarrassed. I really don't want anyone to know."

"What are you talking about?" Was she hiding something? What was she doing? In my new line of work, I had learned that change was usually bad.

She fidgeted with her top and then reorganized the pens, notepads, phone, paper clips, and lamp on her desk.

I waited.

She peeked up at me with those beautiful blue eyes. "Do you promise not to tell anyone?"

At that moment, it no longer mattered what she was doing. She could be the one who shot me and I wouldn't care.

I nodded, not trusting my voice.

She leaned toward me, her face breaking into an excited smile. "Okay, I'll tell you. I've been taking some online courses in computer programming. I wanted to create a more efficient program for myself and our staff."

"You want to program computers? That's great! I had no idea you wanted to do this."

"Well, I've always wanted to work with computers, which is why you see me here behind one all day. I know I'm only doing administrative work, but I get to see and play with how programming works all day.

What I wanted to do was replace the crappy admin programs here and create my own which will be more efficient. You would think a company like this would have top of the line programming, wouldn't you? We still work in DOS."

Confused by her comment, I asked, "What's DOS?"

"See! Exactly my point. It was a popular and useful operating system used in the 80's and 90's. No one uses it anymore, and here we are, stuck using very outdated technology. It's ridiculous. I'm creating a new software program that is compatible with the newer and more powerful operating systems available."

"If I knew what you were talking about, I'm sure I'd agree with you."

"I don't really talk about it much, because everyone just sees me as some secretary, so who am I to write software?"

"Don't say that. I have faith in you. You're smart. And if you've been taking these classes, I'm sure you know exactly what you're doing." I backed away from the computer to give her some privacy. "I won't look at it. I promise. Can you promise to show me when you're done?"

"Sure. Maybe one day you'll be using it. I would love to show you and get your input on it. I just want to finish it first. I need to make sure the financial advisors can use it, too. It'll make things so much easier and more efficient around here."

An arm suddenly wrapped around my shoulder.

I tried not to wince.

"What's up, you two love birds?" Tommy said, standing to my right. "What are we all talking about?"

"We just got done talking about your face and what animal it most closely resembles," Lara said.

"Oh really? I was always under the impression that was a Tuesday discussion. Today is Wednesday. And for the record, I look like a more handsome and more chiseled Brad Pitt."

Lara laughed. "Brad Pitt? Seriously? First of all, Brad Pitt isn't an animal. And second, get over yourself. You look nothing like Brad Pitt."

Tommy turned to me and started posing like a model. "What do you think? Brad Pitt worthy?"

I shook my head at him. "If that's who you think you look like, then sure. Whatever you say."

"See?" Tommy said, turning his attention back to Lara. "Even your boyfriend agrees with me."

"Devin?!" Lara exclaimed.

"What?" I responded.

Tommy smiled and strutted down the hall to his office.

She smiled at me. "I can't believe you took his side. Traitor..." She stood up and leaned over the desk and gave me a kiss. "I'll see you later."

"Bye." I walked to my office.

Once I entered, I hung my suit jacket up on the door hanger and sat down at my desk. I booted up my computer and looked at the pre-market indications. The stock market was looking good today.

And then the phone began to ring. It was a little early for phone calls.

I picked it up anyway. "Hello, this is Devin..."

"Hi, Devin. It's Mitchell. How are you?"

My eyes rolled back in my head. Really? Wasn't it a little early for my grudge-busting exposure therapy? Why was this guy calling me already? I thought our business was done with.

I tried to sound chipper. "I'm good. How are you, Mitchell?"

"I'm good, thanks for asking. You're at work nice and early this morning."

"What can I help you with?" I asked, ignoring his question.

"I'll get right to the point and not waste your time. I'm having some close business associates down to the construction site to show them the work being done and some blueprints and models of the final product. I'd love to have you and Tommy join us."

This was the last thing I needed to do, spend more time with Mitchell. How could I get out of this? "That would be great, except I'm pretty busy today with meetings and catch up work." I lied.

"Oh, that's fine. This was scheduled for tomorrow anyway."

Great. I rolled my eyes again. One more excuse to try. "Oh, okay. Well, I don't think I'll be able to drive down there. I have to bring my car in for inspection tomorrow."

"Not a problem. I have a limo picking up some people. I'll have the driver swing by and pick you guys up."

Excuse number two had failed. Looks like I'll have to see Mitchell again. "Okay, that sounds good. I guess we'll see you tomorrow."

"Great! The limo should be there around noon. I'll see you when you arrive."

I hung up the phone and dialed Tommy's line. The phone rang once and he picked up. "Tommy speaking, how can I…"

"It's me," I interrupted him.

"Oh hey! How pissed was Lara that you sided with me earlier?" Tommy laughed.

"She wasn't pissed. Disgruntled is a better word. Anyway, Mitchell just called me. He wants us to come down to his construction site tomorrow with a bunch of his business associates."

"I'd love to. That be so cool! You told us we can go, right?"

At least one of us was excited about this. "Yes, we are going. He's having a limo pick us up around noon tomorrow."

"A limo? Dude, that's awesome. This guy is amazing. I'm excited to check this place out. This is so cool! I've never been to something like this befo–" A click on the other end of the phone line stopped Tommy mid-word. "Hey, Devin, that's my other line. I need to take this. I'll talk to you later."

The phone line went dead. I put my phone back on the receiver and turned back to my computer. A headline popped up on my dashboard.

The Vigilante Has Resurfaced

I clicked on the link. It took me to an online article about what happened last night. Looks like I'd end up spending most of my morning looking into what people were saying about my return. At least this would keep me occupied while I tried to forget about having to see Mitchell tomorrow.

CHAPTER TWENTY-EIGHT

"How are you feeling?" I asked my grandfather. I came over after work to check on him since he had been bumped and bruised pretty bad last night.

"I'm all right. I've been limping around most of the day," he replied. "But on a positive note, I did find some information for you regarding the pills you found."

"What did you find?"

"It actually made its first appearance about five months ago."

"That long ago? Why haven't we heard about it?" I asked.

"That was exactly my thought. I called my retired friend from the police force, and he said the police have been following it for some time now but have been trying to keep it low key. There's already enough going on in Decker City, they didn't want another reason for people to panic. But a few media outlets have been running the story recently. It's starting to come out."

"Yeah. I heard about it on the news this morning."

"I saw that, too. He also said taking those pills makes you easier and more susceptible to suggestions."

"So kind of like hypnosis?" I replied.

"Exactly like that. He said if you were on the drug, you would get a high and that chemical reaction drops your guard and screws with your willingness to do things. So someone could say 'go do this' and you would without thought or resistance. It's almost like mind control. It's scary."

"Yeah, it sounds like it. Imagine having this drug fall into the wrong hands," I said.

"I'm sure it already has, considering all this violence that's taken place over the past few months. I think whoever is behind all of this has something to do with this drug."

That got me thinking. What if someone was using this drug for their own mind-controlled army? It would make sense why people just started causing panic and destruction out of nowhere. If this drug does what people say it does, whoever is in control of it is a very dangerous person.

"I think we need to get back out there tonight."

I nodded. "I'm going alone."

"Oh no you're not!"

I pointed to his bandaged-up knee. "Look at you. You can't go. What if you need to get away quick? You can't drive."

"I can go. You think I'm leaving you out there on your own? Think again."

I opened my mouth to speak.

"That's final."

My shoulders slumped in defeat. "Okay. But I'm driving this time."

***

We were back on the road. It felt great, but underneath the excitement I was nervous. Now I needed to protect my grandfather and the city. I wished he had stayed home.

I pulled off the main road and backed into an alley. I turned the headlights off. My grandfather and I sat there and listened to the police scanner. Everything we were hearing wasn't big enough for me to go after. A domestic disturbance, a drunk driver, a simple traffic stop.

The police radio became full of static for a split second, the moment someone would call in. "We have a 10-94 in progress on Capital Street between Market and 8th."

I got excited. "What's a 10-94, Grandpa?"

He grabbed his paper with all the police codes on it and ran his index finger down the page until he found 10-94. "It's a street race. Not something for us."

"All right."

Static filled the radio again. "Officer down...officer down...need assistance on the corner of Long Neck Road and 10th."

It was the worst kind of call. My excitement turned to dread.

I hit the gas and spun out of the alley onto the main road. We were only about a mile away. We could get there in about two minutes.

I made a quick right off 7th Street and took Main Street which would put me about two blocks away from Long Neck Road once I made it to 10th street. I approached the traffic light. I had the green. 9th street. Red. As usual. It didn't matter what time of day it was, for me, it was always red. I wanted to just peel out and floor it through the red light but knowing our luck, a cop would stop us, and that would be the last thing we need right now.

Green light. Finally. I floored it. Before reaching 10th Street, I turned down an alley and parked. I reached for the handle to exit the car.

My grandfather grabbed my arm. "Be careful, Devin."

"I will," I jumped out of the car. I threw my hood over my head and stormed out of the alley.

A crack of gunfire filled the air. Then another. And another.

I was a block away now and the gunshots kept happening. I watched for any flashes of light in the darkness. My heart was racing. I could move things, but I wasn't bulletproof. I had learned that the hard way.

I made it to the corner of Long Neck Road and leaned against the wall. I peeked around the corner and a loud gunshot startled me. I retracted my head. I took a deep breath and tried to slow my adrenaline down. Gunfire brought back bad memories. I needed to ignore them and move forward. I took a deep breath and pushed the fear away.

I peeked around the corner again. There was a police car in the middle of the street, perpendicular to the sidewalk. There was an officer ducked down behind his cruiser. His hands shook as he reloaded his weapon as fast as he could. On his left was an officer lying on the ground. He was motionless. My stomach lurched. I couldn't tell if he was dead or alive. To the right of the police cruiser was a dark blue van. It was impossible to know how many shooters there were, but there was a constant barrage of gunfire coming from behind it.

The police officer had his gun ready to go. The shooting from the van stopped, giving the police officer the opportunity to return fire. When he did, I dashed out from behind the corner and dove behind the police cruiser. It startled the officer and he ducked back down and pointed his gun at me. I put my hands up and said, "Don't shoot! I'm on your side!" He nodded, recognizing me and went back to returning fire. I leaned behind him and looked at the officer on the ground. He looked familiar. The name tag attached to his jacket read "D. Reed."

Wait…Reed? He was the officer who saved my life during my car accident. If it wasn't for Officer Reed rescuing me that night, I'd be dead and I wouldn't have this ability. Bile rose in my throat. I did my best to ignore it. Now wasn't the time to grieve.

The gun fire stopped. The officer ducked back down. "Hey!" the officer said. "Are you going to help or what? Do that thing you do! Your magic… or whatever is it."

I nodded my head. They needed to pay for what they did to Officer Reed. I watched through the police window as these criminals decided their next course of action. One guy came out from behind the van and started firing. I flicked my hand up and the guy's gun flipped up in his face and smacked him in the chin. The gun fell to the ground as the guy grabbed his face with both hands. Another guy stood up from behind the hood of the van and was about to shoot, but I threw my hand to the right and the gun left his grip and dropped on the sidewalk.

"He's here!" the man shouted.

The guy with the busted chin came out into the open to reach for his gun. The officer stood up and took two shots. One hit him in his shoulder and the other took out his leg. He collapsed to the ground screaming in pain. I used a pulling motion with my hand and pulled the gun away from the man on the ground and dragged it toward the police car. The officer turned his fire onto the man behind the hood of the van. The man ducked to avoid the bullets headed in his direction.

The officer stood behind the cruiser and waited for the man to peek out again. He had his gun trained in his direction. Before long, the second shooter peeked out again, but he pulled back when the officer fired. The man was trapped.

"Wait here," I told the officer. "I'm going to flank him and draw him to you."

As the officer nodded, I raced out from behind the car and made my way over to the van. I crouched low to the ground to avoid any detection. I approached the van from the rear and peeked around the side.

He was gone. Where did he go?

I turned to my right and he was running down the sidewalk in an attempt to get away. I turned and followed his direction.

He raced down the street and attempted to pull open any door he could to try and escape. Unfortunately for him, each time he tried, he slowed himself down. He made it to the end of the block and turned down 11th Street. I was still a few yards away from the end of the block when a horn came blaring from around the corner.

I made it to the corner of Long Neck Road and 11th Street and the man I was chasing was throwing a driver out of a car. He hit the ground and rolled out of the way. The criminal climbed in the vehicle and hit the gas. He was driving toward me. Fast.

I came to a stop and quickly dove toward the wall to my left as the car came plowing up on the sidewalk in an attempt to run me over. I fell to the ground and rolled over to see the car brush against the building and bounce back to the street.

As the vehicle approached the intersection, the beat up, bullet filled police car came flying up Long Neck Road. He slammed into the driver's side of the criminal's stolen car. The crunching noise of two cars colliding with each other filled the area. Metal and glass instantly scattered the street. The stolen car lifted off its driver's side and did a complete roll and a half before sliding into a store front on the opposite side of the street and coming to a complete stop.

I stood up and ran over to the police car which laid motionless in the middle of the intersection. The destruction that I just witnessed reminded me of my accident. The totaled vehicle. The car parts scattered all over the street.

I reached the vehicle and the officer was slow to move. He pushed himself off the airbag and tried opening his door. It was jammed.

"Hold on, I'll help you out," I said.

The officer wanted nothing to do with my help. He insisted on climbing out the driver's side window as I made it around the car. He fell to the ground once he made it out.

"Stay still," I pleaded with him. "Let me get you some help."

"No," he said as he planted his hands on the pavement, trying to push himself to his feet. "He's not getting away."

The guy in the stolen car started crawling out from the passenger window. He was moving slow. He wasn't going to put up a fight anymore. The officer made it to his feet and limped over to the man crawling out from under the car. He had this under control now.

Sirens in the distance began to make their presence known. They weren't far away now. I had to get going. I couldn't be involved or in sight when they showed up. I went to turn and make my getaway but something stopped me.

Officer Reed. Where was he? Was he okay?

I jogged back to the corner and looked down Long Neck Road. Two bodies laid in the street. One was handcuffed and screaming in pain. The other was motionless. I ran down the street to hopefully find some form of life in Officer Reed.

I ran past the man crying in pain from his gunshot wounds and made my way over to Officer Reed. He was just as I left him. I poked his shoulder. "Officer Reed?" I tried again, this time with more strength. "Officer Reed? Can you hear me?"

"He's dead," a voice came from behind me. I turned around and it was the other police officer. "He saved my life. Those guys opened fire and he pushed me down and took a bullet for me."

This man was a hero. He didn't need superpowers to be special or be called a hero. He saved my life, this officer's life and I'm sure countless others. My heart began to ache. "I'm sorry," I replied.

The sirens were much louder now. I had to leave. "He saved my life, too. A few months ago," I told the officer. I could now see the flashing lights coming down the street. They were about two or three blocks away now. "I'm so sorry. I have to go now."

"Thank you," the officer said. He reached out and extended his hand. I accepted the gesture and returned the handshake. "I'll make sure to tell people what you did and how you helped me."

I nodded and began to run away from the oncoming police cars. At least I knew I had one officer on my side. Still, the ache in my heart wouldn't budge. Tears stung my eyes as I sprinted toward my grandfather's car.

CHAPTER TWENTY-NINE

Shootout Erupts in the Downtown District of Decker City
By Kate Phillips

Gunfire began around 10:15 last night when two police officers came upon a robbery in progress. The two shooters began opening fire when the police arrived, taking up position behind a van in the middle of the street. The police officers blocked the street of Long Neck Road with their police vehicle. The police returned fire until Officer Dennis Reed was struck in the chest. He was pronounced dead at the scene. Both officers would have been killed if not for the Gray Hood coming to the rescue just as the surviving officer was pinned behind his vehicle.

Both shooters have been arrested.

"If it wasn't for Officer Reed, I'd be dead too," Officer Umburger told reporters in a statement. "He saved my life. But I also owe my life to the vigilante, whoever he is. If he didn't show up when he did, you'd be writing about two dead police officers."

The police investigated the van and found multiple containers full of thousands of pills of new drug flooding the streets, Crystal Clear. They see this as a win for the department as these pills will never make it into the hands of the criminals. But the department mourns the loss of Officer Reed, a true local hero.

CHAPTER THIRTY

The door came flying open to my office.

"Yo buddy, have you seen this?" Tommy flipped the newspaper in front of me.

Shootout Erupts in the Downtown District of Decker City, the headline read. I grabbed the paper and skimmed through the article.

"I would love to have this guy's life," Tommy said.

"Whose? The vigilante?" I replied.

"Of course! You see all the fun he's having? He's living the life of a hero in an action movie. It's awesome."

"I don't think you mean that." I ached from my dangerous adventure last night. He couldn't see the bumps and bruises I get from doing what I do and the danger I've been in. He didn't feel the grief of seeing a good man on the ground, never getting up.

"What do you mean? Of course I mean it. This guy in the hood is taking down all these bad guys. He's saving the day-well, I mean saving the night. Wouldn't you enjoy doing what he's doing?"

I shrugged. "I guess I would. I really don't know."

Tommy reached back across my desk and took the paper back. He looked at the article again. "Yeah, definitely not your kind of thing. But I would love to do what this guy does. He's the modern-day superhero!"

"Well, maybe you can learn to develop a superpower and you can fight crime, too," I told him.

His eyes opened wide. "That would be awesome!" His demeanor quickly changed. "But don't be silly, I wouldn't fight crime."

"You wouldn't?"

"Nope. I'd pick up chicks. I'd move things without touching them. They'd all be amazed and want me."

"Sounds like you have a plan."

He turned and walked toward the door. "Now all I need is a way to make them *think* I can do magic." It was never a dull moment when I was with Tommy.

My phone began to ring. "Hello, this is Devin…" I answered.

"Hey Devin, it's Lara. There's a man here who says he's your limo driver and he's here to pick up you and Tommy."

I looked at the clock on my computer screen. It was already noon.

I had Officer Reed on my mind the whole time. The man who risked his life to save mine and countless others was gone.

I wasn't a hero. Officer Reed was.

I rubbed my face, trying to wipe away the memories from last night. I had to put this behind me.

"Okay thanks, Lara. We'll be there in a minute." Mitchell was waiting. I sighed in defeat.

I hung up the phone and yelled for Tommy in the hallway. He didn't answer so I picked up my phone and quickly dialed his extension. It started to ring. "Yeah, hello, Tommy speaking."

"It's Devin. Our limo driver is here."

"Cool, I'll be right there. By the way, I just found a magic trick on YouTube. I want to try it out on our car ride over there. Do you have a deck of cards I can use?"

I ignored him. "I'll see you up front."

I walked out of my office and shut the door behind me. I made my way to the front lobby. There was a man with an all-black attire standing at the desk with Lara. He wore a black chauffeur hat.

"Devin, I presume?" the driver said as he stuck out his hand for a greeting.

"Yes, sir," I shook his hand.

"Your ride is waiting outside. I'll meet you there," the driver said. He walked out the front door and headed toward the elevator.

"Nice guy," Tommy said, and followed him out in the hallway.

I turned to Lara. "I'll be back later."

"Okay. Hope everything goes well. Don't party too hard without me," she said.

"I don't think this is a party meeting. I'll save that for happy hour tonight. You in?"

"Of course I am."

"Okay. I'll see you when I get back," I told her.

She leaned in and kissed me goodbye. I know it wasn't the most appropriate thing to be doing in the office, but it was Lara Scarlette. How could I say no?

I smiled as I met Tommy and the driver at the car. Even Mitchell's shiny black limousine couldn't put me in a bad mood now.

We arrived at the construction site. The entire block was fenced with temporary wiring. This place was going to be massive.

Mitchell was standing in front of the caged area, waiting for us. The driver opened our door and both Tommy and I stepped out of the limo.

"Welcome," Mitchell began. "I'm excited for you to be here. I hope the ride was to your satisfaction?"

To our satisfaction? Who was he trying to impress?

"It was awesome. I've never been inside a limo before," Tommy replied.

He used the word 'awesome' in front of Mitchell. We were professionals and he used the word 'awesome.' So much for being professional this afternoon.

"That's fantastic. I'm glad you enjoyed it." He turned his attention to me. "Devin, nice to see you again." He extended his hand.

"Hi, Mitchell. You too." I returned his handshake.

He extended his arm forward through the opening and said, "Welcome to The Entertainment Galaxy, the future home to all of our city's entertainment needs."

Both Tommy and I proceeded through the opening and Mitchell shut and locked the gate behind us. He jumped in front of us and began leading us down a stony pathway. We entered the door a few feet from the gate's entrance. I was completely blow away by what Mitchell did to this place in such a short amount of time. A marble floor welcomed us as we walked through the front door. A giant gold chandelier hung above us. Reflected light sparkled throughout the building as the sun shined through the glass ceiling. A restaurant was under construction across from the entrance. We could turn left or right once we entered the building. The hallways led to store fronts, other dining experiences and many other entertainment areas.

"This way," Mitchell said as he turned right. The first place I came across was an arcade. A few arcade and pinball machines were already lined up, but wires and building supplies were scattered all over the store. The next establishment looked like a sports bar. Boxes of televisions were stacked in a corner. A huge bar was stationed in the middle of the area with piles of bar stools stacked on top of one another. Across from the bar on the opposite side were store fronts. I couldn't tell what was going in those places. They had tons of boxes within each store. Might be retail of some sort.

Mitchell turned around to us while walking backwards. "What do you guys think?"

Tommy replied, "It's incredible!"

"I like it," I said. I was being honest. This was nothing like what I was expecting.

"Thank you," Mitchell said. He stopped at a door in the middle of the walkway. "This is us here. If you keep walking the way we were going, we have a bowling alley being built at the end there."

"Wow, really?" Tommy said.

"Yes. And at that end," Mitchell said pointing back the way we came, "we are putting in a movie theater. Unfortunately, it's only going to be three screens—it's all we have room for. But we will always get the big blockbusters in our theater."

"That's awesome!" Tommy said.

I winced inside. I hoped it hadn't shown on my face. There he went with that word again.

Mitchell opened the door. "Right this way."

There was a staircase to walk up. At the top of the stairs we turned right, leading us to a giant open area. It looked like it could serve as a giant phone operation center. All it needed was a ton of cubicles and he was set.

A large round table was stationed in the center of the room with three other people standing around it. Behind them was a smaller, rectangular table with a model of the entertainment facility. We got closer to the round table and Mitchell started to introduce everyone.

He pointed to the first man to the left. "This gentleman here is Patrick Malloy. He's my right-hand man. He's been with me from the start. A great business partner." Patrick wore horn-rimmed glasses and had a neatly trimmed five o'clock shadow. His suit was thin and tight fitting, showing off his athletic build. Once again, another guy who looked like he jumped out of a men's modeling magazine. Then I noticed the tattoos. First, there was a neck tattoo that wasn't fully covered up by his collared shirt. A quick double take, looking him up and down again, I noticed small tattoos on a few of his fingers.

Those tattoos didn't seem business professional to me. They screamed criminal.

"Hi." His voice was deep and raspy voice.

Mitchell continued. "This man next to him, his name is Ross Greentree. He's the best accountant money can buy."

"Hello," he said and waved to us. This guy was overweight. A complete opposite of Patrick. He seemed legitimate. He had on a brown blazer with jeans. He was much older than the others. His hair also looked like a bad comb over.

"And finally, Shawn Beiser. He's the contractor responsible for all the work you see here today and will see when it's all complete."

"Hi," he said.

"And these two men here are my new financial gurus. This is Devin," he said pointing to me, "and this is Tommy," he said moving his hand toward Tommy's direction. "These are the men who will help handle all my money and make sure we're all financially successful."

"Hi," both Tommy and I responded in unison.

"So now that everyone has been introduced, let's get this started," Mitchell said as he pulled out a chair to the round table in front of him. "What we have in front of us is a model of the completed center. Stores, restaurants and activity centers are all in the process of being built. Before I move forward with anything else, I want everyone to take a look at what's in front of them and let me know if there's anything that needs to be added, taken away or changed."

Everyone, including Tommy and me, walked around the table looking at the large model. The model didn't show exactly what store went where but it was a generalization such as *bar, restaurant, retail store* or *bowling alley*. The model looked beautiful. There was going to be a ton of places to visit and have fun. I couldn't believe it, I was getting excited to visit this place once it was opened. There was an outside area behind some of the restaurants for outdoor seating, and he had even added a small stage for bands to play. I didn't know how he was going to pull this off, but this place was going to be a huge success.

Everyone seemed to agree that it looked good. I still couldn't figure out where this was going. What was the point of this meeting?

Mitchell asked us to sit. We all took a seat at the table, and he started explaining population size of the city and what numbers he expected to draw in from this place. Mitchell and his accountant discussed how much revenue each location would generate, how much rent for each store front would be, and of course how much richer he will be.

He turned to Tommy and me. "That's where you two come in. I wanted you to meet with my accountant and discuss ways to diversify my portfolio. If this venture is a success, as I assume it will be, I want to duplicate this and bring more ideas to the city and possibly other cities. I'm bringing jobs back to Decker City. I'm bringing entertainment back to Decker City. Many businesses have closed and many people have left. Prices have fallen, big time. My goal is to attract Decker City natives to the downtown area and put this city back on the map where it belongs."

Mitchell then turned the conversation to Shawn the contractor. They discussed time frames on completion and when he can expect to open.

A phone began to ring. The conversation went dead for a moment while everyone reached in their pocket for their phones. Patrick grabbed his ringing phone out of his jacket pocket. He looked at it and then stood up. "Excuse me for a moment," he said. He walked a few feet away to answer his phone.

"Okay, back on topic," Mitchell said to Shawn. "I need an exact date to open. I need a guarantee. I can't make false statements to the public and have it come back to ruin me. They are depending on me. I have a lot riding on this place."

Shawn spoke fast. "Mitchell, I understand. We have well over a hundred people working on this place almost 24 hours a day to get this operational for you. We have been moving at speeds unknown to building before. I've never done something like this in the time you're asking for. You've got to give me some leeway."

Mitchell leaned forward in his seat. "Shawn, I don't have time for leeway. I need a time frame, and I need it now."

Before Shawn could answer Mitchell's intimidating question, Mitchell's assistant, Patrick, walked back over. He stood next to Mitchell, leaned over and whispered something into his ear. Mitchell's eyes became fixed on me.

Why was he looking at me? That was weird.

"Are you sure?" Mitchell whispered back to Patrick, but loud enough that we all could hear. Mitchell looked up at Patrick and his assistant nodded. "Gentlemen, it seems something of great importance has come up that requires my attention immediately. I apologize for the early dismissal, but I need to take care of this. Please excuse me." Mitchell slid his chair backwards and stood up. "Thank you all for coming. You may stick around as long as you'd like and check out whatever you'd like." Without another word, Mitchell and Patrick walked toward the stairs and disappeared.

The rest of us stood up and said our goodbye's and parted ways. Tommy and I toured both ends of the building. The place was turning out to be an incredible entertainment facility. Mitchell was going to make a killing on this place.

As we stepped outside, my excitement was replaced with the nagging feeling that something wasn't right. Why did Mitchell leave in such a hurry? Why all the drama about having us together? Why was Mitchell looking at me?

"Are you gentlemen ready to return to work?" the driver said as we approached the limo. I pushed aside the questions circling my head about the meeting. It was time to go back to the office and enjoy a nice evening out with Lara.

"Yes, we are," I said.

CHAPTER THIRTY-ONE

The rest of the day seemed to fly by. I just wanted to end my day and have a drink with Lara.

I got up from my desk and made my way to the office door. Tommy walked by. "Where are you going?"

"I'm heading over to the bar with Lara now. Want to join us?"

"Absolutely," Tommy said as he zoomed past me. I don't know how he did it. He was always full of energy, and he was always in a good mood. I could never keep up with him.

I walked into the lobby and Lara was waiting by the front door for me. "Come on, slow poke. Tommy probably already made it over there and had a drink."

"The guy is always in a rush," I said as I opened the lobby door. We both walked out and I pushed the elevator button.

"So how was the meeting today?" Lara asked.

"All right, I guess. Nothing special." Nothing special? I was impressed by how everything was coming along, but I couldn't give Mitchell the satisfaction of making me tell others about it. And what was with the end of the meeting?

I pushed those thoughts aside. My evening was going to be fun. I was going out with Lara and Tommy and I wouldn't let Mitchell ruin my night.

After five hours at the bar, we decided to leave. But it was only 10:00. Still too early to go home. Tommy, as drunk as he was, reminded us that we needed to come back to his place and watch "Da Big Leblowski." He had just a few more drinks than he should have and talked about this movie most of the night. He couldn't pronounce the title of the movie properly, but was insistent that we see it. We decided to call a cab to take us all back to his place.

Lara got on her phone and let the cab company know where to pick us up. "Someone will be here in about five minutes," Lara said as she ended her call. She pointed to Tommy, "What's he doing?"

Tommy was trying to climb a traffic light post.

"Dude, get down from there." I walked over to Tommy and grabbed his leg and pulled him down.

"The light was threatening to change color if I didn't climb up and save it," Tommy said.

"And who told you that?" I asked him.

"The fire hydrant."

"Okay. How about you sit down for a little bit before the cab comes. Sound good?" I said.

"Sounds good to me. What about you?" Tommy asked, looking at the fire hydrant. He turned back to me and said, "It's sounds good to him, too." He made it to the sidewalk and laid on his back. He would probably pass out before the cab came.

"What are we going to do with him?" Lara asked.

"We are going to bring him back to his place and make sure he's okay. I'm going to stay with him. You're welcome to join us or I can have the cab take you home."

"I think joining you guys is more interesting than going home. I don't want to miss out on anything else he does." She giggled.

"You can be so evil sometimes," I said.

Lara tilted her head and smiled innocently.

"Just a small town girl…livin' in a looonely worrrlldd. She took the midnight train goin' annnyywhere…"

Both Lara and I looked down at the sidewalk.

"Shut up!" Both Lara and I said at the same time.

"Don't be hatin' on my singin'. Plus, the hydrant requested it," Tommy replied.

Lara and I couldn't help but laugh.

A taxi finally came around the corner and headed in our direction.

I kicked Tommy who was still lying on the sidewalk. "Get up. Our ride is here."

He climbed to his feet as the cab pulled up to the curb. Lara opened the car door as I helped Tommy make his way inside.

My phone started to ring. Who would be calling me now?

I grabbed the phone as I followed Tommy inside the cab. It was an unknown number. Who was this?

I was sandwiched between Tommy and Lara in the cab when I answered the mysterious phone call. "Hello?"

"Hello, is this Devin?" a female's voice responded on the end.

I placed my left hand over my left ear as I spoke into the phone planted against my right ear. "Yes, who's this?" I asked.

"This is…"

"Ohhhhhh we're halfway there….OHHHHH OHH, LIVIN' ON A PRAYER" Tommy began singing at the top of his lungs. Lara reached in front of me and punched Tommy from across the seat.

"Shut up, Tommy! Devin's on the phone."

Tommy quieted down.

"I'm sorry, I couldn't hear you before. Who's calling?" I asked the female voice again.

"This is Joyce from Decker City Hospital. I'm calling to let you know your grandfather has been admitted. He's been shot."

"What?!" I yelled into the phone. "Wait, what happened?"

"I don't know much more other than he's being prepped for surgery right now. You are listed as his emergency contact and I wanted to let you know in case you wanted to come over and see him."

"Yes, I'll be right over. Thank you." I ended the call and I couldn't believe what I just heard. My grandfather was shot. How did this happen? Who would hurt him?

"What was that about?" Lara asked.

I stared forward in my seat, pondering the question. What happened? What was my grandfather doing that got him shot? My heart began to ache.

"My grandfather was shot," I finally said.

"What?!"

Tommy shook his head. "He's been shot?!"

"Why would anyone do that?" Lara cried.

Tommy held his head with his hands. "I shouldn't have drank so much. I can't handle the adrenaline. I feel sick."

"I don't know!" I said. A million thoughts and feelings flowed through my body. But only one made sense.

I needed to see my grandfather.

I needed to know if he was okay.

I needed to find out who did this.

I leaned forward to speak to the taxi driver through the back window. "Change of plans. We need to go to Decker City Hospital."

CHAPTER THIRTY-TWO

I rushed through the hospital doors. Lara and Tommy followed behind me, struggling to keep up because of Tommy's state. He kept apologizing for being drunk.

"Forget it," I said to Tommy. "Just forget it. It's okay."

Lara was helping Tommy get around to make sure he didn't fall and hurt himself.

I approached the front desk. "I'm looking for Paul Shephard, my grandfather. Do you know where he is?" I asked the lady behind the desk.

"Let me check for you. Give me one moment please," she responded.

I was shaking. I felt like I was going to vomit, but it wasn't from alcohol.

"It looks like he's in the emergency area being prepped for surgery. Let me tell one of the doctors you arrived. You can wait in their waiting room down the hall," the woman behind the desk said.

"Thank you."

Lara and Tommy walked into the hallway where I stood.

"You are too fast," Lara said, out of breath from holding onto Tommy.

"Sorry, I just needed to get here. I can't wait any longer."

"I know, I understand."

"Hey," Tommy said. "Devin, I'm here for you, buddy. Anything you need." He gave me a thumbs up. He was trying really hard to not sound or act drunk.

"Thanks, Tommy," I said. I really appreciated both Tommy and Lara being here right now with me. I wouldn't have known what to do if I got this news alone.

"How about we sit down instead of standing here waiting."

"Good ider," Tommy replied, still unable to speak properly.

We sat in the waiting room and were as patient as we could be. Lara brought us both scalding hot coffee from the vending machine. It was terrible.

Tommy groaned in relief. "This is the best coffee I've ever had."

The television was on. It was the local news. We watched, but there were no reports of gunfire. There were no reports of any robberies. In fact, it seemed like a quiet night. Except for where we were now.

Finally, a doctor came walking into the room. "Devin?" he asked.

I jumped to my feet. "Yes, that's me." I walked over to the doctor.

"Hi, Devin. My name is Dr. Engleman. I'm the doctor on call tonight and will be handling part of the surgery on your grandfather."

"How is he?"

"It's touch and go right now. He's lost a lot of blood and the bullets…"

"Bullets? You mean more than one?"

"Yes. He was shot twice. One in the chest and one in the stomach. The one in the chest went straight through. It missed any major arteries and organs. The one in the stomach. Well, it's not good. I'm not going to lie to you so this may seem very blunt. There's a lot of damage. We are doing the best we can, but I want you to prepare for the worst. Let's hope for the best, but I can't promise anything."

Tears welled up in my eyes. My heart was breaking. "So he's going to die?"

"I didn't say that. There's always hope, but like I said, there's a lot of damage and he's lost a lot of blood. It doesn't look promising, but things can always change. We just started a few minutes ago so I can't say for sure which way he's heading. Let me get back in there so I can do what I can for him. And Devin, I'm sorry."

I didn't even know what to say. I blinked and tears streamed down my cheeks. If I lose my grandfather, I'd have lost everyone in my family. I'd have no one left.

"It's going to be a long surgery so I suggest you go home. I will have one of the nurses call you if his situation changes." The doctor left.

I returned to my seat and slumped back into it, unsure of where to go and what to do.

"How is he?" Lara asked.

I shook my head. "The doctors are going to operate on him now. They told me to go home and wait for their call because it'll be awhile."

Lara stroked my hair. "I'm sorry, I'm so sorry."

Tommy spoke up. "I think that's a good idea. Let's get a taxi and we can all go home."

"I don't know if I want to leave. I want to be here when he wakes up."

Lara continued. "I know you do. But you need to get some sleep."

"Sleep? Are you kidding? He's my only living relative, Lara. He's all I have."

Lara wiped away the tears on my face. She was crying now, too.

"I can't leave."

She wiped away her own tears with determination. "We have to be positive right now. Devin, he's going to be okay. I'll call for two cabs. I'll get Tommy home and then come to your place and join you." She looked up. Her eyes were pleading with me. "Please? I want you to take care of yourself. And there's nothing you can do here."

I sighed. She was right. "Okay."

"Good. It's settled." She pulled out her phone, called, and got Tommy to stand before I even stood up. I helped Tommy to the entrance of the hospital. We arrived just as one cab was pulling into the parking lot.

"Devin, you take that one," Lara said.

"No. You have Tommy. Get him home first," I replied.

"You're right, thanks. I'll see you soon." She reached for the door as the cab pulled up. I helped Tommy get in the car. Lara turned back to me before she got in and kissed my cheek. "Go home and relax. Don't worry so much. I'll be over soon." She got in the car and the cab began to drive away.

My phone began to ring. I pulled it out of my pocket and once again, an unknown number. This must be the hospital again. I started walking toward the entrance when I answered the phone. "Hello?"

"Hello, Devin…" The mysterious voice on the other end dragged out the *hello*, almost sounding creepy.

"Who is this?" I asked.

"I'm surprised you don't know my voice by now."

"Mitchell?"

"See? It didn't take your detective skills long to figure that one out."

I pulled the phone away from my ear and looked at the time. It was almost 11:00 pm. I placed my phone back against my ear. "Why are you calling me right now?"

"Is that how you talk to all your clients? Never mind. I'll cut right to the chase then. I was calling to see if you got my package."

"A package? What package? What are you talking about?"

There was a pause on the other end.

Silence.

"Hello?" I said.

Finally, he responded. "I see you're at the hospital, so I'm guessing you got it."

What was he talking about? How did he know I was at the hospital? Was he here too? Could he see me? And then suddenly it hit me.

"You son-of-a-!"

"Whoa there. Relax, buddy. Actually, I probably shouldn't call you my buddy. We are more like…enemies."

"Why did you do it? What did my grandfather do to you? What did I do to you?"

"You see, your little heroics around this city have been pissing me off. It's been causing me a lot of grief. A lot of my money and time wasted. A lot of my drugged-up minions have been tossed in jail. A major shipment of mine is in police custody. I have some people not happy about that. And at the center of if all, is you. Well, actually, I'm at the center of it, but so are you."

"What are you tal–"

"Don't play stupid with me, Devin. I know it's you. I know you're the hooded creep running around the city at night. I have my proof so stop denying it."

I was full of anger right now. First, he shoots my grandfather and now he knows I'm the guy under the hood.

"How do you know?" I asked.

"Oh come on, it was easy. I had my guys knock off the same convenience store for about a week. First of all, the cops suck around here. Even after my donation, they still can't do their jobs. But whatever, at least they are on my side. So anyway, I knew the hood was bound to show up. Either him or the cops. The hood won. Lucky you. I had surveillance around the area, which I'm guessing you didn't know about, and I watched where you came from and where you went. I saw you come from an alley before you ran into the store. I got the license plate number and had my assistant hack the Department of Motor Vehicles to find out who the plate belonged to. And what do you know, it came up under the name Paul Shephard. And then I thought, you know what, that name sounds awfully familiar. And of course, I didn't think a 79-year-old was underneath the hood. So a quick online search found me the information I was looking for–his grandson, Devin Shephard."

"So why shoot him?"

"I'm assuming by shoot him, and not the phrase *kill him*, means he's still alive. Ugh. What a stubborn old man. Anyway, why did I shoot him you ask? Because you've stood in my way long enough. You've taken people from me. It's my turn to take someone from you. Actually, you're lucky I'm being generous. I could have gone after your girlfriend, too."

"You stay away from her!"

"Don't worry. She's my leverage now. You see what happened to your dear old grandpa? If you don't stop what you're doing, if you don't stop trying to play the hero…she's next."

"Don't you dare touch her!"

"Oh please, Devin. It's my turn to ask you a question. How do you do what you do? You know, that magic you apparently possess."

I ignored his question. "You will pay for this. If my grandfather dies, it's murder. I'll make sure you go to jail for a long time."

"Come on, you think this is the first time I shot someone? You think I've never murdered someone before?"

"I'll go to the police. I'll tell them it was you."

"Ehh. It's all hearsay. You have no proof. No evidence was left at your grandfather's house, I made sure of it. Patrick is a *very good* assistant. And do you really think the multimillionaire who's trying to turn this city around by building a place everyone can and will enjoy, by bringing jobs and people back to this city and of course by making a very large donation to the police department is going to commit such a terrible crime? Like I said, the police are on my side. They don't like the Gray Hood. And for safe measures, in case that didn't sink in, if you do decide to take that chance and go to the police, I'll unmask you. I'll tell everyone who is under that hood."

"Maybe I don't care," I said. I was bluffing. I don't want the world to know who I am. Like Dr. Kane said, if people knew what I could really do, they may turn against me–if they haven't already.

"Well then, we will just have to see, won't we?"

And then the call disconnected.

It took every ounce of energy not to crush my phone in my hand or throw it against the wall next to me. I wanted to kill Mitchell Quinn, for threatening me, for threatening Lara and for shooting my grandfather. I was against killing, but he deserved to die. Still, I didn't think I could actually go through with something like that. I didn't think I could be a murderer. Being a murderer would make me no better than Mitchell.

He was a murderer. I wasn't.

I took a deep breath, trying to calm down.

No.

Not murder.

Justice.

He needed to be brought to justice. But if he's alive and in custody, what's to stop him from telling everyone who I am? I didn't know what to do. I usually talked to my grandfather about these problems. Now, I have no one. I couldn't tell Lara or Tommy.

Wait. Dr. Kane. That's who I can go to. Maybe he'll know what to do.

My cab arrived. I hopped in and gave the driver directions to Dr. Kane's office. I picked up the phone and dialed his number, hoping he would answer.

CHAPTER THIRTY-THREE

I sat on the front step outside Dr. Kane's front door. He had a second office that was an old house he had transformed. I was there for about 20 minutes when headlights appeared down the street. The vehicle turned into the extended driveway and parked outside the house. The headlights blinded me for only a moment until his car turned off.

Dr. Kane stepped out of the vehicle. "Devin? Is that you?"

"Yeah," I answered.

He walked up to the front door, fidgeting with his keys in the dark. "Have you waited long?"

"No, just a few minutes."

He found the key and unlocked the front door. We entered a waiting room and he turned on the lights. "Would you like something to drink? A glass of water?" Dr. Kane asked.

"Sure," I said.

He walked off down a hallway and I stood there waiting for him. A faucet turned on and then off. Dr. Kane reentered the waiting room with a glass of water for me.

"Thank you," I said, taking the glass.

"Let's go into my office where it's more comfortable," Dr. Kane said.

We walked down the hallway until it dead ended into a closed door. Dr. Kane pulled out his keys again and unlocked the door. He flipped on the light switch and walked around his desk to his black leather chair. I sat down on the sofa that leaned against the wall. I took a sip of the water and placed it on the table at one end of the sofa.

I explained what had happened. From my grandfather's shooting to Mitchell's threatening phone call.

Dr. Kane was somber. "I think you should go after Mitchell. You're the only one who can stop him and expose him."

"But if I do, he'll go after my girlfriend," I said.

"Then ask her to leave town. Make her go somewhere far away. Make sure she's safe before you go after him. Does she have friends or family that don't live around here?"

I had to think for a moment. She never mentioned any friends from back home.

"Oh! Her parents," I said.

"So convince her to go to her parents for a few days while you figure out how to stop Mitchell."

This may work. I just had to convince Lara to go see her parents, which I know she never really enjoyed doing. But this was for her own safety. I felt horrible that I couldn't tell her. I know she would just tell me to go to the police if I told her I knew who shot my grandfather and that the guy is coming for her next. But if I didn't contact the police, I knew she would. I couldn't risk that. I had to stop Mitchell on my own.

"So how can I help?" Dr. Kane asked. "What can I do to help you stop this guy?"

I thought about the question for a moment. But I had no answer. No one ever asked me if they could help me. I was always doing this on my own.

"I don't know," I told Dr. Kane. "I don't want to put you in danger, too. My grandfather was shot and my girlfriend's life is being threatened. I don't want to put anyone else in harm's way."

"Let me decide what kind of risks I want to be involved with. Besides, he doesn't know about me. All he knows is about your grandfather and your girlfriend. And I have my own reasons. I want to get that sadistic psycho for what he did to my friend Howard a few months ago."

"You're right. But what can we do?"

"Your first step is to get your girlfriend out of town. Then you have the freedom to go after him."

"But what do I do when I find him? I can't kill him and if I take him to the police, he'll expose me."

He pondered that for a moment before he finally said, "I don't know, Devin. I really don't know…"

CHAPTER THIRTY-FOUR

"Hi, this is Lara. Leave a message."

This was the second time I called Lara and I still got her voicemail.

"Lara, it's Devin. I'm not going back to my place tonight. Something came up. Anyway, I need you to do me a big favor. I need you to go visit your parents this weekend. You to have to leave right now. I really need you to trust me on this. I'm sorry I can't explain more. When you come back, hopefully everything will be solved and I can tell you what's going on. But in the meantime, I really need you to head up to your parent's house. Please."

I held the phone in the palm of my hand, staring down at it hoping she would be calling me in the middle of leaving the message. Nope. I put the phone back up to my ear. "I don't know why you're not picking up now and it's worrying me. I have to go. Let me know when you get there. Goodbye."

I placed the phone back in my pocket and turned on the ignition to my car. I needed my hood. I needed to find Mitchell. I needed to make him pay for what he did.

I grabbed my hooded shirt and quickly left my grandfather's house. No need for communications this time since my grandfather wasn't going to be coming along. The thought of that made my heart ache. This was the first time I would be going without him. It just seemed wrong. It felt empty.

I needed him in this adventure. This was our adventure. This was something we built and worked on together.

I couldn't wait any longer for Lara to get back to me. I had to go after Mitchell now.

I got in my car and headed out to find Mitchell. I knew he'd be waiting for me. He was not a stupid man. And he couldn't possibly think that I wouldn't come after him after he threatened Lara. Beyond that, I needed to get Mitchell before he got to Lara.

And I knew where he'd be. His new entertainment facility.

I parked the car about two blocks away to avoid suspicion. From the distance, I could see that there were still construction crews working on the building. Like Shawn had said, 24/7.

I walked toward the facility. The streets were nearly empty. It was now well after two in the morning and the only people out right now would be the people going home from the bar. Hopefully, there wouldn't be anybody I would have to worry about.

I passed a group of people who stumbled out of a bar. They were all laughing hysterically.

At the corner of Mitchell's construction site, I stopped.

This was it. I threw the hood over my head and sprinted down the block to the front of the building. The entrance was barricaded with the locked gate from earlier. Mitchell wouldn't be standing behind it this time waiting to let me in. But chances were, he was waiting inside. I started my ascent to the top of the gate.

I jumped from the top onto the ground on the other side. I stayed in a crouched position to make sure I could avoid detection. I waited for a moment, still and in complete silence. No one appeared. I stayed low and ran across the path to the front door. I pulled the handle down and the door slowly opened.

I made my way into the building and came to the crossroads. Both corridors seemed empty. There were some faint rumblings of machines working in the distance.

Looking down both walkways, I remembered from the earlier meeting that Mitchell turned right. I did the same. I stayed close to the sides of the storefronts to avoid detection.

After a few steps, a door opened near my location. Three men walked out and headed toward me. I ran into the arcade they were building and hid behind a machine. The men's voices grew louder as they came closer. I peeked out from behind the machine as they walked by. They were talking about building codes. It was nothing important to me.

They passed the arcade. Their voices soon became distant. I crept toward the front of the store and peeked in the direction that the men had been walking. They had disappeared.

It was clear. I left the arcade and continued my way down to the door Mitchell had entered during our meeting.

Upon arriving at the door, I reached for the doorknob. The door flew open, knocking me backwards onto the floor. A man walked out. Patrick Malloy, Mitchell's right-hand man.

"Hey! Don't move!" he yelled pointing at me. His suit jacket was open just enough for me to see the gun holstered by his side.

If he was here, Mitchell was here. I needed to get past him and get to Mitchell.

I pushed my hands forward toward Patrick and he stumbled backwards onto the door behind him. This gave me a split moment to get to my feet and rush toward him. He reached for his gun, but I grabbed his arm and threw it back against the door. He kneed me in the stomach and knocked the wind out of me. It loosened my grip on his arm and he shoved me backwards into the middle of the corridor.

He grabbed his gun from his holster but before he could aim it at me, I flicked my hand upwards and his gun flew out of his hand and landed a few feet from him on the floor. He stood there for a moment, unsure of what to do next.

He stared at me and then back at his gun. He turned and raced for it. I jumped back to my feet and chased after him. He reached it first and attempted to bend down to pick it. Before he could, I waved my hand at the ground and the gun slid further away from him. He was barely able to fully stand back up before I tackled him to the ground.

I landed on top of him and sat up. I went to throw a punch but Patrick lifted his arm to block it. He lifted his legs and tossed me over his head. I rolled over and made it to back to my feet almost instantly. He stood back up and charged toward me. He lifted me off the ground and we went into the wall behind me. Plaster, wood and paint chips fell to the floor. While I was still in his arms, he retracted from the wall and ran me into it again. My back was aching with pain. He pulled me out of the hole again and I started elbowing the spot between his neck and shoulder blades. By the third time, he loosened his grip and I slid off his body.

Once I was on my feet, I threw a solid right hook into his jaw and he stumbled backwards. I charged at him and rammed my shoulder into his stomach. He was a few inches off the ground as I kept running with my shoulder in his stomach. A few steps later I connected with a glass door, opposite Mitchell's office door, which shattered upon our contact. He slammed onto the ground covered in shattered glass and my momentum made me lose my balance. I stumbled over him, landing into a clothing rack which came tumbling down on top of me as I fell to the ground.

I moved the clothing rack off me and turned over to find Patrick. He was moving slowly, covered in glass and blood. I didn't have time for this. I grabbed one of my zip ties and one of his hands. I attached it to the unbroken door's handle. He wasn't going anywhere and my battle wasn't with him. My job was to find Mitchell.

I hunched over, keeping my right hand on my lower back as I walked out of the clothing store. My back was killing me. I limped back to the door Patrick had exited. Mitchell must be hiding upstairs. I reached for the handle and swung the door open with such force, I thought it came off its hinges. I headed up the stairs and crept around the corner of the large room.

It was empty.

I stood up from my crouching position and walked over toward the large table which sat in the center of the room. I kept an eye out for some unsuspecting attacker, but no one was there.

There was something on the table as I walked closer. It was a piece of paper. I picked it up and it was addressed to me.

Devin—I see you don't take my threats seriously. You are one stubborn idiot. And you just cost the safety of your darling girlfriend. I'll see you soon. I'll see her sooner.

I rubbed my thumb across the ink. It smeared.

Mitchell had just been here. Patrick had been a distraction so he could escape. Rage started to build inside of me. I had him. I knew he would be here and I missed my chance.

I slammed my hands down on the table. I grabbed a chair to my left and tossed it across the room. I threw another one on the right. It crashed against the wall, breaking upon impact. There was a bookcase full of files in the corner of the room. I reached out and pulled my hands toward me. The bookcase came crashing down to the floor. Binders and papers spilled out everywhere.

I left, heading for the stairs to return to the main floor. I needed to find Lara before Mitchell did. He had a head start, but I could catch him.

I opened the door when I got downstairs. There was a group of people around Patrick, helping him up and patting him on the back.

"There he is!" one of the guys yelled.

They ran toward me. I pushed my arms forward and the first guy in the line abruptly came to a stop like he ran into a brick wall. He tumbled backwards and fell back into the guy behind him who then fell like a domino piece. The two guys behind him tripped over each other and lost their balance as they fell to the ground. One push took down four guys. I even impressed myself.

I started to run toward the entrance as the men gathered back to their feet.

"Stop him!" they yelled as I sprinted away from them.

A man came out from around the corner of the entrance. As I approached, I pushed both my arms to the right. He stumbled and fell. I was able to jump over him as I ran past him. I pushed my arms forward and the front doors opened immediately for me to easily exit.

Once I made it into the open, I sprinted toward the fence and hopped over it. As I landed on the ground, the door swung open and the men chasing me came flooding outside. Their conversations became muffled as I ran down the street back to my car.

I couldn't believe I was *this* close to getting Mitchell. If Patrick wasn't at the door, I would have had Mitchell. I had to find him before he found Lara and did any more damage to my family, my friends or this city. The only place I had left to look now would be Tommy's place. I just hoped I would make it there before Mitchell and any of his associates did.

CHAPTER THIRTY-FIVE

I f only traffic would just part like the Red Sea, I could have been at Tommy's place by now. I did my best to obey the traffic laws, but I broke more than my fair share on my way to Tommy's apartment.

After what seemed like an hour, I was on Tommy's street.

I looked for an open spot, but it was so early in the morning that they were all taken. I decided to double park, not caring since Lara's safety was more important than parking my car.

I started toward Tommy's place and pulled my phone out of my pocket again to see if Lara had responded to me yet.

Nothing.

I called her again.

Ring...

Ring...

Ring...

"Hello, this is Lara's cell phone." A male voice answered the phone on the fourth ring. It sounded like...

"...Mitchell," I said. I could feel my blood start to boil. The hatred for this man was growing by the minute.

"Hey there, buddy. I hope I have your attention now," he said.

I stopped in my tracks right outside the front door to Tommy's building. He had Lara's phone. That meant he had Lara.

"What do you want?" I asked.

"What do I want? Hmm...how about exactly what I asked from you earlier–leave me alone. Stop doing your superhero stuff. I told you I would get your girl if you came after me. Someone doesn't listen very well."

"Fine. I'll stop. Let her go."

Mitchell laughed into the phone. "Oh Devin, it doesn't work that way. She's my leverage now. You didn't listen to me earlier so this is to make sure you listen to me now. Stop. Ruining. My. Business." He paused. "She's mine until further notice. And if you decide to not listen to me again, I'll make sure I finish the job this time, unlike your stubborn old grandfather."

The phone went dead.

"Mitchell!? ...Mitchell!?" I screamed into the phone. But it didn't matter.

Killing Mitchell seemed more likely every time I talked with him. I had to find Lara. But how? Hopefully Tommy had some answers.

I put the phone back in my pocket and quickly entered Tommy's building, heading toward his apartment.

I knocked on Tommy's front door. It immediately swung open. Tommy stood there in a tee shirt and boxers. His eyes were drooping. He looked awful. "Dude, not so loud."

"Sorry." I walked into his place and noticed the mess he had to clean up. A lamp was shattered on the floor. Chairs were turned over. A table was flipped. Little things, such as books and papers were scattered all across the floor. "What happened here?"

"I was passed out," Tommy replied. "I don't think I've drank that much in a long time."

"Do you remember anything that happened?"

He walked to the sofa and sat down. "The last thing I really remember was playing pool. Then I remember you saying we were going to my place to watch a movie and I've got nothing after that. I don't even remember coming home."

He was useless. I needed a clue, a hint, anything to help lead me to where Mitchell was and where he was keeping Lara. I started scanning the room, looking for anything.

"But the dream I had was weird," Tommy started to say.

I stopped. "Yeah?" I answered, still looking around his apartment.

"Well, I dreamed that people came into my apartment and wrecked everything. There was a girl screaming. Then I woke up in my apartment and it was destroyed."

"Wait," I stopped searching the apartment and focused on him now. "You said you dreamed this was happening?"

"Yes," Tommy replied. "Now that I think about it, I don't think it was a dream. It felt like a dream. I guess I was just so drunk that I must have thought it was."

"Do you remember anything else? Did you see any faces? Did they say anything?"

Tommy shook his head. "No, I don't remember anything else. I just laid there and watched. Like I said, I was drunk and thought it was a dream. There was screaming, too. But you know how in dreams when you try to scream and nothing comes out? I felt like maybe I was screaming but I couldn't and yet I still heard screaming. It was weird. Was I robbed?"

Lara. They came here and took her.

"Do you remember Lara bringing you home?"

"No, but now I wish I had." A smile appeared on his face.

I was not in the mood for jokes. I stared at him with glaring eyes.

"And now I wish I didn't say that. It's the hangover, I didn't mean it." He didn't know what was happening. I couldn't be angry at his ignorance.

"It's fine. I just have a lot going on right now," I told him. I didn't want to involve him in this. He was already in no shape to be helping anyway.

"You have a lot going on? Look at my apartment!" he started to yell. "Ouch." He leaned his head forward into his hands. "No yelling."

"You don't remember going to the hospital last night?"

"The hospital? No. Did I injure myself?"

"My grandfather was shot."

"Oh dude, really!? ...ouch. No yelling," he said again, clutching his head with his hands.

"He's been in surgery. The doctors don't know what to expect yet."

"I'm sorry, Devin, really. I didn't remember. I hope he's okay."

"Me too," I said. "I need to get going. Are you going to be okay here by yourself?"

"Yeah, I'll be fine. I'm just going to lay back down and sleep it off. I'll clean up when I'm feeling better. I hope everything is still here."

I turned to walk from his living room toward the front door.

Tommy said, "Keep me updated on your grandfather."

"I will. Thanks." I turned back to the front door when I stepped on something. I lifted my right foot and there was a pack of matches on the ground. Tommy didn't smoke. I bent over and picked them up.

The Prime Time. It was a local club that was usually pretty busy at all hours of the day. A perfect cover for Mitchell and his people to conduct business in the public eye and not seem shady.

The matches could have come from one of the people who grabbed Lara. I couldn't know for sure, but it was all I had.

I put the matches in my pocket and left Tommy's apartment.

CHAPTER THIRTY-SIX

made it back to my car and plugged in the direction to the club when my phone chimed to life. It was a voicemail. When did I miss a phone call?

I unlocked my phone to listen to my new voicemail, eager to see who it was.

This message is for Devin. It's Dr. Engleman, the surgeon who operated on your grandfather. We spoke briefly. I was calling to let you know we finished with the surgery and he should be waking up soon. I think in his condition you should be here when he wakes up. I look forward to seeing you soon.

This was good news. My grandfather was waking up soon. I had to get to the hospital. I had to see him. I had to talk with him. My grandfather was the only one who would know what to do.

I rushed through the hospital doors and went to the front desk. "I'm looking for my grandfather, Paul Shephard. Do you know what room he's in?"

The lady at the desk looked down at her computer and pounded on her keyboard in front of her. She looked back up at me. "Fourth floor, room 413."

"Thank you," I said and continued down the hallway to the nearest elevator.

I waited at the elevators for what seemed like an eternity. I hope people don't have to wait this long for these elevators in an emergency. It almost seems like it would be hazardous to their health.

The elevator dinged and the doors slid open. I stepped inside and hit the button for the fourth floor. The doors closed and I started moving. Within seconds, the elevator dinged. Second floor. The doors slid open and a doctor walked on holding a medical folder. He pressed the fifth floor and went back to his reading. The doors shut and we began to move again. And once again, the elevator dinged and stopped. The doors slid open and two women came walking on. Of course, I would be forced to stop at every floor.

Finally, I reached the fourth floor. The elevator doors opened and the two women walked out first. I followed behind them. The elevator doors shut behind me. I stood in the middle of the hallway trying to figure out which way to go. I found the sign on the wall behind the two women. 413 was to the left.

I walked by a lot of rooms before I found my grandfather's. I walked in and his eyes were open, watching the television. "Hey, Grandpa," I said as I approached his bed.

"There's my boy," he whispered. "It hurts to talk so don't mind my crappy voice. I sound like a cat scratched my vocal cords, then found a mouse somewhere inside me and went chasing for it all while scratching up everything inside of me."

Even in his condition, he was still trying to make light of the situation. I smiled and nodded at him.

"Don't smile and nod at me, you look like an idiot."

And he was still able to make fun of me.

"How are you doing?" I asked.

"Well, after the cat incident, I could be better. The doctor was just in to look at my vitals."

"Do you know what happened? Can you remember anything before you were shot?"

"Not really." He winced in pain and tried leaning back in his bed. He took a deep breath and the pain must have past. He started to seem more relaxed. "I don't remember anything. I was making a sandwich in the kitchen and then I heard a bang and I was out. I guess a neighbor heard the gunshot and called the police."

"It was Mitchell. He did this," I told him.

His face had a confused look on it. "What? No. That's impossible."

"I'm serious."

"Why would he do something like that? It makes no sense."

"He knows who I am. He knows what we've been doing. He wants me to stop so he went after you and now he's kidnapped Lara."

"I don't understand…"

"He's the one who's been behind the attacks in this city. I think he's the one who's been bringing in that drug. He's profiting off the destruction of our city. He sends his people in and they run out the businesses. Prices fall and he comes in and buys everything at a deep discount. Right?"

"I don't know where you're getting all this from, but I think you've let your hatred for this guy cloud your judgment."

"He even called me and confessed to shooting you. He just kidnapped Lara. Why don't you believe me?"

"Okay, okay. I believe you. I just don't understand all of this. Maybe it's the drugs I'm on. I know he was a bully but now he's some sort of… criminal king pin?"

"Pretty much. I tried finding him a few hours ago but he got away."

"Can't you just go to the police with this information?"

"I can't. He said he would tell the public who I was if I went to the police. If I told his secret, he'd tell mine."

A knock came at the door. We both looked and Dr. Engleman came walking in. "I'm glad to see you're awake. How are you feeling, Mr. Shephard?"

"I feel like a cat scratched my–" my grandfather started to say before I interrupted him.

"He's in pain," I said. "Can you do anything for him?"

"That's to be expected. You were just shot, Mr. Shephard. Twice. It's going to be a long road to recovery. You're very lucky to be alive. But you're not out of the woods just yet. We still have to watch out for clotting. You were experiencing some issues during the surgery which require us to keep a very close eye on you."

"Nothing I can't handle," my grandfather said, followed by a furious coughing fit.

I handed him a glass of water.

The doctor told us he would be back in an hour to check on him again. He left the room and my grandfather looked at the television screen. He had a puzzled look on his face.

I turned to see what he was looking at. I couldn't believe it. They were doing a news report on Mitchell's entertainment center. I reached for the remote to turn the volume up.

"This was supposed to be a place full of entertainment and fun. Until something unexpected happened here a few hours ago," the reporter said. I could feel the bottom of my stomach drop.

This wasn't going to be good. A surveillance video started running on the screen.

"The vigilante interrupted a meeting between Patrick Malloy and the gentlemen who owns the building, Mitchell Quinn. You can see here the Gray Hood attacks Patrick in this video. According to Mitchell, this attack was unprovoked. Patrick claims he was trying to defend himself. The Gray Hood threw Patrick through one of the glass doors of the clothing store across from Mitchell's private room. You can see the vigilante tie him up and leave him behind. Patrick was treated by the paramedics on the scene for his injuries and is expected to make a full recovery."

The video made me look like the bad guy. The video was edited in such a way you don't see Patrick come after me. All they showed was me attacking Patrick and throwing him through the glass door.

The screen cut to a shot of Mitchell being interviewed. "I don't understand why he would do such a horrible thing. He destroyed a wall, a glass door and injured my assistant. He also went into my private office and destroyed my furniture."

The surveillance video reappeared on the television and showed me slamming down on the table and throwing the chairs across the room. "I have personally supported him in the past, but I can't accept this behavior. Our friends and families can't accept this behavior from this vigilante. As of now, the police have my full cooperation in catching this guy. And I ask you, the people of Decker City, if you see him out there, be careful. To assist with the capture of this vigilante, I'm putting a reward on his capture. $50,000 will go to whoever can arrest the man under the hood. He is not to be harmed. I want…*this city* wants justice for what he's done."

I turned off the television to avoid hearing anymore of his lying.

"You want to tell me what that was about?" my grandfather asked.

"Not really."

"From what I saw, you got caught. And well-edited to seem like you're the bad guy in all of this. Why did you go there?"

"I needed to find Mitchell. I needed to make him pay for what he did."

"And when you found him, then what? What were you going to do, kill him?"

"It doesn't matter, because I never saw him anyway."

"You can't kill him. Then you're no better than him. The hooded idiot is better than that."

My grandfather was right. And I didn't have any intention of killing him. I just wanted to beat the living crap out of him and have the police come sweep him away and put him in jail for the rest of his life. But he'd talk if that was the case. Maybe if people knew the truth about him, they wouldn't believe him. Although having that accusation pointed at me, whether people believed it or not, would still stick with me. I couldn't have that.

"I really haven't thought it through. All I know is I wanted to find him and beat him at this game. I'll figure it out when I get there. And I'm not the hooded idiot."

"Yes, you are," he said with a smile. "You need a plan–" my grandfather started to say before he leaned back again and his smile faded into a painful look on his face. His teeth clenched. His eyes were squeezed shut. He was sucking in air through the little gaps between his teeth.

"Grandpa, are you okay?" I asked.

He finally came back down from his episode. He took two deep breaths before he answered me. "I'm okay. Look, I'm going to try and get some rest. I'm really tired."

"Is there anything you want me to bring you?" I asked.

"Yeah. On your way out, just grab one of the nurses to help me get comfortable in this awful bed. It's like I'm lying on concrete here. Don't they know I've been shot?"

I started to smile. "Yes, Grandpa. I'll make sure your bed is like you're lying on a comfy white cloud."

"That's the spirit!"

"I'll see you later, Grandpa. Feel better."

"Thanks. And Devin…" he called to me as I was about to walk out of the room. I turned to face him. "Go get your girl back. And when you find Mitchell, duke him a couple times for me."

I nodded. "I will." I turned and walked out of my grandfather's hospital room.

I made it to the elevator and pushed the button to go down. It was time to go check out this club and see what I could find there.

CHAPTER THIRTY-SEVEN

E ven in daylight, the club was busy. The bright, neon sign on top of the club was flickering in the daylight; not that anyone could possibly notice, nor were they even looking.

I parked in the lot and started to walk in. A bouncer greeted me at the door asking for my I.D. Once he handed it back, I made my way inside. It was like going from day to night. The club was dark. Some strobe lights and wall lighting managed to light up the place enough to walk around and see where I was going. The loud music made for a difficult time listening around me.

As I made my way through the dance floor, no one looked familiar. I needed to find the offices.

I walked up the ramp off the dance floor and onto a walkway which led to the bar area. Once I got to the bar and sat down at a stool, I spun around to look at the entire club.

"May I help you?" the waitress behind me asked.

I turned around to face her. "Oh, hi. I'm actually just looking for someone."

"Maybe I can help. Who are you looking for?"

I didn't expect this. I thought she would have left me alone. "I don't know."

She looked puzzled by my answer. "You don't know who you're looking for?"

"It's a blind date," I lied. "Never met her before."

"Oh, okay. Good luck."

"Thanks," I replied.

I started to stand and walk toward the dining area next. As I stood up and took one step forward, a man in a black suit bumped into me. A tall man with a scar down the left side of his face. At first glance, he looked intimidating. He had a look about him that this man was someone I didn't want to mess with. Nor did I have the time to.

"I'm sorry, my mistake," I said.

"You better watch where you're going, kid," the man responded.

Kid? Really?

I let the comment go as I didn't want to argue with the man. Plus, I had other things I was interested in. The man brushed past me and walked toward the dining area. I stood there staring at him, amazed that some people could be as stuck up as he was.

Who did he think he was?

He walked into me.

Idiot.

Just as I was about to turn my attention away from him, he sat down at a table. This just got very interesting. The man sitting across from him was Patrick Malloy. His face was bandaged up from our encounter a few hours ago. He had a bandage across his forehead and a few butterfly band aids on his cheeks and chin. The man in the suit with the scar down his face was talking to Patrick, waving his hands and bumping his chest. Then he points in my direction.

No.

I can't have Patrick see me here. I jumped onto the dance floor and got lost in the crowd. Both Patrick and the man in the suit looked toward the bar area, but they returned to talking with one another. I stood on my toes to see what was going on. Patrick slid something to the man. An envelope? Was it money? Drugs? I couldn't get close enough to see.

I realized I couldn't do this part alone. I needed some help. I couldn't get over there because Patrick would recognize me. But he wouldn't recognize Dr. Kane.

I walked out of the club. Daylight hit me and blinded me. My eyes soon adjusted to the change in light and I made my way to my car. I got in the driver's seat and pulled out my phone. I needed Dr. Kane's help.

A silver car pulled up next to me. I looked over at the driver. Not Dr. Kane. It had been about twenty minutes by now. He told me he'd be here in fifteen minutes. I started getting anxious.

A few more minutes passed.

There was a knock at my window. It made me jump in my seat. I turned to the passenger window and Dr. Kane was waving for me to unlock the car door. I unlocked the doors and he got in.

"I didn't mean to scare you," he said.

"It's okay," I told him.

"So tell me what's going on?"

"There's this guy in there, Patrick, he's one of Mitchell's main guys. He may have other people in there, but I had to get out before he spotted me. He was meeting with some big guy in a suit."

"What do you want me to do?" Dr. Kane asked.

"Just watch Patrick. He's sitting at a table by the dance floor, across from the bar. You'll know it's him by the bandages on his face."

"Courtesy of you, I presume?"

I nodded my head. "He knows who I am. I can't risk being caught. Lara's life is now in danger. Mitchell has her."

"How did that happen?"

"He must have had people watching her. He's using her as leverage so I don't come after him."

"Obviously he doesn't know you very well."

"I'm not letting him ruin my life by almost killing my grandfather and kidnapping my girlfriend, threatening her life. He will pay for this."

"I agree. I'll go inside and see what's going on."

"Be careful," I told him.

He nodded and got out of the car. I watched him step into the darkness through the doorway. One moment he was there. In the next moment he was gone.

This better work.

It had to work. I didn't have any other ideas. I had no other way of finding Mitchell.

Who was the guy in the suit? What was he doing with Patrick? Hopefully Dr. Kane could find out.

Ten minutes went by.

Then fifteen.

Twenty.

I took my phone out almost a million times to text Dr. Kane but thought better of it. Another minute ticked on by.

Screw texting, I wanted to go in there and find out what was going on. It was killing me that I couldn't be involved in this.

Finally, I saw Dr. Kane walk out of the club. He took a few steps away from the entrance and then started to hurry back to my car but stopped halfway and waved to me.

Is he waving at me to get out?

He furiously waved at me again, bringing both hands toward him. I got out of my car as he started to hurry back to his car. I decided to follow and rush to his car. I got in the passenger seat and he says, "Get down."

I tried to peek around really quick before slouching down in my seat.

"Stay down," Dr. Kane tells me.

"What's going on?" I ask.

"Your guy was getting ready to leave. I rushed out of the club so we can follow him. Maybe he'll lead us back to Mitchell and hopefully where Lara is being held."

It was a good idea.

"Here they come," Dr. Kane said.

"What's happening?" I asked from the bottom of the seat.

He peered out the windshield and said, "They are standing by the front entrance. They just seem to be waiting."

"For what?"

"I don't…oh wait. A limo just showed up." He paused while he continued watching.

"And?"

"The guy in the suit grabbed a suitcase from the trunk and gave it to Patrick. The guy in the suit just got in the limo…It's driving away. Patrick is walking to his car. You can come up now. I think you're safe."

I sat up. Dr. Kane pointed to the car pulling out of the parking spot a few cars over to our right. "There. That's him." Once Patrick's car drove out of the parking lot, Dr. Kane turned on the engine and began to follow him.

"What happened in there?"

"Just looked like conversation to me. They had a drink and picked at some food. Nothing really exciting."

"Before I left, I saw Patrick pass something to the man in the suit. Did you notice anything like that?"

Dr. Kane shook his head. "Sorry, no."

I sat there as Dr. Kane followed Patrick's car at a distance. We made it on the highway after a few back roads. Where was he going? I just hoped he was leading us to where Mitchell was and hopefully to Lara's location.

We drove by the spot where my accident happened. I turned and looked out the window at the new guardrail.

It seemed like my accident happened so long ago. So much has happened between now and then. I would have never imagined my life turning out like this. I enjoyed and embraced my ability, but it also seemed to lead to destruction. My grandfather was gunned down and my girlfriend was kidnapped.

Patrick got off the highway and took the exit toward the river front. We took the exit and continued to follow him. He led us toward the docks where ships come in and out. Warehouses lined the streets.

Patrick turned into a parking lot and parked his car. We kept our distance and parked on the side of the road. We watched as he opened his car door and walked toward the warehouse in front of him. He pulled a key chain out of his pocket, unlocked the front door and stepped inside, shutting the door behind him.

"Do you think Lara and Mitchell are inside?" Dr. Kane asked.

"I don't know," I answered. "We need to find out though. We need to wait and see if Mitchell comes out or shows up."

As I was about to open the passenger door, a limo turned the corner in front of us and headed our way. I quickly closed the door and slid down into my seat. Dr. Kane did the same. As the limo approached, it turned into the same parking lot Patrick pulled into. I sat up in my seat just a little bit to peek out the window and check on what was happening.

The driver stepped out of the vehicle and walked to the back of the limo. He opened the back door and stood behind it. A leg reached for the ground, followed by another. A full body emerged from the limo but was facing the warehouse. He shook the driver's hand and began to walk toward the warehouse doors. The driver shut the back door and got back into his limo and proceeded to drive away. The man knocked on the warehouse doors and within seconds they opened up. He walked inside and briefly turned around to close the doors.

It was Mitchell. He was here.

"That's him," I told Dr. Kane. "That's Mitchell."

"So what do you want to do?" Dr. Kane asked.

What I wanted to do was charge in there. I wanted to take down Patrick and Mitchell and whatever operation they were running within that warehouse. I wanted to get Lara back.

But I needed to be smart about it.

Just because Mitchell knew who I was under the hood doesn't mean everyone did. What if there are cameras in there? What if someone else sees me? I can't risk that. I needed my hood. I needed my communication equipment if Dr. Kane was going to be working with me. I wasn't prepared.

"Would you be comfortable watching over the building for me?" I asked. "I need to go get my stuff."

"How do you plan on getting back?" I saw Dr. Kane's expression instantly change. He realized the answer to his own question the moment he asked it. "You're taking my car, aren't you?"

I nodded my head. "I'll be right back. You can hide in that alley over there. It'll give you a view of the door to make sure they don't leave. And if they do leave, let me know."

Dr. Kane sighed. "You better be careful with my car. I'm not thrilled with this plan. You better be back quickly, too."

Of course I'd be back quickly. Lara was in there. I needed to get her back.

He opened the driver's side door and stepped out. I crawled across the middle console and sat in the driver's seat. Dr. Kane closed the door and made his way over to the alley. He tucked himself behind some boxes and trash bags. I started his car and sped off toward the highway.

CHAPTER THIRTY-EIGHT

I drove back to my grandfather's house. I didn't want to keep Dr. Kane waiting long. I also didn't want Lara to suffer any more than she already had. I prayed Mitchell hadn't hurt her. She didn't deserve to be involved in this mess. Neither did my grandfather. It was between me and Mitchell. I needed to make sure I got Lara back safely.

I pulled into my grandfather's driveway. The police tape with the bold black words, "Crime Scene – Do Not Cross" spanned the entire circumference of the house. My throat filled with bile and I wanted to vomit.

I shoved my emotions down deep. I got out of the car and sprinted to the front door, ducking under the tape. Once I was inside, I ran upstairs to my bedroom and opened my closet. There was another gray hoodie hanging there. I put it on. I knelt and opened a small chest on the floor, taking out two small ear pieces. I stuffed them in my pocket. Closing my closet door, I ran back downstairs.

As I came to the bottom of the stairs, I caught a glimpse of the kitchen. I took a step toward it.

That kitchen held a lot of fond memories for me. Growing up and eating my grandfather's horrible cooking, reading comics at the kitchen table and more recently discussing my new ability. That kitchen now also held a disturbing memory, a hateful one. It's the place where Mitchell shot my grandfather and left him for dead. The stained floor was more than I could bear to look at.

Rage filled me. I wanted to punch a hole through the wall, but I fought against it. I needed to focus this rage against Mitchell. He needed to be stopped. He needed to be punished. He needed to be brought to justice for his crimes.

I turned and headed for the front door, now prepared to take on Mitchell.

"Dr. Kane? Dr. Kane?" I walked around the alley looking for him.

A box tipped over and his head popped out from behind it. "Over here," he said. I made my way over to him and ducked down with him. "Another vehicle showed up so I had to hide back here. It looked like some of Mitchell's security or something."

"How many of them?"

"Maybe four. Could be five. I ducked down because they started looking around so I didn't get a clear view."

"That's okay. We need to stay here until it gets a little darker out. We can use the nighttime to our advantage."

"So what's the plan?" Dr. Kane asked.

I reached in my pocket and handed him one of the ear pieces.

"Here," I said, handing it to him. "Put this in your ear. Once it's in, you'll hear a beep. That means it's on. We can communicate this way."

Dr. Kane placed the ear piece in his ear. "What do you want me to do?"

"Stay outside. I don't know what's going to happen in there and Mitchell and his crew don't know you're helping me. I want it to remain that way. I also don't want to put you in harm's way in case something bad happens inside. Plus, if I get hurt, I need you to fix me."

"I don't like you going in alone, but I trust you know what you're doing. If you need me, let me know and I'll come in and help."

I focused on the warehouse's front doors, waiting for the moment to strike.

This is it, Mitchell. This is where it ends.

CHAPTER THIRTY-NINE

The sun was beginning to set. Dr. Kane and I sat back in the alley behind the boxes watching the entrance making sure Mitchell and his crew didn't leave. We hadn't seen any indication that Lara was in there with them, but we had to assume if Mitchell, Patrick and some of his gang were present, she had to be there, too.

"Ready?" I asked Dr. Kane.

"Ready," he replied. Our plan was to go inside the warehouse, find Mitchell and stop him. It wasn't much of a plan, I had to admit. Given our lack of information on what was inside, it was best for us to keep our options open.

My number one priority was getting Lara to safety. A very close second was taking Mitchell down.

Once I found Mitchell, I needed him to confess to his crimes. I had my phone ready to record whatever happened in that warehouse. If I could get him to admit to his crimes, that would be all the proof I needed to put him away. Unfortunately, that would come at a cost–losing my secret identity.

It was the chance I had to take. I couldn't let my secret hold me back from doing what was right. Lara needed to be saved and Mitchell needed to be stopped.

It was time.

I ran across the street. When I got to the side of the warehouse, I ducked down behind a giant dumpster.

"Can you hear me?" I whispered to Dr. Kane, talking into my ear piece.

"Yeah, I hear you."

"Okay, good. When I go in there, I'll distract them. You make your move and head over to where I am behind the dumpster. Wait there until I say so."

"Okay," he responded. "Good luck."

I kept low and crept around to the front door. I pulled out my phone and tapped the recording app, getting it ready for when I need to record. I needed to get Mitchell admitting to his crimes. This may be the only way I get the proof I need. I hoped this was going to work.

I pulled on the handle on the front door. It was unlocked. I slowly pulled the door open and slid inside the warehouse.

Inside, there were dozens of pallets scattered across the floor. They were full of boxes and wrapped in plastic. There was a walkway above me which wrapped around the entire upper level. A staircase extended up the back of the warehouse. At the top of the stairs was a single door.

A shadow moved past the glass. Someone was in there. I took another glance around the entire warehouse. There were only six guys on the floor. Patrick and Mitchell must be upstairs in that room. Hopefully Lara was there as well.

I hid behind a pallet next to the entrance. Footsteps grew louder. Someone was coming my way.

"Did one of you knuckleheads leave the door open?" a voice said.

A couple of faint no's came from around the warehouse.

The footsteps were louder now. They were coming closer.

A man walked by me and reached for the front door. He peeked outside for a moment and then pulled his head back inside and closed the door. As he turned around, I tackled him to the ground. Before he could even acknowledge the attack, I threw a hard right fist at his face. The back of his head bounced off the cement below us and his eyes shut. His chest was still rising and falling. He was unconscious. He wore a military vest. He had a set of handcuffs attached to his belt. I took them off and cuffed one side to his hand and the other to the bottom of the pallet.

Five guys left.

I peeked above the pallet. There were two guys talking to my right. One of the other guys was walking up the stairs. Another was standing outside the upstairs room. Where did the other one go? I continued to frantically look for him.

"Hey!" a voice came from above me. I looked up and one of the men was standing on the walkway staring down at me. He went for his gun on his belt. This was going to get loud fast. So much for the quiet entrance. The other men now had their attention on me.

The moment he took his gun out of his holster, I shoved both my hands up toward him and the gun flipped out of his hands straight up in the air. I turned to the guy on the staircase and reached out toward him. I pulled both arms toward me as if I was playing tug of war with a giant rope. The man tumbled forward down the staircase. That should at least slow him down.

The gun bounced on the walkway above me, metal bouncing on metal. I looked up and the guy reached down to pick it up. I sprinted toward my left and hid behind another pallet just as he pulled the trigger. Bullets started flying. I turned to make sure it was clear behind me, but the man guarding the door come running down the stairs with his gun trained on me. As I was about to make my move, a bullet came bouncing off the box above my head, spraying dust and shards of the box remains all over me. It made me duck and hesitate with my attack. The man coming down the stairs finished his descent and started running toward me, gun drawn. I looked up as the man on the walkway came closer. I reached up and pulled my arms forward. The man lost his balance and was pulled toward the railing. He tilted off the side of the railing and came crashing down on top of the pallet in front of me.

The door to the office opened. "What's going on out here?"

There he was. Mitchell stood at the entrance of the doorway. He looked down at the destruction I was causing and then he looked right at me. He pointed at me. "Kill him! I don't care how you do it! Make sure he's dead!"

The man running at me fired one shot. That's all he was about to get off before I threw both my arms to my right and he went crashing into a pallet, knocking over all its contents inside. Pills in little plastic bags spilled across the floor.

Crystal Clear. A whole warehouse full of it.

A bullet whizzed past me. I ducked and hid behind the pallet with the man still laying on top of it. I peeked behind it and Mitchell was outside the room shooting at me. He didn't care the man was in my way, he kept firing, possibly hitting the man above me. He stopped shooting after a couple of rounds.

"Get him! He's over there!" he shouted to the remaining two guys pointing in my direction. I peeked around the pallet but a bullet hit the wall behind me. Mitchell was keeping me pinned back here while the two guys made their way over.

I turned back toward the other side and peeked around the pallet and one of the men was making his way over. I couldn't see where the other guy was. I focused on the guy I could see.

Mitchell stopped shooting. Out of bullets.

The man had his gun pointed at me. I flipped one hand up in the air and the gun left his grip. As he tried fumbling for it, I pushed both my arms out toward him. He fell back and slammed his head against the cement floor. He'd feel that for a few days.

"Don't move," a voice behind me said. Then I heard the clicking of the hammer being pulled back. I could feel the cylinder of the gun planted against the back of my head. For a split moment, I thought about trying to make a move. But having a gun against the back of your head makes you think otherwise. "Boss, I got—" he started to say before he was cut off. A loud thud came from behind me. The man fell and landed next to me with his gun sliding across the floor. I turned around and Dr. Kane was standing above me, holding a large piece of wood.

"Thought you could use some help," he said.

I stood up and looked back at the room where Mitchell was standing in front of. He wasn't there. I turned back to Dr. Kane. "These guys have handcuffs on them. Make sure each one of them is handcuffed or tied to something and remove their guns."

He nodded and started his mission.

I turned back toward the room and Mitchell came walking out with Patrick.

"Patrick, get him!" Mitchell yelled.

Patrick came running down the stairs and I followed by charging toward him. We met the second he touched the floor. I pushed both arms forward and he went crashing back into the staircase. I jumped on top of him and started to throw punches.

Before I hit my third punch, he tossed me off of him. He stood tall as if he felt no pain at all and came toward me. As I was trying to stand up, he kicked me hard in the stomach and knocked the wind out of me. "Your stupid powers won't save you this time," he said. I was on all fours as he punched down on my lower back. I winced in pain and collapsed falling flat on my stomach. He bent over and tried to grab my hood when I heard footsteps running toward me. Dr. Kane leapt and took out Patrick.

I turned over and sat up. They were both rolling around on the ground. They came to a stop as they rolled into a pallet. Patrick was first to get to his feet. Dr. Kane was a little slower trying to get up. Patrick kicked Dr. Kane into the pallet. He clutched at his side and curled up into a ball. Patrick brought his foot back and kicked him again. The third time he brought his foot back, I reached out toward Patrick and pulled with both my arms. Patrick's planted leg came flying back off the floor and both legs were air born. He tried to reach forward to protect his fall but it was a too late. He came crashing down on his face.

I got up and went over to Dr. Kane. "Are you okay?" I asked as I tried helping him up.

He held his side, aching in pain. "Might have a broken rib, not sure." He looked down at Patrick. "What about him?"

I looked down at him. I could hear him sighing in pain. He wasn't moving all that much. "He'll live," I said.

"Devin!" Lara yelled as Mitchell brought her out of the room. He held her against his chest with one arm wrapped around her neck. He held a gun at her head in his other hand.

"Shut up! Your idiot boyfriend down there has a hearing problem. He doesn't listen to anything I tell him to do, which is how you ended up in this situation. So blame him for all of this."

"Let her go," I said.

"Why? You took out my men, severely injured my partner and you want me to let her go? What do I get out of that?"

"Nothing."

"Well, that doesn't seem all that fair now does it?"

"Fair? You want to talk about fair? You left my grandfather for dead after you shot him. You kidnapped Lara. You have spread violence and chaos all over this city. You have released a drug that has criminals committing acts of violence because you planted the idea in their head. So you still want to talk about fair?"

I pushed the record button on my phone.

Mitchell seemed to ponder that for a moment. "When you put it that way, you make me seem like such a bad guy. First of all, Paul Shephard had it coming."

He was admitting it. I smiled and peeked at the phone. The audio meter indicated that the phone was picking up every word.

Mitchell continued, faking a wistful tone of voice. "He looked so helpless when I broke into his house and shot him. Poor guy. And kidnapping Lara, she was easy. I debated on grabbing Tommy, too, but it wouldn't look good if multiple people from TruGuard suddenly went missing.

"As for the violence, get over it. That happens in every city. If it wasn't me, it would've been someone else. I just did it to get ahead of the competition. Simple, really. Run some businesses out of town, buy everything for cheap and rebuild for huge profits. You would have done the same thing if the opportunity presented itself to you."

"No, I wouldn't."

"Ehh. You're probably right. You're too much of a goody-goody with that hoody on."

I had enough. I needed to get that gun out of his hand. I needed him to take his attention off me for just a moment and I could get the gun away from him.

"I had to clean up your mess around Decker City," I began to tell Mitchell. You've caused so much destruction and pain." I pointed to Dr. Kane. "One of your dumb criminal friends broke into a pharmacy and shot a friend of his."

Mitchell turned his attention to Dr. Kane. "Is that true?" he asked him. "Did one of my guys shoot your poor friend?"

As Dr. Kane began to speak, I lifted my hand up to flick the gun out of Mitchell's hand. The gun went up in the air. So did Mitchell's hand. He brought both back down. "You think you can outsmart me?" He lifted his hand up holding the gun. "Tape." He wrapped the gun around his hand with packaging tape.

Suddenly, Lara threw an unexpected elbow into Mitchell's stomach. He released his grip around Lara and clutched his stomach. She took the opportunity to sprint toward the stairs and rush down them. Mitchell regained his breath and held up his taped-up hand and gun combination. He was only able to fire one shot before Dr. Kane grabbed one of the security men's guns and shot back. Mitchell ducked down and kept his hand above his head and fired blindly in our direction.

I grabbed Lara as she made it to the bottom stair, screaming. I pulled her behind a pallet while Mitchell kept shooting.

"Are you okay? Did he hurt you?" I asked her.

"I'm okay. I'm not hurt."

"Good. Stay here."

The gun fire kept going on for a few more seconds. The bullets stopped flying from upstairs. Out of bullets again. I peeked above the pallet and he was running back into the office.

Dr. Kane fired another two shots before his clip was out, too.

"I'm going after him," I told Dr. Kane. "Stay here with Lara."

"Okay," he said.

"What?! No! Don't leave me," Lara pleaded.

I turned to her. "I have to. I promise, I'll be back. I need to make sure Mitchell pays for what he's done. I can't let him get away."

I jumped to my feet and started toward the stairs. I sprinted up the stairs, taking two at a time. Once I made it inside the room, he was gone. The window was open in the far corner. I rushed over and looked out the window. He was getting in a car parked behind the warehouse. Sirens could be heard in the distance. The police wouldn't make it in time.

I hurried back out of the room and raced down the stairs. Dr. Kane was sitting on the floor with Lara. I sprinted past them and headed out the front door of the warehouse. Just as I exited, a car sped past me. It was Mitchell.

If only I could move things heavier than I could lift, I would've flipped his car and that would've been it.

I got across the street and into Dr. Kane's car. I turned on the ignition and the car came to life. I put it in drive and slammed on the gas.

CHAPTER FORTY

Car horns were blaring from every direction as I chased Mitchell down the highway. The speed limit was 65 mph but I must have been doing close to 90 mph just to keep up. Swerving in and out of traffic in a high pursuit car chase was something I never thought I'd be doing, especially after my accident. But I had no fear right now. My focus was on Mitchell and him alone.

Mitchell was about five or six cars in front of me. I know he could see me, because we were the only two cars speeding in and out of traffic. Mitchell's brake lights lit up. The cars behind him slammed on their brakes as the red lights flashed in my face. I had to swerve out of the way to avoid hitting anyone.

Two of those cars in front of me collided. One car ended up rear-ending the other. Mitchell was trying to slow me down. He purposely caused that accident.

The lane in front of me opened up as some cars moved to the shoulder to check on the two cars involved in the accident behind us.

I floored the gas pedal. I was about four car lengths behind Mitchell when he swerved into the middle lane, causing a car to swerve out of the way and collide into another car driving parallel with it in the left lane. That car spun out of control and came to a stop after crashing into the median. I sped past them and was hesitant to continue pursuing this close. I didn't want anyone else to get hurt.

I decided to try something before I dropped back. I continue accelerating toward Mitchell. We were now about a car length apart. I pulled up behind him and tapped the rear end of his car. His vehicle shook a little, but it wasn't enough to slow him down. He sped up.

We were now at speeds close to 100 mph. Death wasn't a concern of mine. I knew I had already died once. I had come to terms with it. If this is what I had to do to stop Mitchell, then it had to be done.

I pulled around to the passenger side of his car and rammed the side of it. I fought to keep the steering wheel aligned. I turned the wheel again into his vehicle. Scratching metal noises filled the airwaves as our cars drove attached to one another, side by side. Once again, I fought to keep my wheel aligned with the road. We pulled away from one another and I decided to hit his car one last time and take him out. As I went to steer into him, he slammed on his brakes. My car missed the attack and spun right into the median and flipped over.

Knocking.

More knocking.

What happened?

I opened my eyes. Everything was upside down.

More knocking. I turned my head toward the noise. Someone was knocking on the driver's side window. He was upside down too.

The car accident.

I was hanging upside down, still attached to my seat belt. A pedestrian was knocking on the surprisingly unbroken window asking if I was okay.

Mitchell. Where did he go?

I reached for the seat belt release and pushed the button. The belt released and I dropped to the ground, which ended up being the roof of the car. I reached above me and grabbed the handle to open the car door.

The door swung open and I rolled out of the vehicle. I got to my knees and finally made my way to my feet. My body ached. The pain from the accident started to register. I looked around, not knowing where exactly I was or how long I was out for. There was a street sign above me.

Broad Street. Next exit.

"Where did that other car go?" I asked the guy standing next to my car.

He had a startled look on his face as he pointed toward the exit. Was something wrong with my attire? I looked down and I didn't see anything wrong. Suddenly someone in the distance screamed, "That's him! That's the vigilante! Get him!"

The reward money.

I turned to the man next to me. "Give me your keys," I told him. He hesitated at first but then reached into his pocket and handed them to me. "Which car?"

A mob of people started rushing toward me. I turned back to the man. "Please, I need your help. I'm not the bad guy." He pointed to a car parked on the side of the road. I thanked him and took off toward the car.

"Stop him!" yelled one of the men in the mob.

I unlocked the car and hopped inside. I started the engine and hit the gas. The tires screeched on the pavement as I floored the pedal. The exit was immediate and I took it to get off the highway.

As I sped down the ramp, I came to a dead end.

If I turned left, I would head toward the stadium and some small city homes. If I turned right, I'd head into the entertainment district where all the stores were.

I turned right.

———

I pulled up to Mitchell's new entertainment center. His car was parked sideways on the sidewalk with the driver's side door still opened. It was as if a drunk person parked it.

I got out of the car and walked toward the gate. It was still open.

I jogged past the gate and to the front doors. I reached for the handle. It was unlocked. The door opened and I stepped inside. The door echoed throughout the building as it slammed shut.

The building seemed empty. At every other time, there were workers here.

It just seemed too quiet.

I headed to Mitchell's office.

Reaching the door, I took a deep breath. The adrenaline had my heart pumping fast. This had to be it. This was where I would put Mitchell's plan to an end and stop him for good. I reached for the handle and pulled open the door. A gust of air came flying out at me, making me stumble backwards. I fell to the ground, covered in a white foam. I looked up and Mitchell came charging at me with a fire extinguisher in his hands.

He threw it down toward me but I rolled out of the way. The extinguisher bounced off the ground and rolled down the hallway. Mitchell took no time to continue his attack as he started kicking me before I could make it to my feet. I curled up to block most of the attack but on his fourth attempt, I reached out and grabbed his leg. I pushed him backwards and he fell to the ground. I was able to climb back to my feet while Mitchell did the same.

He came at me with a right punch. I backed away in time. I followed up with a right fist to his stomach. I could hear the air leave his lungs. He bent down and grabbed his stomach. I got him in a headlock. Mitchell threw multiple elbows into my stomach.

I released my grip on his head. He followed up with a left punch to my face. The punch caught me off guard and brought me to my knees. Mitchell took advantage of this and threw a knee into my face. I fell back onto the ground, now seeing stars. I felt liquid run out of my nose.

"At least you're putting up a good fight this time. A few years ago, you only managed to get one shot in. I'm impressed. Now get up," Mitchell taunted.

I brought my hand to my nose and wiped away some blood.

"I said get up!" Mitchell grabbed the front of my sweat shirt and pulled me to my feet. He shoved me backwards into the taped off area behind me. I fell into the tape and ripped it on my way to the floor.

Mitchell walked over to me, but I threw both my arms forward and he fell backwards. This gave me the moment I needed to climb back to my feet.

Mitchell was faster. He was up and charging at me again before I could even turn toward him. He hit me from behind and we both went through a table.

I was better than this. I knew how to fight. How was he beating me?

Mitchell climbed off me and got to his feet. "Get up," he said.

I rolled over and grunted from the pain. I climbed to my feet and tried to shake off the pain.

"Pathetic," he said right before swung the table leg at me. He struck me on my left shoulder. I grabbed my shoulder and turned away from him. He swung again and struck me in my back. The pain brought me to my knees.

"You took out so many of my men. No one gave you a challenge. Except for me. I knew I should have killed you when I had the opportunity."

I turned my body to face him. "What are you talking about?"

"You were shot a few months ago, were you not?"

How did he know that? I never told him how I hurt myself. And then it hit me. In that store. It was him.

"You shot me?"

"And one of my guys wanted to finish you off, but I said no. I wasn't about to start my work here by killing the vigilante of Decker City. The bullseye that would have given me would have had the whole city out for blood. They all loved you. But now I turned the city against you. You have no friends here anymore. They would praise me for taking you out now. So I've changed my mind about killing you."

He brought the table leg back behind his head and swung down at me. I threw both hands up and stopped his movement. He looked stunned by the sudden motionless of his arms. I moved my arms to the right and the table leg slipped out of his grip and landed by the entrance of the store. He went tumbling down as well. I stood up, staring at him.

Now I stood above him. "Get up."

His eyes were glaring with such evil behind them. His lips sneered at me. He rose to his feet and charged at me. I sidestepped him and pushed him back to the ground. He slid outside the store entrance. I walked over to him as he climbed back to his feet. He turned toward me as I threw a right jab at his face, making him stumble backwards.

He made his way to his feet again and stood at a distance from me. I pushed both arms forward and he lost his balance, falling down to the floor. I walked over to his stumbling body trying to make his way to his feet again and kicked him back to the ground. He made his way on all fours and looked up at me. I threw a punch downward at him and he collapsed to the floor. He was slow moving now.

"You won't win this, Mitchell. The police will arrest you and you will spend a long time in prison."

Laying on his stomach, Mitchell said, "Then the whole world will know who you are. You'll just have to kill me to keep that secret silenced."

I got down on one knee and bent over toward him. "I'm not going to kill you, Mitchell. I don't care if people know who I am."

"Wrong choice," Mitchell said before he turned over and sliced my leg with a knife he had hidden. I grabbed my wound and screamed in pain. I fell backwards and sat there gripping my leg. Mitchell rolled over and stabbed me in my right shoulder. Before I even registered the pain, I used my left arm and disarmed Mitchell by waving the knife away from him. It went flying down the long hallway, bouncing off the floor away from us.

I sat on the floor, bleeding and in a lot of pain. I held my left hand over my right shoulder's stab wound. I looked up at Mitchell and he held a gun at my head.

"You don't have to do this," I tried to tell him.

"Yes, I do. You've already caused me enough destruction. You didn't listen to me. You didn't stay away when I told you to. This is your fault. Not mine." He pulled back the hammer of the gun.

I couldn't disarm him this close. I would risk him pulling the trigger before I could make my move.

At least I had all of this recorded. I had Mitchell admitting to his crimes–the acts of violence around Decker City, the kidnapping, the attempted murder of my grandfather, the drugs, and now the murder of me.

"Any last words?" he asked.

"Go to hell."

"You first."

I closed my eyes and let the darkness take over as I waited for the end.
BANG

CHAPTER FORTY-ONE

The gun went off.

I tensed as I anticipated the bullet striking me. But it was as if nothing happened. I felt no pain.

Was that it? Did I die?

I opened my eyes and Mitchell stood in front of me, staring down at me with his eyes wide and glazed over. The gun fell from his hand and dropped to the floor. Mitchell's body crashed to the floor.

I looked down at his lifeless body, stunned.

I looked up and saw Officer Umburger running toward me.

"Are you okay?" he asked as he helped me to my feet.

I put the weight of my body on my good leg as I stood up. I used my left hand to continue putting pressure on the hole in my shoulder. I stared at Mitchell's body lying motionless on the floor and said, "Yeah, I'll be okay. Thank you. How did you find me?"

"I was the first to arrive at the warehouse. I figured out the rest. It was pretty easy to follow the trail you guys left behind."

"I'm glad you showed up when you did. I thought he was going to kill me."

"I'm just paying you back for saving my life. I've seen you in action. I've been a part of the dangerous situations you constantly throw yourself into. You're one of the good guys. And I protect the good guys."

I felt honored knowing someone would do that for me. I've been sticking my neck out for everyone and doing what I could for this city. It felt good knowing people counted on me and that I could count on them in return.

"I need to call this in though," Officer Umburger warned me. "The police will be here within minutes of my call, if they're not already on their way. If I put this together, you know others aren't too far behind me. You need to get out of here. I'll clean this up. And don't worry, I'll try and help clear the bad press you've been getting."

I pulled my phone out of my pocket. "Maybe this will help." I stopped the recording and played back a moment where Mitchell was confessing to kidnapping Lara and terrorizing the city.

Officer Umburger smiled. "That will help." He pulled out a card from his jacket pocket. He handed it to me. It had all of his information on it–phone number, email address, physical address. "Get that recording to me and I'll make sure it gets into the right hands. I'll make sure the police department clears you of any wrong doing."

"Thank you." I took the card and stuffed it into my pocket. I turned and started limping down the hall.

"Take care of yourself," Officer Umburger said.

Being stabbed was almost as bad as being shot, but I needed to get away from the building. As I exited, I realized my grandfather wasn't waiting to pick me up. I was so used to him being there that I hadn't thought past this point. Dr. Kane and Lara were with the police back at the warehouse. I couldn't go walking down the streets like this.

I limped past a store that had some items scattered throughout its messy area. As gently and quickly as possible, I took off the hoodie. I threw it in the large trash can and covered it up with trash. A jacket laid behind a fold out chair, tucked in a corner. I made my way over to it and put it on. For now, it would cover up the blood.

As I made my way out of the store and back toward the entrance of this giant place, I pulled out my phone and called for a taxi. I couldn't drive in this pain. I made sure to request the pick up at least a few blocks away from here.

Once I had exited Mitchell's entertainment center, I limped down the street to my pickup location. I started to hear the sirens in the distance. I made it to the end of the block and the sirens grew louder and louder. The flashing lights lit up the area from between the buildings. Police cars began to swarm the front of the building. Officers jumped out of their vehicles. They charged into Mitchell's entertainment facility. I sat on the sidewalk and watched everything from a distance.

I pulled out my phone again and dialed Dr. Kane's number.

"Devin! Are you okay? What happened? Where are you?" Dr. Kane said.

"I'm okay. But you've got some patching up to do."

My taxi pulled up to the warehouse. Before I could take one step away from the car, Lara came running toward me. She threw her arms around me and gave me a huge hug. As much as I wanted to enjoy that moment, the pain in my shoulder prevented it.

"Ow!" I screamed.

She let go. "I'm sorry! I knew you were hurt! Dr. Kane told me everything." Tears streamed down her face. "I was so scared. I thought he was going to kill me. And then when you went after him, I thought you weren't coming back." She sobbed into her hands.

"I'm okay, Lara," I said. "Don't worry. We're okay now."

"Do you know how incredibly lucky you are that the police officer arrived when he did?!"

"Oh yeah. I do. You don't need to tell me how lucky I am."

Lara turned around as if she was looking for someone. She turned to the right, and then to her left. She looked behind her. Then she stared at me. "If you weren't hurt, I'd punch you so hard right now," she told me.

"Why?" I asked.

"Why didn't you tell me you've been the guy in the hood running around Decker City?"

I knew this day would come. Especially when Mitchell kidnapped Lara. There was no getting around the reason why she was taken. I had to tell her everything. "I–"

"Devin, are you ready to go?" Dr. Kane asked me as he came walking out of the warehouse.

I turned to Dr. Kane and said, "Yes, the cab is right here." I turned my attention back to Lara. "I will tell you everything, I promise. Come with me back to Dr. Kane's place and we can talk then."

She glared at me. "You're lucky I love you." Then she leaned forward and kissed me.

CHAPTER FORTY-TWO

We arrived back at Dr. Kane's office. Both Lara and Dr. Kane helped me inside and laid me down on a bed. "It doesn't look all that bad," Dr. Kane told me. "Give me thirty minutes and I'll have you sewn up. Let me get some supplies. I'll be right back." He walked out of the room and left Lara and I to ourselves.

"You have this thing about making me wait for your incredible stories, don't you?" Lara asked me.

Thinking back to the car accident, I made her wait a day to hear that story. "Luckily, you only have to wait a few minutes this time."

She waved her hands telling me to *hurry up and tell her already.*

"Remember when I got into my accident?"

From there, I told her everything. It was such a relief. I didn't have to keep it a secret from her anymore.

At the end of the story, I said, "I'm sorry, Lara. I never meant to hurt you or keep this from you. I never wanted to lie to you. Please don't be mad."

"Mad? No. I'm not mad."

"You're not?" I asked.

"No, not at all. I'm dating the Gray Hood, the vigilante. My boyfriend has superpowers and just saved the city from an evil madman. You're a hero. You've got to be crazy if you think I'm mad at you. I'm freaking excited. This is like the coolest thing ever!"

"I'm glad you're taking this so well." I laughed, but then I stopped. "Ouch."

"Oooh!" Lara said, "Don't laugh if it hurts."

I looked into her eyes. The most beautiful eyes I had ever seen.

How did I get so lucky? From a dweebie office bum to a near-death experience, and now with the most beautiful girl I'd ever seen leaning over me, squealing in sympathy.

And she loved me.

It was a good day.

Well, it was a bad day turned good.

The door opened and Dr. Kane walked in. He began placing all his tools on a table in front of him. He wheeled it over to my bed side. "Okay, let's get started."

***

I fell asleep once he finished my stitches. Lara slept on the sofa out in the waiting area and Dr. Kane slept in his office chair. I woke up and used my left arm to push myself up. My body hurt, a lot.

I was thinking that I would be taking a break from this vigilantism for a while. Mitchell was dead. Patrick and most of their crew was arrested.

I could finally rest.

One thing still stuck with me though. Who was that man with the scar Patrick was talking with, and what did Patrick give him?

Just as the thought entered my head, I shoved it out. I'm done for a while. I needed to get better. I needed to heal. I could deal with that another day.

I needed to see my grandfather. He doesn't even know what happened yet.

I swung my legs off the table and tried to stand. It hurt to stand, but I felt like I could get around all right.

I limped to the waiting room and sat down next to Lara. I placed my hand on her head and brushed my fingers through her hair. She slowly opened her eyes and smiled at me.

"I'm going to visit my grandfather in the hospital. I didn't want to leave without asking if you wanted to join me."

"Yeah, I'll come." She rolled onto her back and stretched out.

"I'm going to leave a note for Dr. Kane. Can you find us a ride?"

"Sure," she replied.

I sat down behind the receptionist's desk and opened the drawers looking for something to write with and something to write on. I found a pen and just grabbed a white sheet of paper from the printer behind me.

> *Dr. Kane,*
>
> *Thank you for everything that you've done for me. I owe you big time for helping me with Mitchell. You put yourself in harm's way when you didn't have to. Thank you. Lara and I left to go visit my grandfather in the hospital. And if I owe you any money for the medical services you provided, please let me know so I can reimburse you. Also, sorry about your car.*
>
> *Devin*

"Taxi's here," Lara said. I left the note on the desk and left Dr. Kane's office.

CHAPTER FORTY-THREE

Lara and I walked side by side throughout the hospital. I used her to lean on from time to time to help relieve some of the pressure off my injured leg. As we walked into my grandfather's room, his eyes lit up. "Hey Devin."

"Hi, Grandpa, how are you feeling?"

"Never mind how I'm feeling. Who's this pretty lady standing next to you?"

"Grandpa, I want you to meet Lara. Lara, this is my grandfather."

She began to walk over to his bedside to shake his hand but forgot I was using her for support. I lost my balance but caught myself before I fell. She quickly turned around, "Oh, I'm so sorry. I forgot." She grabbed me and I put my arm around her for support.

"Don't let this knucklehead trick you, come introduce yourself. He can take care of himself."

"Thanks for the support, Grandpa. Don't you want to know what happened?"

"Nope. Pretty girl in the room. Sorry, but she's got my attention now."
He turned to look at her. "So you're Lara. It's very nice to finally meet you.
This idiot over here has talked nonstop about you for years."

I could feel my face flush red of embarrassment. I gave my
grandfather a wide-eyed stare, trying to tell him to shut up. He nodded
toward me and said, "See? Now he's trying to get me to stop talking. Am
I embarrassing you?"

He always knew how to do this. He didn't care who he embarrassed.
He loved to have fun.

I knew he wasn't trying to make me feel bad. "No, not at all." I lied.

Lara looked at me. "You're blushing." She started to laugh which in
return made my grandfather start to laugh. "Don't worry though, it's cute."

"Cute? You guys make me sick." My grandfather let out a loud coughing
fit which lasted for a few seconds. "Sorry about that. It keeps happening.
Anyway, Devin, you said you had a story for me. What happened?"

Lara and I sat down in the guest chairs in the room and we told him
everything that happened since I last saw him.

"So Mitchell is dead?" he asked.

"Yes," I replied.

"Good, he got what he deserved then." My grandfather started
coughing again.

"Do you want me to get the doctor?" I asked.

Once he finally calmed back down, he said, "No. They should be
here any minute to give me my medicine anyway. But wait a minute, you
distracted me. Pretty girl." He turned back to Lara. "Let's ignore him for a
moment. Talk to me. Tell me about yourself."

She smiled at him. "I work with Devin. I'm the receptionist at the
office." She stared at the ceiling for a moment, thinking of something else
to add. "I don't know what else you want me to say."

"Likes? Dislikes? Where'd you grow up? Got any single friends?"

She smiled again. "My likes, huh? Well, I like long walks on the beach,
especially with older gentlemen like yourself–"

My grandfather interrupted. "Devin, I like this girl. Be careful I don't
steal her for myself."

Lara continued. "I like sports. Devin and I watch most of the same TV
shows together. I was born in Decker City, but my dad was relocated for

his job so we had to move to Mapleton. I came back after college, because Decker City will always be my home."

"So you grew up in Mapleton? Were you there when that alien debris fell from the sky?" my grandfather asked.

"Okay, first of all, it wasn't alien debris. It was some asteroid that broke up in our atmosphere," Lara started to say. "And second, no, I wasn't there for that. That happened like twenty or twenty-five years ago. I moved there when I was in elementary school so I missed that event by a few years."

My grandfather looked at me. "I'm telling you, it was alien."

I shook my head. "You're a crazy old man."

He smiled and then said, "I know."

He started coughing again. This time more intense than before. He stopped and threw his head back against his pillow. His eyes squeezed shut. His teeth clenched.

"Is he okay?" Lara asked.

"I don't know," I replied. "He did this the other day when I saw him and came out of it within seconds."

Seconds past and nothing changed. He began to shake violently.

"Get the doctor!" I yelled to Lara. She rushed out of the room and I sat on the bed side with my grandfather trying to control him. "Hold on, Grandpa, the doctors are coming. Everything is going to be okay."

Lara ran back into the room with three doctors and a nurse trailing behind her.

"Stand up and move out of our way please," the one nurse said as she began checking his vitals.

Lara grabbed me and helped me move out of their way. She helped me walk to the edge of the room by the doorway. I watched the doctors scurry to help my grandfather.

Everything is going to be okay.

CHAPTER FORTY-FOUR

I stood motionless, watching my grandfather from a distance. As they continued to work on him, Lara stood by my side. She grabbed my hand and squeezed it. She leaned in to me and told me that everything was going to be okay. I knew she cared and meant it. I knew she was also trying to make me feel better.

It didn't work. Nothing could make me feel better.

Everything seemed to move at a slower pace. I wanted everything to be over with. I wanted everything to go back to normal. I wanted to go back to a happier time where my grandfather was healthy and having fun. I wanted him to be cracking jokes and making fun of me like he always did. I wanted him to be by my side again when we took to the streets to stop crime.

I didn't know what to do with myself. Ever since he went to the hospital, I've been busy trying to take down Mitchell and his gang. Now that it's done, I'll have time again. My grandfather and I always spent a lot to time together. I was going to miss that the most.

I saw Tommy approaching. "I'm sorry for your loss."

"Thank you," I said. It seemed to be the robotic reply I had for everyone. He turned to face the grave as the workers continued to lower my grandfather into his final resting place. I still couldn't believe it. The only family I had left was gone.

I was alone.

Many of my grandfather's friends had come to pay their respects. It was nice knowing there were so many people who knew and cared for my grandfather. Even Dr. Kane stopped by.

By now, most of the people had already left the cemetery. Only Lara and Tommy stood by my side. My best friends were here in this most tragic moment of my life.

"Are you ready to go?" Lara asked me.

I nodded. "I'm going to have the limo take me to meet with my grandfather's attorney and then take me home."

"Okay," she agreed. "Are you going to be okay?"

"I'll be fine." Was it true? I didn't know. I felt numb. "I'll let you know how everything goes." She leaned in and gave me a gentle hug, careful not to reinjure my stab wound. She followed it up with a kiss.

Tommy reached out for a handshake. "I'll settle for this. I don't feel comfortable kissing you, too."

It made me smile. I definitely needed that.

"Thanks for coming, Tommy. I really appreciate it."

"Let me know if you need anything."

I nodded as he walked off toward his car.

I was left alone for the first time in a long time. Probably ever. I didn't know what came next. Could I just go back to work? Could I return as the Gray Hood after all of this? Doing so the first time around put Lara at risk and got my grandfather killed. I didn't think I'd ever put the hood back on again.

First things first. I needed to visit my grandfather's attorney.

I walked over to the grave and looked down at the casket at the bottom of the hole. I grabbed some dirt and tossed it in the hole on top of the casket.

"I love you, Grandpa. I'll miss you."

"Devin, it's a pleasure to finally meet you. I just wish it was under better circumstances."

"Me too," I replied while reaching to accept his welcoming gesture.

"My name is Randy Jones, and I'm the attorney representing your grandfather's estate. I'll make sure this meeting is quick. I know this is probably the last thing you want to be doing right now." He waved his hand forward toward a chair placed in front of his desk.

I walked over and sat in the chair.

He sat down behind his desk. "There's really not much to go over. You were his only family. All other family relatives have passed away. You're the only Shephard left."

The only one left. Alone. Empty.

A lump formed in my throat. I relied on my grandfather for so much, and now he was gone.

"Now don't think of that as a bad thing. Because if there were others, you'd have to share his entire inheritance with the family. And believe me, I've seen what money can do to people. I've seen families get in fights over inheritances or personal items from their recently passed relatives. I've seen siblings sue one another over their parent's wealth. Things can get ugly sometimes so you're lucky you don't have that problem. Don't get me wrong, I'm not saying having no family is a good thing. Sometimes it just makes things easier when you only have to deal with one person getting everything and not splitting up an entire estate."

Did he just say everything?

"I'm sorry, I don't quite understand. What do you mean by 'one person getting everything'?"

"My mistake. I didn't mean to make things confusing for you. Your grandfather had a will. It's a document that—"

"I know what a will is," I told him.

"Okay. So in his will, he designated what happens to everything in his estate. His property, the items in his house, his investments and money. And it all goes to you. Of course, once Uncle Sam gets their cut, then you get the rest." He picked up a paper in front of his desk and ran his finger down the page. "It looks like you'll be receiving just shy of twenty-two million dollars."

I was stunned. Twenty-two million dollars? I never thought I'd see that kind of money in my life. How did my grandfather have twenty-two million dollars? I knew he sold his businesses and was a successful investor, but I never knew what he actually made. He never acted like he had that kind of money.

"Wait a minute," I said, trying to collect my thoughts. "I get twenty-two million dollars?"

"Twenty-one million, nine hundred and fifty-two thousand, eight hundred and ten dollars to be exact. And seventy-two cents. But yes, it's all yours. And his property is yours, too. I know that'll be a nice upgrade from your apartment he told me about."

"He told you about my apartment? Were you guys close? When did you and him last talk?"

"We spoke every now and then. I saw him about a week ago when he was in the hospital. He called me and asked me to come see him just in case something like this were to happen. Your grandfather planned accordingly. He was a smart man."

I couldn't have agreed more. He was the smartest man I knew. I learned everything from him. From his dorky comic collection to the world of finance and investing. I owe all the success I have to my grandfather. Without him raising me the way he did, I don't know where I'd be. Especially when I discovered my ability.

"I don't plan on you filling out all the paperwork today, so what I'm going to do is give you this folder," Randy said while raising the manila folder for me. "It has all the paperwork inside. I put 'sign here' labels on everything you need to sign. If you want to go through it together at a later date, I'd be happy to help you out." He slid the folder across his desk. I reached out and took it.

"Thank you, Mr. Jones."

"You can call me Randy. And it's my pleasure." He stood up.

I stood up as well as he walked around his desk to walk me to his door.

"Thanks for coming in. If you have any questions, feel free to call me anytime. I put my card in there for you so you'll have my contact information."

"Thanks," I said, walking out of his office. He shut the door behind me. I stood with my back to the door and just held the folder to my chest.

Sure, the money was going to go a long way for me. I could leave TruGuard and never work again. That would be nice. But I enjoyed my job. I liked working with Tommy. I enjoyed seeing Lara every day. It gave me pleasure knowing I was helping others.

And now I had a house. No more rent. I didn't have a mortgage to pay.

If Grandpa was alive, I would've been so excited. But if I could have my grandfather back instead, I'd choose that in a heartbeat.

All the money in the world and the biggest house wouldn't fix the heartache and emptiness I felt. I knew enough about loss to know that would never change. The pain would mellow with age, but it would always be with me.

I walked out of the office building and got back in the limo. I told the driver to take me home. I wanted to get changed out of my suit and just lay in bed the rest of the day. I wanted to sleep today away. Hopefully tomorrow would be a better day.

CHAPTER FORTY-FIVE

Shootouts, Car Chases & Bad Guys...Oh My...
By Kate Phillips

The streets of Decker City were lit up with crime-fighting and heroics this weekend. It started out as a shootout in the docks, escalating to a daring car chase which left multiple people injured and one dead.

As usual, The Gray Hood is at the heart of this investigation. Around sunset on Saturday evening, The Gray Hood entered the warehouse on the 1800 block of Woods Road. According to the police, The Gray Hood entered the building to help rescue a hostage who was being held by the business magnate, Mitchell Quinn. It's still unknown why Quinn kidnapped the woman—her name is not being released for her protection. Mitchell's guards opened fire on The Gray Hood, but The Gray Hood emerged unharmed. Mitchell then attempted to escape via car which led to the chase between Mitchell and the vigilante.

Their dangerous antics led onto the highway where Mitchell swerved his vehicle into and at other vehicles, trying to hinder the vigilante's chase. Six vehicles were damaged during the chase which reports claim were at speeds of close to 100 mph. Ten people were injured during the pursuit.

The Gray Hood crawled out of his flipped vehicle and hijacked another to continue the chase.

The incident ended at Mitchell's Entertainment Galaxy. According to Officer Umburger, who was on the scene, Mitchell had a gun pointed at The Gray Hood. Officer Umburger opened fire on Mitchell, and Mitchell was fatally wounded.

New evidence from a digital recording has been released which proves that Mitchell Quinn was far from the magnanimous philanthropist and businessman he pretended to be. He admitted on the recording that he was responsible for organizing the recent crime waves that have rocked the city. He was also guilty of multiple crimes including kidnapping, murder, attempted murder, and drug smuggling. He had tried to frame The Gray Hood to secure his evil scheme. With this new evidence, the police have dropped all charges against The Gray Hood.

At a recent press conference, Police Chief William Conway has this to say. "As of today, the charges have been dropped for the Gray Hood. Now, just because the charges have been dropped and he's been helping us catch these bad guys, I want to make something very clear.

"First, I want to thank you, whoever you are, for your help and your service. And second, acting as a vigilante is a criminal act in of itself. I want to remind whoever is under the hood that should we ever catch you, we will have to arrest you. Although I don't see my police force strictly enforcing that rule after what you did and have been doing for the citizens of Decker City."

Cleanup has begun to repair the damage caused by the chase on the highway and at the entertainment center. It's unknown whether the multimillion dollar building will open now that it's owner has been revealed as a mastermind criminal.

Talks are underway to determine what to do with the property.

CHAPTER FORTY-SIX

I had slept for fourteen hours last night. I think that was the longest I've ever slept.

Today was a new day. Today was the day I would go to my grandfather's house for the first time since the night Mitchell died. It would be my house once I sign the papers.

It felt strange calling it my house.

I still couldn't believe my grandfather was gone. I couldn't believe the estate he had left me.

I knew it was my house now. I knew I now had close to twenty-two million dollars, but I didn't feel any different. I didn't feel richer. I still felt like the same me.

I rolled out of bed and took a shower. I got dressed and began my journey to my new home.

I opened the door to my grandfather's house, 'my' house, and stood in the entrance for a moment. I dropped my bag.

I was drained and beaten.

I had officially lost everyone in my family. All I had now were memories.

I looked down the hallway to the kitchen and remembered all the times he tried cooking for me. His ability to pick up the phone and order in was a much more satisfying and tasty experience. I smiled as I remembered the time he almost set fire to the kitchen by trying to host a Thanksgiving dinner for the two of us.

I stared at the kitchen floor, looking for any signs of my grandfather's blood. I was relieved that there was none. The cleaning crew had done their job after the shooting.

I squeezed my eyes to hold back the tears.

Kicking my bag to the side, I walked into the house. I closed the door behind me and headed toward the kitchen. Standing in front of the bay window, I stared toward the forest that acted as a divider between the neighbors, all of whom who were at least a few hundred feet away. It was so quiet.

My eyes moved to the backyard. Fresh laid sod covered the area where the construction had been going on.

Where was my grandfather's pool?

I reached down, unlocked the door and stepped outside.

I stood with my hands on my hips. This made no sense. What had he really been up to?

The only thing different was that he had moved the shed. It was pressed up against the house on the left.

Why in the world would he move the shed?

I walked over to it, hoping it would solve this mystery.

My heart began to race.

The shed was now made from reinforced steel.

He remodeled the shed? Who does that? And where did the giant hole in the backyard go?

The shed looked like it could be a bomb shelter, but it wasn't big enough to be one. I banged on the side of it and it was solid. I walked to the front and looked at the door; it was locked with a touchscreen keypad. Interesting.

I reached for the handle and pulled it.

Locked.

My attention turned to the digital keypad. It required a passcode. I stared blankly at the screen. After a moment of thought, I decided to go for the obvious, a commonly used password by everyone. I typed in my birth date. I finished the combination, pushed # and red light appeared on the screen followed by a short half second buzzer sound.

That obviously wasn't the right combination. He couldn't have made it that easy…or could he? It didn't discourage me. I quickly pressed the screen to the combination of my grandfather's birthday. I pushed # once I finished the combination. Just like before, the red light appeared followed by the buzzer. Wrong again. I tried both of my parent's birthdays. I was wrong both times. I tried the numbers of the house address, my apartment numbers, the year he sold his business, his phone number, my phone number, our favorite numbers and any combination from those numbers. Nothing worked.

This was really getting frustrating now. What numbered combination would he have used? Would it be something only he knew, or could I figure this out?

In a rage of anger and frustration, I grabbed the handle and pulled as hard as I could. It didn't work. It didn't even budge. I turned around and leaned back onto the door behind me. I collapsed to the ground and held my head in my hands.

I was defeated.

After everything I just went through, this stupid door would be the thing that beat me. I had no idea what the combination was and had no way to ask my grandfather.

Wait. I lifted my head out of my hands and sat straight up. "That's it!" I exclaimed out loud.

Names.

I stood up and peered at the keypad again. It was a password not a numerical code. I took out my cell phone so I could line up the letters with the numbers on the keypad. I then typed in my name.

3…3…8…4…6…#

Red light and the buzzer sound.

I typed my grandfather's name. I was wrong again. I added last names to the mix. I tried my parent's names.

Everything was wrong. What was the code? What was I missing?

I started tapping my foot in irritation. I had to get this door opened.

I looked around the yard for anything that might help me get inside this shed. If my grandfather was here, I knew he would be teasing me. He'd be laughing at me, making fun of me, calling me names.

And then it hit me like a ton of bricks. It was so obvious, and it was something only I could have known. I smiled as I traced the numbers down on my phone to correspond with the letters of the password. I began pushing them.

4...6...6...3...3...3...4...3...4...6...8...#

The screen flashed green and I heard the bolts unlock.

The door pushed toward me only a matter of inches. I reached for the handle and pulled the door open.

CHAPTER FORTY-SEVEN

"Hooded Idiot," I said to myself, shaking my head as I walked inside. He was still teasing me about that, even in death.

The shed was dark except for a bit of sunlight peeking through the opened door. There was a wire hanging in front of me, attached to a light bulb above. I reached for the wire and pulled it down. Immediately, light filled the inside of the shed. I began to look around as a loud *BOOM* filled the room. I jumped as I turned around to locate the source of the noise. The door shut behind me.

I brought my attention back to the surroundings of the room. It looked just like any other shed. There was a hose nicely wrapped and hanging on the wall. A shovel was placed to the right of the hose. There was a shelf on the wall across from the hose which housed a few pairs of gloves, and a tool box. I walked over to the tool box and opened it up. There was nothing out of the ordinary inside. It had a few different sized screwdrivers, a hammer, a wrench and some other equipment I'd probably never use since I had no idea how to use it anyway. I closed the box and continued my search.

Where did the motorcycle go? Last time he brought me in here, before the remodel, my grandfather had a motorcycle in here. Now it was gone.

Things just didn't seem right.

There was a broom placed against the wall in the far corner. Above it was my old bicycle. I smiled at the sight of it. I can't believe he kept that thing all these years. I walked over to the bike and admired it. I used to ride this bike up and down all the streets when I was younger.

I reached out and grabbed the handlebars as old memories flashed before me. I used my right hand to reach out and squeeze the brake when and suddenly the floor shook. I looked down at my feet and noticed I was standing on a discoloration on the floor. The entire floor was a solid steel, except where I was standing. Where I stood, the floor had a darker metallic color.

I knelt to better examine the floor. Upon closer observation, this wasn't just a discoloration. I was standing on a platform of some sort. I stood back up but just as I did, the floor moved again, and this time it moved down.

The mysterious platform descended beneath the ground level. Before I could even move or jump off, I was being taken underground on some kind of elevator. The ride lasted about nine or ten seconds before the platform came to a stop. The darkness of my new environment consumed me. There was water flowing somewhere. Was it above me?

Just as my eyes started becoming accustomed to the dark, I took one step off the platform and lights began to illuminate one by one, like street lamps coming on at sunset.

As they flickered on, the first thing I noticed was a huge screen at the end of the room. It must have been almost the size of the wall. In front of it was a long table, hosting three computer monitors. To the right of the table was a large, empty glass display case that went from the floor to the ceiling. Opposite the glass casing was the home to what seemed like servers for the computers. This place seemed a little extreme for a bomb shelter.

What is all this for? It was frustrating to know that I couldn't get a direct answer. My grandfather was the one who had this built. He had all the answers, but I couldn't ask him. I had no choice but to keep searching.

The big wall screen came to life. Then the center computer monitor lit up. They both blinked once and then displayed a large "play" button. In a part of my mind, I thought for a second that my grandfather was just going to pop out and surprise me, telling me this was all one big joke. Maybe it was all just a dream.

Of course he didn't.

Although that was what I wanted most, I took what was in front of me.

I walked toward the computers. I pulled out the swivel chair which was tucked underneath the desk and sat down. I looked around the room one last time to make sure I was alone—and I was. I reached for the computer's mouse and clicked "play."

"Hello, Devin," my grandfather said as he appeared on the wall monitor.

Tears spring to my eyes. I wiped them away.

The video continued. "As cliché as this may sound, if you're watching this, it means I'm probably dead. This also means you managed to find your way down here all by yourself so on a positive note, congratulations!"

He had a sarcastic way of congratulating me. Even in death, he could still make me laugh. He had a smile on his face, which faded when he started to speak again. He was laying down while talking to me. He must have recorded this while in the hospital in the event he never came home.

"I'm so proud of you. I know you had a crappy hand dealt to you, but you have managed to keep your head on straight. You're a good kid. Now on to the good stuff.

"I'm sure you're wondering 'what is this place'? First of all, I have to apologize for the secrecy. I couldn't tell you what I was doing. I wanted it to be a surprise for you when the time came. I'm just sorry I couldn't be there to see your face and show you around myself.

"When you called me the night you got into your accident, I didn't know what to expect. I rushed down to the hospital as fast as I could. I was so worried something horrible happened to you. You were—and are—everything to me. You were all I had left of your mom—my daughter. I know I don't show that side of me very often, or even at all, but I need you to know that I love you very much.

"When you came home that day from work and told me what happened and what you could do, I was scared. I thought something was seriously wrong with you. I wanted you to be normal and grow up and have a normal life. A part of me was a little scared knowing what you could do. I'd never seen anything like it. Then I saw how you embraced it. You took control of it and learned what you could do with your ability.

"I know I may have pushed you into that life and got a little carried away and excited for you. I became a little jealous. With all the things you could have done with your new ability, you used it for good. You used it to help make Decker City a better place. By taking those steps to make the city safer, you have taken on a great responsibility. People are going to depend on you. They are going to need you to protect them from all the evils out there. They are going to rely on you to help keep this city safe. And you are going to be a hero to them. And you're my hero, too."

I paused the recording. I felt so honored. My grandfather said he was proud of me and told me I was a hero. Of all the stories and comics I had read growing up, I never once imagined this happening to me. Best of all, my hero, my grandpa, said I was *his* hero.

I resumed the video. "So," my grandfather continued, "every hero has a secret identity. Yours is just being yourself. It's you. Continue going to work. Don't do anything to jeopardize your ability and raise suspicion. You are special. You can't let people know who you are and what you can do. Who knows what they would do to you if they could get their hands on that special brain of yours.

"And speaking of secret identity, what does every superhero need?"

He asked the question that I couldn't even answer. My mind was already going crazy right now trying to understand all of this. I tried to understand where he was going but I couldn't even concentrate with everything going on. This was all way too much to take in.

"There's a button underneath the table," he said as he paused for a moment. It gave me time to roll my chair toward the table. I slid my hand back and forth underneath the table until I finally came across a small button. "Press it," my grandfather finally said.

I pushed it.

A noise came from my right. The large glass display case began to turn on the inside. The wall spun to reveal a life-sized mannequin in a dark silver hoodie with black pants and black boots. Black gloves finished the attire.

"If everything worked properly, and hopefully it did, you should be looking at your new attire," my grandfather continued to say. "You're now The Silver Hood. No more Gray Hood. Gray is too plain. *Silver* is the way to go. It looks better. It sounds better.

"Also, no more worrying about injuries. The outfit in front of you has been handcrafted and equipped with Kevlar. It's bulletproof. Well, it should be. I wouldn't suggest trying so don't go try and get shot…again.

"Everything, including the hood, pants, gloves and boots are made from Kevlar. You should be a very well protected walking machine in that attire."

I stared at it, smiling ear-to-ear. Bulletproof? After what happened with Mitchell and my grandfather, I really had no desire to put the hood back on. But after seeing all of this, how could I say no?

In the back of my mind, I heard Tommy's voice. "Whoa, that's cool, Dude." I wish I could tell him.

My grandfather continued. "And to be able to use that suit, you need to know where the criminal activity is happening. I have linked into the police department and there's a program on the computer that will activate when there's a call into the police. A map will pop up and show you exactly where the crime is taking place. Think of it like an automatic criminal tracking GPS system.

"So how can you possibly get there quicker than the police you ask?"

I waited for him to tell me.

My grandfather looked excited. I could tell he was loving this. "There should be a small switch next to the glass casing holding your suit. Push that button. Don't worry, I'll wait."

I stood up and walked to the remote on the wall. My grandfather was humming some of the Jeopardy theme song in the meantime.

The remote was encased in a small metal box on the wall. I reached forward and flicked it in the upward position. More noise began as I could feel motors humming from all around me. About ten feet behind my computer chair, the floor parted into a black hole. Suddenly, the missing black and gray motorcycle from the shed rose from the black hole. Above me, the ceiling began to open. Sunlight quickly spread throughout the room. The ceiling dropped down like a ramp. The motorcycle spun to face the ramp.

"How's that for an entrance? Or an exit? I guess it'll be used as both. I don't know. You'll figure it out." My grandfather looked confused on the video screen as if he didn't know exactly how it would be used either. "I really hope everything is working, otherwise this video is probably looking really stupid right about now. But I'm still going to continue as if everything is working to plan. I really just have one last thing before I end this video. What else does every hero need?"

I had no idea. My grandfather just surprised me with a new outfit, a way of tracking crimes, a hidden motorcycle in the floor and a secret passage in and out of this place. If he was asking me a question right now and expecting an answer, he would be sadly mistaken.

"Every hero needs a secret hideout. This place is *your* secret hideout. It has everything you need to continue your crusade, your adventures, your work to make Decker City a great place to live. Go make the city better. Maybe when you're done with this city, move on to another. I'm proud of you, Devin. So proud of you. I'm going to miss driving you around while we hunted for criminals. Decker City needs the hooded idiot." A smiled appeared on his face.

"Go out there and make a difference." The screen shuttered and went blank.

I was humbled by everything he'd given me, everything he had done for me. He had set me up to become a hero for this city. He gave me the funds to do whatever I wanted and needed. He gave me a protective suit. He gave me a secret hideout. He gave me quick transportation. I had everything I needed, except him.

I would be the hero this city needed. I would do it for my grandfather.

I stared at my new suit. I wanted to go out and try it, but my injuries prevented that. It would be some time before I could get back out on the streets again.

I felt excitement rising in me as I thought about that day. One day soon.

Maybe I couldn't stop crime yet, but my injuries didn't stop me from trying on the suit. I took it off the mannequin and put it on. It looked awesome. I felt strong.

I couldn't wait to try it out. I couldn't wait to figure out the rest this place. I couldn't wait to get back on the streets and fight crime again as The Silver Hood.

Today was definitely a new day.

About the Author

Justin Richman has had a fascination with superheroes and science fiction since he was a child. He has memorabilia from both the DC and Marvel universe all over his home office which help give him inspiration to write. He graduated from Temple University, majoring in Risk Management, Insurance & Actuarial Science. Currently, Justin owns two business franchises and resides in Harleysville Pennsylvania with his wife and son.

Morgan James
Speakers Group

www.TheMorganJamesSpeakersGroup.com

We connect Morgan James published
authors with live and online events
and audiences who will benefit
from their expertise.

CPSIA information can be obtained
at www.ICGtesting.com
Printed in the USA
LVHW11s2313270918
591666LV00001B/265/P